D R E A M

TALES FROM THE PIKES PEAK WRITERS

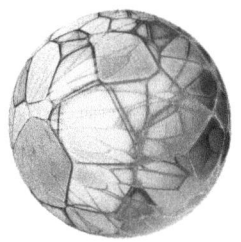

Jean Alfieri • Steven Anderson • C.E. Barnes
Lou J. Berger • John M. Campbell
John Christenson • D.J. Davis
Rick Duffy • Marlene Fabien Stiles
Karen Fox • Lawrence Good
Ronnie Graham • Matthew Heneghan
Scott Kerby • T.R. Kerby
Lauren Lang • John Lewis • Gregory Mattix
Peter McQuade • Tracy Mitchell
P. James Norris • Cepa Onion
Barbara Preslier • Uchechi Princewill
Sandy Reay • C. S. Simpson
Benjamin X. Wretlind

EDITED BY:

EDWARD T. RAETZ

DEBORAH L. BREWER

KATHIE SCRIMGEOUR

JENNY KATE

COPYRIGHT

TABLE OF CONTENTS

Introduction

Your climate control is broken, the engine is overheating again, and the traffic has come to a dead stop amidst a swarm of horns. To top it off you're late for work. In a heartbeat, you find yourself in another place, another time. Just for a moment, your mind takes a break. Your subconscious decides to get out of the traffic and set sail along a coast of white sand beaches and palm trees. Later that night, you wake with a jolt but don't remember what startled you. Your thoughts are racing as sweat beads on your forehead. What was it? Is someone there? Are you afraid to go back to sleep?

Whether you are awake or asleep, dreams take your mind and open it to a kaleidoscope of dreamscapes you never knew could exist. In a blink, the dream can transform from a bloody war to a little boy escaping his troubled childhood with his action figures.

In this second anthology from the Pikes Peak Writers, you will take a journey through the creative minds of the twenty-seven writers who penned the following works based on a simple one-word prompt - *Dream*. Let yourself experience worlds in a spirit-filled house, on a pirate ship, or teeter on the precipice of Hell. Then, with the turn of a page, walk through the beauty of far-off lands, watch purple ducks on a yellow pond, or run with terror through a town filled with monsters. Enjoy this stroll down a crooked path that could hold your worst nightmare or your most beloved wish. Be careful what you wish for, a genie may be lurking in the labyrinth of your mind waiting to be set free.

–Kathie Scrimgeour

House of Dreams

By: Steven Anderson

My house is haunted. No one would question that truth. The spirits of previous residents sit at the table with me while I eat dinner, and drift through the family room when I watch TV in the evenings. Why they stay wasn't obvious when I first became aware of them. Or I should say, when they first allowed me to become aware of them. I've come to believe that many houses are haunted. The spirits of those who once called a place home decide to remain for a while.

I can understand that with the Third Street house. It's perfect. Cross the road, and a fine hiking trail climbs the foothills through protected open space. Stand by the family room's big windows on a summer evening and marvel as the city lights sparkle to life in the valley. Step out on the broad deck and admire the stars.

I intended to remain long after my physical body became dust, which is why the notice of Eminent Domain from the City of Boulder was so terrifying. The ghosts and I examined it around the dining room table, and started to make plans for how to save our home.

Nels Bradford tapped the letter with one fat finger. He built the house in 1926, the culmination of his dream to spend each evening with a fine cigar and glass of port while contemplating his business empire in the valley beneath his feet. "See here, Eaton. This woman, this Sarah Patterson with the Board of Supervisors. You must speak to her and find out who's behind this nonsense. Engage a barrister and submit a petition of appeal. If nothing else, drag it out through the courts until they tire of the fight."

Alisha Cavender floated closer to peek through my shoulder. She was the most ethereal of the ghosts, often more a shimmer than a woman. She'd bought the house with her husband in 1966, and sold it after his death at the second Battle of Quang Tri. The story went deeper than that, but she never talked about it. The *Daily Camera's* archives said she'd been forced to sell after a jury convicted her of blowing up a Marine Corps recruiting office.

She touched the letter, making it flutter as if a gentle breeze had passed over it. "All this to flatten the road? Robert, the courts are not the answer, and you know it. Go next door and talk to the Beckers tonight."

"Tonight? It's late, and I–"

"Tonight, Robert. Then the Mallards and the Keplers. They must have received the same letter. Organize. March down to the Courthouse *en masse*."

"Alisha, I'm not sure seven upset homeowners constitute a *masse*."

She passed through me, leaving a cold tickle in my chest. I coughed. "Please don't do that."

She solidified. Her corporeal self had died an old woman in Austin in 2015. Her spirit looked about thirty, dressed in a blue floral maxi-dress with little rainbows. She had round framed glasses perched on her nose, and she'd tied her blond hair up with a scarf. I'd seen the look before. Mrs. Alisha Cavender, University research librarian, scowling at another slothful undergrad wasting her time.

"You can't let this letter sit on the table. You have a responsibility."

"I know I do. To the house. To all of you."

She glared at me, the blue eyes behind her glasses narrowed to slits. "To hell with us."

Nels pulled the stump of a cigar from his mouth. "Damn it, Mrs. Cavender. Don't say that."

"To hell with us," she repeated. "This is about Robert. And it's about Brenda."

Buying the Third Street house had been Brenda's dream, a quiet retreat in a noisy world where she could feel safe. When the ghosts first started appearing to me after Brenda's death, I expected her to be among them. Alisha explained it to me. Brenda still lived in my heart, and no one, not even a ghost, can be in two places at once.

"All right. I'll go tonight."

Alisha faded to mist, vanished, and reappeared a moment later outside on the deck to watch the shadow of the mountains stretch eastward across the city.

Nels remained at the table, the glow of his cigar bright behind a swirl of smoke. "Picketing and making a fuss won't get the job done, Eaton. I met Emma Ghent in 1892. Even let her put a stack of her suffragist fliers in my store." He puffed smoke into the air above him. It vanished, leaving no scent of his Cuban tobacco to linger in the house. "Appealing to people's better angels never changed a damn thing. Miss Ghent knew real change happens in the legislature and the courts. Find yourself a good lawyer, son. Deals made behind closed doors are where this started, and where it will end."

I stuffed the letter in my pocket and walked next door.

Linda Becker answered my knock, as surprised to see me as I was to be there. They were good neighbors, and I felt bad about not being as social since losing Brenda. Linda and Peter had watched the house for me when I'd traveled to Delaware to bring my wife's flag-draped coffin home, and they'd brought me a casserole my first night back. More importantly, they stayed and ate with me. We talked of inconsequential things; how the flowers were starting to bloom, the Chautauqua summer concert schedule, and the beauty of the evening. It helped me understand that life went on, no matter our losses.

Linda opened the door and I stepped into the foyer. "Robert. I don't think I've seen you in months. How have you been?"

I answered with a polite lie to excuse myself from ignoring people who should be my friends. "Busy. Like always."

"I'm sure. The hectic life of a professor."

"I taught two courses this spring, and finished my research on silver mining in Boulder County." I smiled. "Now all I need to do is write the book."

She smiled back, having no idea of the pain involved in turning notes into peer-reviewed prose. "We just opened a bottle of wine. I'll get you a glass."

"Thanks." I followed her onto their deck and shook Peter's hand. Their view isn't as perfect as mine. They'd let the aspen grow too tall, and the angle looking out over town is subtly wrong. I sat, and he poured wine into my glass.

"So, Robert, what brings you out from your fortress of solitude?"

I heard the gentle rebuke. "You're right. I need to get out more." I placed the letter on the table and smoothed out the wrinkles. "You got one too?"

He shrugged. "It's not a surprise."

"I was surprised."

Linda stood behind me with her hand on my shoulder. "You really do need to get out more. Don't you remember a few weeks back when that car hit the Minter's kid in front of our house?"

"Bumped is what I heard. That car couldn't have been going more than five miles per hour. No one goes faster than that. You can't see anything on the other side of the hill until you're over the crest. Minter is behind this?"

Linda sipped her wine and didn't answer, at least not in words.

"Minter," I repeated. "I don't know him. What's he like? Can we get him to drop it?"

"Not a chance," Peter told me. "He wants to sell next year when his kids are out of the house. A normal street will boost his listing price. This way he gets the city to pay for it."

"Right," I said. "No changes on his side of the street. We lose our front yards."

"It's only twelve feet. They can't take it from the upslope houses, like Minter's. It'd make the driveways too steep."

"Of course it would. His property stays the same. They'll gut ours. I paced it off before I came over. My big pine will have to go. Then they'll run a bulldozer through the rock garden that Brenda... that I've been tending. I added moss rose this year. It won't make it through the winter, but it adds color, you know?"

Linda smiled a sad smile for me. "I know. I went with her when she picked out the initial plantings. I'll miss seeing all the butterflies."

"We can appeal. Will you support me if they want some extra names?"

Linda answered before her husband could object. "You know we will."

I left my wine unfinished, too angry to be social any longer. They walked outside with me to the edge of the yard. Peter looked up and down the dark street, streetlights not having been part of the original design. "You like this?"

I closed my eyes and listened to the distant city sounds and the soft murmur of wind in the trees. "Yeah. It's perfect."

"Look, Robert. Minter's a lawyer, and he has friends. Don't bother with the Mallards and Keplers. They're already planning how to spend the city's money. It would be better if you just went along with the whole thing. Understand?"

"Sure." I scuffed my shoe in the loose dirt beside the road where a normal neighborhood would have a smooth concrete sidewalk. "Tilting at windmills. It's stupid, but I have to try."

Linda gave my cheek a little kiss. "Don't be a stranger, win or lose."

"Thanks."

David Fielder waited for me on the couch, a plume of cigarette smoke rising and fading above him. "So, my man. Done wasting your time?"

I sat opposite him. "Yes. I don't understand my neighbors. We have this special place here, and they're ready to sell it out."

"It's progress. Bigger, better, faster. That's the Boulder I know. The whole mellow, Earth-Mother-chic mountain town vibe is for the tourists. There's cold steel in the government, just like every government. Take the cash, my man. In a few months, you won't even notice the difference."

"I thought you loved this house as much as the rest of us."

"They ain't changing the house." He gestured out the windows. "Best view in the world. The chicks dig it like no other. The effect it has on them is like a dream come true. I wanted to reinforce the deck, put a sweet hot tub out there, but then the whole... well, you know."

I knew. David made his first million before turning twenty-five from flipping real estate and selling a little coke on the side. He'd been well on his way to his second million when his BMW drifted wide speeding down the canyon and collided with a county snowplow.

"I can't do it. When I walk out the front door, I expect to see her, fussing at the weeds, calling to me to pick up something for her on my way home."

He took a deep drag on his cigarette and blew a smoke ring I thankfully couldn't smell. "Look, you teach history, right? When did anyone ever beat history? You grab it by the horns, and you humpin' ride it. You want to go talk to Sarah Patterson? Too cool. But don't ask her how to stop the wheels of progress. Tell her you want more. More money. A bigger wall. Some plants, and rocks, and shit, if that will make you happy."

I chuckled. "I can hear Brenda telling me that. She'd make a better rock garden than the one we have now. And no more fighting a steep, icy hill in the winter."

"Damn straight."

I nodded, and then shook my head. "I don't know."

"Yes, you do. Either you make history, or you become history. The Erhard seminars taught me that. And one other thing. If this Sarah chick is fine, invite her up here for dinner and a close inspection of the property. Show her the view."

***

Over the next week, I became convinced that Sarah Patterson wasn't real. She didn't respond to voicemail, email, or my online request for a review. I scoured the boulderco.gov site looking for a way to reach her. Or go around her.

That led me to the Planning & Development Services page, and the application for Individual Landmark Designation. If I couldn't get a review of the Eminent Domain ruling, maybe I could block it by claiming historical significance. I called the number for the Historic Preservation staff. The voice telling me that no one was available to take my call sounded familiar. Maybe Sarah had done all of the city's messages. She had a nice voice, assuming she existed at all. I left a message, sent an email, and waited.

I stepped outside a few days later to pull weeds before the heat of the day and to contemplate how to stop the mule deer from snacking on my new moss rose. I reached for a clump of weeds they'd left untouched.

Alisha moved as a helpful shimmer of sunlight in the shade of the trees. "Robert, that's not a weed. It's *Aurinia saxatilis*. It's supposed to be there."

"Are you sure?"

"Thin them if you must, but I think they're pretty."

I took off my gloves. "I'll let them live. They'll all be gone in a few weeks, anyway."

Alisha floated closer and became almost solid. She wore a black shirt and pants, her blonde hair tucked inside a black watch cap. The clothes matched what she'd worn in an old Boulder PD photo from the night an empty recruiting office had exploded. She'd lingered to make sure no one entered the building; that no one would get hurt. It had cost her. The police responded faster than she'd expected. Alisha never made it home to Third Street that night or ever again while she was alive.

She put her lips next to my ear. "Are you desperate yet, Robert? There's something I need to show you."

I followed her to the basement. She paused in the darkness under the stairs. "I haven't told you how I lost the house."

"You mean how you blew up the Marine Corps? I know."

She looked into my eyes and a smile touched her lips. "Do you?" Alisha didn't seem embarrassed by what she'd done. Her smile reflected defiance, and a touch of pride. "Look at the bottom of this step. See how it's a little fatter than the rest? Pull on the bottom of it."

I pulled, and a narrow shelf slid out. I caught the book that fell free and turned it over. "*The Anarchist Cookbook*? Seriously, Alisha?"

"I felt just like Montag in *Fahrenheit 451* when I built that shelf. Isn't it wonderful?"

"I don't think blowing up city hall will save our front yard."

She touched my arm, and I imagined I could feel the warmth of her hand. "Robert, I always knew you were a rebel at heart."

"I said I'm *not* blowing up city hall."

"No, you said you didn't think it would do any good. But, if you thought it would do some good, you'd already be looking at my notes on page 118."

I flipped through the pages, reading what Alisha had added in the margins. "I should burn this." A thought came to me, a justification for saving it. No one had written about the more violent players in the anti-war protests of that time in Boulder's history. I could do a paper, maybe something bigger. I placed the book back on the shelf and slid it into place. "I won't burn it. I'm not a fireman."

"What are you going to do, Robert the Rebel?"

"I'll keep trying to appeal, and I'll keep working down my list of attorneys. No one wants to talk to me."

"The establishment *wants* this to happen. You'll still be waiting for the phone to ring while they maim our home. Here's what I would do." She reached for the hidden shelf.

"You ended up in jail for ten years."

She hovered close to me. "It was worth it. They never did reopen the office I destroyed. I like to believe I kept at least one young man from dying in a rice paddy."

"Big difference between that and Brenda's rock garden."

Alisha faded to mist and then reappeared in a blue prison jumpsuit, her hands bound in front of her. "Is there? When the government comes for you, and they say they own your life, you fight them. Fight hard in the small battles and the large ones might never come. This house is my dream, Robert; built on the boundary between the city below and the mountain above, between man and God. But you can't straddle that line forever. They called my husband to war, so I went too."

"I'm not desperate yet. I'm not you, Alisha."

She raised her hands, palms up, and the chains binding her clinked softly.

I stared at the translucent pale skin of her wrists trapped inside chromed steel. My phone buzzed against my leg and made me shiver. "Someone's calling back. Maybe I won't have to… get desperate."

Alisha dimmed and vanished. I touched the green icon. "Eaton here."

A woman's voice answered. "Professor Eaton?"

"Yes. This is Professor Eaton."

"Meet me at Snarf's on the Mall at 1:30."

"Who is this?" No answer. "Hello?" My phone chirped three times, telling me the call had ended.

***

The lunch rush at Snarf's had passed by the time I got there. I opened the door and scanned the crowd looking for someone looking for me. A woman made eye contact and gave me a little wave with two fingers. She was dressed professionally, white blouse and dark skirt, with sunglasses perched stylishly on top of short, brown hair. She gestured for me to sit. I didn't.

"You called me?"

"Yes, Professor. Sorry to be so weird about it, but this whole thing is weird, the way people are acting." She glanced around the café. "Please sit."

I pulled out a chair and sat on the edge.

"I'm Sarah Patterson. You probably don't remember me, but I took your Introduction to Boulder History class a couple, no, like ten years ago. Wow. Hard to believe it's been that long." She smiled, and crushed her napkin into a tight ball.

"I'm sorry, Ms. Patterson. I don't remember you. That would have been my first year teaching. I don't remember much about that year, other than being terrified the whole time."

"Were you? You seemed confident, like you knew everything about the city, and were friends with the people who used to live here. I didn't do anything very memorable in your class, but it changed my life. I'd planned to go to LA or New York when I graduated, but that semester convinced me to stay here. You know, kind of keep the history going? Maybe shape it a little?"

"I'm glad you enjoyed the class. Now, about my house."

"My boss doesn't want me to talk to you."

"They told you to ignore my application and all my messages?"

Her nose wrinkled. "Not exactly? Not in writing. And it really doesn't matter at this point. They pushed construction way up in the schedule, so there's no way you'll get a hearing in time to stop it. But, you deserve to know."

I folded my arms. "Go on."

"It's nothing bad. They didn't tell me to do anything illegal. I'd have refused, or quit, or something if they had. It's just weird, the way they rushed the decision to file for eminent domain. Mr. Minter is kind of a big deal, I guess, and he called in a few favors to get it done quickly. And his son really was hit by a car because Third Street is unsafe, so I can understand some urgency."

I shook my head. "The kid skinned his knee. You really think it's unsafe?"

"Yeah. But not for long. We'll reduce the grade, and add sidewalks, curbs, and a bike lane. All to code. Your neighbors seem happy. They'll get a city check to compensate them for the right-of-way we're taking. You're the only one." She crushed another napkin into a ball. "Complaining, I mean. It's going to happen, Professor Eaton. Maybe I can get something extra added to your package?"

"Have you been up there?"

"On Third Street? No. I wasn't part of the survey. I've seen the pictures."

"It's not the same." I stood. "Come along, Ms. Patterson. We're going on a field trip. A history field trip."

Her eyes widened. "I'm supposed to be back at my desk in a few minutes."

"This won't take long. You can follow me in your car."

"Um, I don't have a car."

I held my hand out, imploring her to come. "You need to see it. It's special. If they're going to destroy it, you should see it with your own eyes first. Please."

She took my hand, as though expecting me to help her up, as though it was the right thing for us to do. The warmth and softness surprised me. I held her hand gently, and for longer than I should have. An involuntary muscle memory. It had been a long time since anyone had held my hand other than in a perfunctory greeting.

"OK. But I really don't have much time."

Sarah settled herself into the Jeep's passenger seat and slid her sunglasses down onto her nose. I had the roof off, not having anticipated I'd have anyone riding with me.

"Do you need a hat?" I asked. "I have an extra you can borrow."

"No thanks." She ruffled her hair. "I keep this short because it's easier with my bike helmet. Works in the wind, too."

"Practical," I told her. "And it looks nice."

She blushed. Or it may have been the sun on her cheeks.

We drove northwest, winding through residential streets with neat sidewalks and wide bike lanes. Sarah kept her hand out the window, feeling the air.

"I'm going to take us up Evergreen. I'd normally use Dellwood since I'm on the south side of the hill, but I want you to experience going over the top."

19

She nodded, not looking at me, staring straight ahead. It made me feel like I'd kidnapped her. "Thanks for doing this. It means a lot to me, to have someone see it and understand what will be lost."

Evergreen reached a dead end. I turned hard left, and downshifted into first gear. The nose of the Jeep pointed at the sky as we climbed the hill.

Sarah leaned her head out the window to see if there was still road under us. "This is nuts. How has this been allowed?"

We crested, and the nose tipped down far enough that the seatbelts locked. I stopped and set the hand brake. "That's the wrong question. The right question is, 'why not?' Why not have an absurdly steep hill and front yards that end in a bit of gravel and poorly maintained asphalt?"

Sarah looked behind us, as though concerned we were blocking traffic. "It's not safe. None of it. It's a miracle no one's been killed."

"We could stay parked here most of the day and no one would care. Kids play up here all the time. It's safe enough." I let go of the brake and we coasted to a stop on the gravel in front of my house.

"I don't want it to change. All the streets in this part of town used to be like this. Well, without the hill. No streetlights. No curbs or sidewalks. Not much traffic. Now you're going to rip it out along with twelve feet of my yard and replace it with a theme park version of what small mountain towns used to look like. Do you understand, Ms. Patterson?"

She nodded. "I do. You're a historian. History is being erased. It's going to be different. It has to be different. I'm sorry."

I sighed, frustrated that I'd yelled at the one person who might be able to help me. "I'm sorry. That had more anger than it should have. It's not your fault, and I'm grateful to you. You came, you looked, and you listened. I don't want you to think I'm crazy."

She smiled. "I don't think you're crazy, Professor. Passionate, is all. Can I see the rest of it? Your email mentioned a garden."

"Are you sure? You said you didn't have much time."

She unbuckled, and moved her sunglasses back to the top of her head. "I'm already late. What are a few more minutes? My boss can only fire me once."

"Right." I gave her a tour, even though I didn't know the names of most of the plants.

"This whole thing is pretty. It must have taken a lot of planning and hard work."

"My wife did most of it."

Sarah blinked at me a few times. "Oh?"

"Brenda had the vision. I had the strong back. I try to keep it looking nice, now that she's gone."

"She's gone?"

"She served as a Captain in the Air Force, stationed at Bagram. They needed a woman to talk to some of the Afghani women one night. She went. She wasn't supposed to, but she went anyway. It wasn't… They…" I shivered at the memory of the cold, precise wording in her Bronze Star citation. "Anyway, Brenda was killed."

I knelt to pull a dandelion that hadn't been there in the morning. It shouldn't be so hard to talk about Brenda, not after two years. I'd talked to other people about her, even my students. One-on-one with Sarah hurt almost more than I could stand.

She moved close to me, as if she wanted to take my hand again. "This is about her, isn't it? Losing the garden she built."

"That's part of it. I see her when I look at it. But she lives in here." I tapped my chest. "It's a place your bulldozers can't reach."

"My bulldozers? Please, don't say that. I wish I could find another way."

"You could approve my appeal."

"It's not so simple. There are a whole bunch of people above me that want this to happen. They don't let me play with their bulldozers."

I stood and brushed dirt from my knee. Sarah's eyes were a darker brown than Brenda's, but they gave me the same feeling of being able to see straight through me. I hate that feeling. And I had missed it.

A couple of butterflies explored the flowers, moving quickly from one to the next. They passed into a shimmer of light, and flew frantic circles around each other. I smiled at Alisha, wondering what she was up to.

"Professor?"

"Yes? Sorry. First butterflies I've seen this year. Look at them dance."

Sarah watched them, a half-smile on her lips. "The way the light shines through the big pine, it's beautiful." She tipped her head, trying to see something that wasn't there. "Professor, I've seen your street, and I know what your rock garden means to you. May I see your house? The inside?"

"The inside? My house isn't part of your eminent domain filing."

The butterfly-induced smile still touched Sarah's lips and glowed in her eyes. "Please."

21

"Sure. But I don't want you to lose your job. You can always come back."

Her eyes widened. "No. Now would be better. You might not want to see me ever again after the bulldozers come. I'll make up something to tell my boss." She took her phone out from somewhere in her skirt.

"You have pockets. That's rare."

She grinned while she typed. "I added them myself. I hate carrying a bag. There. I'm sick, and I went home."

"Very devious. I like it."

"Thank you, Professor."

I shook my head. "Just call me Robert. You haven't been my student for years."

"You always called me Ms. Patterson in class. Please, call me Sarah."

David appeared by the front door as I unlocked it, the top three buttons of his shirt undone. "A delightful afternoon, isn't it, my man? She seems a little uptight, and like she's spent way too many hours in the library. Just your type." He laughed. "Try her out on one of your margaritas. She's a tiny thing. You'll have her wobbling in no time."

Sarah couldn't hear him, or see the leer he gave her. She stepped inside, and examined the portraits in the hallway. "Family?"

"In spirit. These are all the people who have lived here. It's kind of a hobby, or maybe a quest. I wanted to track them down and learn as much as I could about them."

"As one does."

I shrugged. "Occupational hazard for a historian."

"Tell me their stories."

"This is Nels Bradford, the home's designer and builder. He made his money selling supplies to the local miners. He always said that's where the real money lay, not in digging for ore. He died in 1946, just as Boulder started to boom after the war." I glanced at where he stood by my shoulder. "I've always imagined it made him bitter to die when business was picking up."

"Damn right I'm bitter. I could have been a millionaire if I'd lasted another ten years. And you." He poked his cigar at me. "Teacher. I could teach you how to make real money. There's no great trick to it, you know."

"This one next to him is his eldest son, Joshua. He lived here until 1966. He didn't have his father's head for business, so the Bradford fortune was gone by then."

22

"Bah," Nels added. "The fool thought he could just keep doing what I did. Times change, that's what I should have hammered into his thick skull. Moron."

Sarah moved to the next photo. It showed a young couple on their wedding day, the groom in the Dress Blues of the Marine Corps, his bride in white, long blonde hair braided. "Alisha Cavender." I touched the glass over the faded image. "And Paul. He died at Quang Tri."

"Quang Tri?"

"Vietnam."

"Oh."

"Alisha sold the house a couple of years later."

A cold mist passed through me. "You can tell her. It's OK. I like her."

"In February of '73, Alisha blew up a building near campus that had a Marine Corps recruiting office on the first floor. She did ten years in Federal prison for it."

"Really?" Sarah leaned forward for a closer look, as though trying to see a penchant for violence behind Alisha's round framed glasses. "I like her."

"Me too."

"Oh, who is this one? He's like someone out of an old movie."

"David Fielder. You wouldn't like him. He lived fast and hard, and took advantage of everyone that ever trusted him. He lived the bad boy lifestyle, and died young the same way, his car upside down at the bottom of Boulder canyon in 1985. But he loved this house, so I guess he wasn't all bad."

"Wow. He's pretty."

David shook his head at me. "Robert, my man, you don't know jack shit about women, do you. Take some risk. Be the bad boy."

When we turned the corner, Sarah walked ahead of me, paused at the big windows, and then opened the door to step onto the deck. "I don't think I'd ever get tired of this view."

David whispered in my ear. "It's the magic view, man. Use it."

"It makes me smile every time I open the blinds or step out here." I stood at the rail with Sarah, and pointed. "Bradford Flour, Feed & Coal right there on the corner of Main and Twelfth Street, where the parking structure is now. I imagine old Nels standing here in the 1930s, smoking one of his cigars, and admiring how his building looked in the afternoon sunlight."

"You haven't changed, Professor. Robert. You still do it to me. You still make me feel that continuity, that we're all part of the story. It's why I stayed in Boulder, and it's why you have those pictures on your wall. You told us that history is a relay race. We take the baton, carry it as best we can, and pass it on. It stuck with me, and wow, do I ever feel it standing here with you. I'm not doing so good with my baton."

"It's not easy balancing the past and the future. Oh." A shiver went through me, from the back of my neck and down my arms. I smiled at her. "Sarah, you're doing fine."

"I am?"

"Yes, and I'm an idiot." I rubbed my eyes, pushing hard. "I hate it when David's right." He stood next to me, looking smug.

"Who? The pretty bad boy in the picture?"

"Yes. No. Um, some other David. But Nels, what Nels said is the key. His son never understood the need to change after the war. The mines had closed. No one used coal any more. They were building homes in the suburbs. Joshua took the baton from his father and stood in the middle of the road, afraid to move. Just like me."

Sarah's forehead wrinkled in confusion. "So, you're OK with us taking twelve feet from your yard?"

"No, I hate it. I'd give anything to stop it. But, if I can't stop it…"

"You can't."

"It won't kill me." I stepped closer to her. "I want the city to replace the rock garden. And plant a new tree. A big one, not one of those little home improvement store things."

"I'll see what I can do."

"Good. I feel less desperate. I think it's going to be OK. Thank you for coming up here with me. You and the others helped me see I'm being a fool."

"They're real to you, aren't they, those people in the pictures. I mean, like they're still alive."

"Sure. When you get to know someone's life, what they said and thought, how they lived, it's easy to imagine they talk to you. In a way, it's harder to believe they can't."

Sarah nodded. "My mom used to talk to her grandma like that. Ask her for advice and stuff. That's not too crazy."

We watched the city together, and listened to the rumble of it. It seemed far away from Third Street. And very close. "Sarah, I can take you home now. If you want me to."

It took her a moment to answer. "Not yet. I'd like to hear more about the people in your pictures. I love those kind of stories."

We sat in the old wood Adirondack chairs Brenda had found at a thrift store. She'd spent a week of evenings sanding off all the splintery bits. They creaked a little, and one had a stain on the arm that no amount of sanding and paint could hide. They were perfect.

Sarah and I made dinner together, finding rice, and chicken, and some seasonings that I'd forgotten I had, but Sarah managed to find. We ate outside, despite the evening chill, and it was very late when I loaned her a coat and took her home in the Jeep.

I walked her to the door of her apartment, and she offered me her hand. When I touched it, we both realized that a handshake wasn't enough, and not what we wanted.

We lingered over our first kiss. Sarah leaned back in my arms to take a breath, her eyes still closed. "We can't do this. Not now. Not yet." She scrunched her eyes tighter. "I have to prepare a new comp package for you in the morning, one with what we talked about. And then walk it around for approvals. Six approvals. If we're seen together, like this, if anyone suspects we were like this, it will get hideously complicated."

"What do you want me to do?"

She smiled, a wicked sort of twisting of her lips. "This. What we're doing. But we can't. For now, stay away. Don't call. Don't text. I'll let you know the moment, the exact moment, I think we can see each other. Assuming you want to see me."

"I know you were in my class, but I feel like I just met you today. You're amazing, and I want to see you again the moment, the exact moment you think it's safe for us to be together."

She looked up and down the empty hall. "No one has seen us tonight. Would you like to come in, just for a few minutes? I bought a new kind of ice cream yesterday. Blueberry cheesecake. If you don't have some of it, I'm afraid I'll stay up and eat it all myself."

"Ice cream? That's right. I remember now. You wrote your term paper on ice cream, how there used to be ice cream trucks driving around in the summers, and why that changed."

She smiled. "You wrote on the front of it that you learned something new, and I'd written the best paper on ice cream you'd ever read."

"It's still true. You didn't just research what other people had written. You went and talked to the old drivers and the guy who owned the creamery. I think I also wrote that you were sharp, insightful, and tenacious."

She took my hand and pulled me into her apartment. "You did."

***

I made plans to leave town before the bulldozers arrived. The crews would block the road in front of the house anyway, and I feared the sight of them smashing the garden would push me to desperate measures. Alisha whispered to me about how to disable diesel engines, and how much explosive force I'd need to launch a ten-ton piece of construction equipment twenty feet in the air.

Nels seemed to have decided that we were overdue for a change. He talked to me of plans to redo the backyard and expand the kitchen. David's main concern was that I'd let Sarah slip through my fingers, a worry that troubled me too. She'd gone silent, as she said she would. Still, it felt like I'd come close to something great, only to have it pass me by. Maybe I should have seized the night and stayed after we finished the ice cream. But that wasn't who I am. If Sarah wanted a bad boy, she'd have to look elsewhere.

I'd survive seeing Third Street once they'd finished their work, but I couldn't watch it happen. I asked Linda and Peter to let me know if anything came up that required me to make a decision, then I left for a camping spot high above Boulder to wait for Sarah's call.

She texted me at the end of the week. The crews had finished their work, and she wanted me to pick her up before going home. She wanted to be with me when I saw it for the first time.

I came down out of the mountains and met her on the corner by the courthouse. She waited until we were far away from her office before sharing an all too quick kiss.

"You're smelly," she told me.

"Sorry. No showers in the high country above Caribou."

"No, you smell like campfire. It's good."

"That's my clothes. What's inside them needs a long shower."

"Really? Drive up Evergreen the way we did last time."

"Sure." We reached the corner of Third Street. I turned left and stopped. "The hill is still here."

Sarah put her hands to her cheeks in mock surprise. "Oh, no. How did that happen?"

"And there's a Do Not Enter sign."

"I guess we need to circle back to Dellwood." She had her hand over her mouth, trying to hide her smile.

"What did you do?"

"You'll see."

I turned from Dellwood onto Third. "Road looks nice. Bike lane. Sidewalk on just one side?"

"Uh huh. We only took six feet, not twelve, so don't park in the bike lane. But look. Look there."

"My tree."

"Your tree. It's right on the curb. Sorry. We had to move part of the rock garden, but just a little. And you have a One Way sign in your yard. And a 5 MPH sign." She shrugged. "I did the best I could."

"How did you do this? I don't know how to thank you, how to even begin."

"We'll think of something. As to how, well, I have a friend whose job is to look for ways to save the city money. Do you know how much it would've cost to flatten that hill? We saved thousands. Tens of thousands. Thousands more than any favors Mr. Minter could call in."

"Sharp," I told her. "And insightful."

"Don't forget tenacious."

"I won't. How many people did you have to piss off?"

"I let my boss take credit for the cost savings. She's been there so long that people don't mess with her. She'll get a bonus for saving the city money. You get this."

"And Sarah? What does she get?"

"I'd like to come up here once in a while to see the house, if you'll let me."

"It's pretty in the fall when all the leaves are changing."

"I'd like to see them."

"And in the winter, the city becomes so quiet when it snows. It's magical."

"Yes, that too."

"And this time of year, well, you've already seen what that looks like."

"Just once. I want more. Will you show it to me again and tell me more stories about the people who lived here?"

"I'll introduce you to them. They're an interesting bunch."

I pulled into the driveway past the big pine. Sunlight sparkled where Alisha and Brenda danced with the butterflies in the warm afternoon light.

Steven Anderson

Steven Anderson is the author of the *Reunification* series of science fiction adventure-romances and other speculative tales. A passionate fan of science fiction since age six, Steve began creating his own worlds once he was old enough to pick up a crayon. He put his creative skills to work as an aerospace IT professional for many years before writing full time. Steve lives in Colorado Springs with his wife and an aging collection of parts that's sometimes a car. He can often be found somewhere in the Rockies exploring local history and scenic wonders.

Dream Harvest

T.R. Kerby

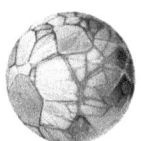

The heels of my sensible shoes *click, clack* on the scuffed tile of the vacant hallway. Grey walls, devoid of decoration, stretch into a pinpoint distance. Grey lockers line the tunnel. The paint matches the fabric of my suit. A size too large for my thin frame, but issued to me by the Corporation.

A figure steps from behind a steel door and comes to meet me. His suit is the same color and cut as mine. I shift the box I'm carrying to one arm in order to shake the bony hand he thrusts toward me. "John Smith. I'm the principal here. Welcome, Miss Jones."

"Thank you."

"Right this way."

I follow him through a solid, windowless door into a classroom. The teacher dips his head to me and scurries out. The principal closes the door behind them.

A chalkboard with simple words covers the front wall. A row of closet doors and a cabinet claim two more. On the final side, high windows let in natural light and frame a bank of blinding white clouds as they scud across an azure sky. I pull my attention from them to the curious faces that stare up at me from behind miniature desks.

The children wait patiently. There is no clamor or whispers. They are attentive and perfectly behaved. I smile to mask my own misgivings. A few smile back.

I place the box on the desk. Inside, an assortment of brilliantly colored hats contrasts sharply with the dull Corporate greys that mark everything else. I lift one above the lip of the plastic container and hold it up for the children to see. I spin the toy helicopter blade that sits on top. The children giggle.

"You guys want to play a game?" I ask.

Heads bob with excitement and wonder.

"Line up and come pick a hat."

They scramble into orderly lines that are too perfect and too practiced for mere six-year-olds. They wait, evenly spaced, for permission to approach. When I step aside, they advance, one at a time, and choose a hat from the box.

There are more colors than they normally see in any given day: blues, reds, greens, yellows, a couple orange, purple, one pink. They study the array with wide eyes and cautiously select one to carry back to their desks with the reverence of a sacred object.

When all the children have made their choice, I sit on the corner of the teacher's desk and instruct them to put them on. They grin wildly and break into open laughter as they stick them on their heads and regard one another. Their joy is contagious and I catch myself joining in as I plunk a bright purple cap atop my own head and spin the blade.

"Now we're going to start the game," I tell them. "We'll go around the room and I'll ask you each a question. There is no right or wrong answer. Just be honest."

They become serious now. This is school. Questions. A test, perhaps.

I tap the screen of my handheld computer and bring up the program. It shows me a layout of the room from above, each child seated at their desk, and the corresponding signal from the colorful cap they wear.

When it is fully booted up and ready, I lift my gaze to the child directly in front of me. He watches me with intense hazel eyes, and I smile to set him at ease. The program indicates his name is Benjamin.

"Benjamin, what do you want to be when you grow up?"

He seems surprised by the question and his expression turns thoughtful. My computer display shows a revolving disk over his position in the room. The helicopter blades on his yellow cap rotate slowly. "A scientist," he says. "I like space."

"Space is fascinating." I touch my index finger to the revolving disk above Benjamin's image on my screen.

He flinches and blinks several times. When his features relax, his eyes are not as intense.

"What kind of scientist?" I ask.

"I will design interstellar ships for the transport of Corporate goods."

"What an excellent idea!"

I shift my attention to the child behind Benjamin. My program tells me her name is Daina. "What do you want to be when you grow up?"

She scratches at the felt cap where it touches her forehead. "I like dressing up."

"A fashion designer maybe?"

"Yes! A dahsigner!"

I don't correct her minor mispronunciation. It doesn't matter. I touch the revolving disk. Daina twitches and goes still.

"What kind of fashion?" I ask.

"I will make Corporation issue clothing."

"That's a grand plan!"

When I have pushed the button on the final child, I collect the brilliantly colored caps and return them to the box. I don't say goodbye to the children when I leave. They won't remember that I was there.

Back at my workstation, I line up the pre-cooled glass jars bearing the Corporate logo. Dreams are fragile and have a limited shelf life if not properly stored in a climate-controlled environment. The first cap I fish from the plastic box is the bright yellow one. I peel back the felt covering and the harvested Dream swirls inside the nanoplastic container like an oil slick on water. Iridescent blues, purples, and silver sway under their own power. I pop the latches on the container and lift off the lid.

The Dream has a slight odor, like almonds heated over a fire. They all smell and look slightly different. With the sample spatula, I scrape the Dream into one of the containment jars. After I cap the jar, I hold it up to the vacuum tube and it is sucked from my hand. Where they go from here is not revealed to me. My computer terminal pings, indicating the Dream has been processed and properly catalogued.

Dreams sell for unimaginable sums on the Black Market. No one could possibly buy one on Corporation salary. The temptation to steal them is high, but the likelihood of getting away with it is minuscule. I've never entertained the thought. Disappearing into the bowels of the Corporation and never being heard from again isn't something I've any desire to experience. The last containment jar speeds away into the ether.

What Dream did I once possess that led to my appointment as a Dream Harvester? Sometimes I sense it at the edge of my mind, scratching, some vestige of it left behind like an infected sliver. If I focus too hard, it vanishes.

Like everyone else, I take the grey Corporate bus home. It growls through canyons of featureless concrete inhabited by equally featureless people. We blend into a single, dingy organism called the

Corporation, whose only purpose is to churn out products for profit. Individuality is detrimental to the whole and is discouraged by threats and beatings or imprisonment. If one persists in their delusions, they vanish. No one asks where they go. It's safer to conform and live a pretense of a life rather than have even that meager gift taken from you.

The bus stops at a light and waits as a grey stream of humanity flows across its path. A shining black car crosses the intersection, and the people stop to stare, their heads turning as one to watch the glimmering behemoth glide past. Ownership of private transportation is forbidden, except to the top executives. The light changes, but no one moves until the car is out of sight, then they trudge on their way and the bus lurches forward.

Guards patrol the streets, bristling with weapons. What did they once dream? Cameras mounted on poles swivel their cyclopean eyes to take in every detail. Who operates them? I've heard most are dummies, placed to keep us in line, but not actually functional. Rumors are dangerous. People who spread them, or believe them, disappear in the night.

The bus stops several blocks from my place and I walk. There are fewer cameras here and no guards. A wooded creek flows behind the houses. Where does it go, and where does it start? If I traced its course to the headwaters, where would I be?

I often sit beside its burbling waters and contemplate my cage. There seems to be no key to unlock the bars that imprison me as a facilitator of the Corporation's crimes. I see no way off this chessboard that includes a happy ending.

Sometimes, when I sit by the water, I search for the Dream, but I've never found it. Who bought my Dream, and what did they do with it? If my Dream teases at the periphery of my mind, does everyone else's do the same? Could we reclaim them somehow? What would happen if we did?

The summer sun splashes orange and red streaks across the darkening sky. Tomorrow will be another visit to a Corporate-run school. More Dreams collected. More children released from the burden of striving, the heartache of failure. Harvesting is a noble profession.

So they tell me.

My key turns in the lock and I push open the door to the apartment. Grey carpet insulates the floors and grey drapes block out the glaring streetlights. The Corporate chosen nanny crosses my living room, her sweater draped over her arm. "Have a good evening," she says as she leaves.

"Mommy!" My six-year-old daughter, Kala, races into the room and flings herself into my embrace. I squeeze her close and inhale the scent of child. "Can we play with the colors now?"

I decided years ago that they had not bugged my home. If they had, they'd have arrested me long before this. "Of course, baby." In my room, I shift aside the nightstand, lift the loose board, and retrieve the contraband Crayons from under the rubber-banded rolls of paper that constitute my daughter's art collection, never to be displayed on any refrigerator. She takes the Crayons, a gift from her Corporation-delegated father, a lower-level executive like myself, and races from the room.

Her father slipped them to me on the day we learned I was pregnant and would not see one another again. He didn't tell me where he'd gotten them, and I didn't ask. Where is that man now? Sometimes I miss his sad eyes and gentle nature, despite never knowing his name. The risk he took to provide our child with something vibrant and bright spoke of his character. In another world, we might have married, laughed together, and planned birthday parties and vacations, but that is not this world.

I shower and change into a sweatshirt and jeans before joining the daughter he was never allowed to meet.

She sits cross-legged on the floor in front of the coffee table. The scattered box of Crayons presents a wild spatter of color. Green, red, and yellow streak across a sheet of cheap paper. An amoeba-shaped sun dwarfs a crooked building. Slashes of short green grass. Two stick figures dressed in purple, holding hands. One tall. One small.

"See my drawing?" Kala asks.

"It's wonderful."

"It's us."

"I thought so."

"Want to draw with me?"

"Sure."

I sit at the low table and she hands me a fresh piece of paper. The empty white space twists my gut and a lump forms in my throat. She thrusts several Crayons in my direction. "Here, Mommy." She flings color onto the intimidating whiteness with abandon, making wide strokes with utter confidence and freedom. Glee lights her features as she bites her lip and tips her head to consider her artwork. A strand of brown hair falls into her eyes and she brushes it aside.

She is the most beautiful thing I've ever seen.

I swallow the lump. "Kala, what do you want to be when you grow up?"

35

She glances up with earth-rich eyes, and the smile that splits her face shatters my heart. "An artist." She says it with the certainty of a Corporate associate. "What do *you* want to be?"

"I'm already grown up."

She shrugs her tiny shoulders. "So."

So, indeed.

I want to be brave. I want to be strong. I want to be fearless. I am none of these things.

But I *am* a mother.

And tomorrow I will visit her first-grade class.

It is a cruel test of my loyalty. The Corporation will be watching me. They will suspect. The flare of the streetlights seeps under the dismal curtains. They are probably already watching.

Or perhaps their power has made them complacent. I've been an exemplary employee. Never been ill or late. Never botched a Harvest.

Where would we run? I've heard rumors, of course. That somewhere exists, far in the wilderness, where the Corporation doesn't bother to go. Where people live like they once did. Where children keep their Dreams.

To the north, the rumors say. The rumors might be only that. Or they might be false leads to lure the less faithful and the outright rebellious. A trap.

My daughter chooses a red crayon and looks up at me. "This is my favorite one."

I focus on the rounded crimson tip and the room tilts. Heat swims up my legs, weaves through my ribs, flushes my cheeks. The crayon blurs. Suddenly, it is there.

The Dream.

Rising like a phoenix from ashes, it rushes through me, surging, overwhelming and undeniable. It slams the breath from me.

"Are you okay, Mommy?"

I grasp the edge of the table and nod.

The Dream.

Free will. Free choice. Freedom for my child. I am a Mother.

"Want to go on a trip?"

"Where?"

"I don't know exactly. An adventure. We'll have to walk. It'll be very hard, but it'll be worth it." *If we make it…*

"Can I take my Crayons?"

I engulf her hands in mine. "Absolutely."

T.R. Kerby

T.R. Kerby has led a life of thrilling adventure with interesting people in exotic places… so what if most of it was in her imagination?

Her weaknesses include chocolate and rescuing lost souls, mostly animals, but sometimes people. She currently lives in the Rocky Mountains with some of her rescues including her husband, two dogs, and a herd of horses.

She has written or co-written eight novels and her short stories have been selected for several anthologies including *Fantastic Realms* and *Fresh Starts: Tales from the Pikes Peak Writers.*

You can find her at www.trkerby.com and on Amazon at www.amazon.com/T-R-Kerby/e/B07JDZGNQ3.

Dream Crush

Cepa Onion

Me and my BFF Yasmin were singing our arses off, when Obsolete
Membrane pulled us out of the audience and onto his light-splashed
stage. Well, his security dude did.

Now we're singing those same arses off *with* OM, as we OMers
call him. He's shorter than I imagined. But that doesn't matter, because
I'm practically wetting myself. As his real, live, honeyed voice swirls
around me, OM's bourbon-sweet breath is hot next to my face, my
actual face: "Girl let me take you/Girl let me make you/Girl let me
wake you/Up."

Oh, I'm woke, all right. So freakin' woke. How's this not a
dream?

I reach over to hug my BFF—just to share the moment, to make
it forever ours. But the girl dancing beside me isn't Yasmin. She looks
like my friend, with her silky, black hair and tall, dark body. Same pink
OM Tour T-shirt, too.

But it's not her.

I whip my head toward the crowd to find Yasmin. It's way too
dark. A million cell phones blip the blackness—aimed at me and this
Yasmin-lookalike and rock god OM.

He throws an arm around me and fake-Yasmin. The audience
roars so loud my bones vibrate. OM's body heat smells like French
fries. Sexy, deep-fried fries.

And Yasmin's missing it. My euphoria fizzles. I'm up here
without Yasmin. This is unfair—like I'm cheating on her. But I could
swear OM's guard had pulled us both on stage.

OM's song slams to a close. He gives us a final squeeze before dismissing us to the security dude. Although OM applauds us, his face looks kinda smirky and fake. Like I just showed up to deliver pizza and now he wants me gone. Ouch. But maybe I'm being too sensitive.

Where the hell is Yasmin?

The guard leads us off-stage. Fake-Yasmin walks backwards, her eyes pinned on OM. But I'm looking for the real Yasmin. I still don't see her. Did she freak? Is she mad? Maybe off somewhere crying because I got pulled up and she didn't?

I know that's where I'd be.

I squeeze through the crowd, back toward my seat. People paw me like I'm famous. Like OM's greatness has rubbed off and they want it, too. Oh, this would be so much better if it were me and Yasmin.

We've followed OM since we were both thirteen—for three years. Fueled by hot McDonald's fries, we fan-girled at him on Insta over his birthday selfies, his beautiful DUI mugshot, and even his wickedly tragic attempt to grow a beard.

He never replied. But we knew he saw our posts. He always reads stuff from his fans. Like once a bunch of us told OM to update his photo and he did—almost the next second.

Hey, maybe Yasmin got invited to a private backstage blowout and is waiting for me!

I text her. *Where R U?*

In the lobby, she responds. *Next to G6 exit.*

OM starts his beautiful ballad, *"Must."*

RU sick? I ask.

No.

Mad?

No.

Get back in here, I text. *UR missing MUST!*

See you after, she replies.

WTF? Yasmin loves *"Must."* It's like OM wrote it just for her. That song literally saved her after all that horrible stuff with her stepbrother. I shudder at the memory.

OM's sweet ripe voice fills the air. "Victims of heartbreak/ Casualties of lust/Staring at the future/But only seeing dust/Still we must, we must, we must/Find a way we can trust."

For the first time, the song fails to touch me. *I have to see Yasmin.*

I push from my overpriced seat and jog through screams and darkness to exit G6. Yasmin said she wasn't upset, but something must've derailed her. She probably got jealous that I was chosen—even though I swear we both were. Or did the security guard get all pervy

40

and touch her? Yasmin's therapist said crap like that could "trigger" her. I swear if he ruined her dream-come-true, I'll come back here with a machete.

Outside the exit door, I see Yasmin, crouched on the dirty floor under the bland white lobby lights. She looks down as her thumbs dance across her phone.

"Hey," I say gently kicking her. She stands and smiles at me, so welcoming it hurts.

"I'm sorry," I blurt. "I thought he pulled you up, too."

"He did," she says more to the floor.

"What happened?" I curl my fist into a ball, ready to pound the guard's dream-crushing face.

"I didn't want to go," she says.

I grit my teeth. "What did that guard do to you?"

"Chill, okay? Nothing. I just changed my mind."

"But OM is, like. He's our *everything*, right?"

She doesn't answer.

"And oh my God, his sweat totally smells like French-fries."

"Cool." Yasmin smiles, but her umber eyes tell a different story. She looks like someone who almost jumped off a cliff and pulled back at the last second.

OM's muffled voice presses against the walls. I recognize the song as "Turning my Dream Wheel Again." It's Yasmin's second favorite song. And she's missing it. Confusion riles me more. I reach for her arm.

Yasmin yanks it away. She shakes her head. I notice her lip's quivering.

I'm so hit by Yasmin's sadness that I can barely hear the music.

"Hey," I say, extra soft. "What's wrong? Why don't you want to meet OM?"

"Because I can't—" She breaks off. Is she going to cry?

"Why not?" I whisper.

Yasmin gazes at me with tear-filled eyes. "Because, it's the *dream* that holds my heart together. I don't want to lose it."

OM's smirky dismissal of me off-stage and his fake applause hits me like a thunderbolt. The thunderbolt that my insightful BFF Yasmin wisely avoided.

"Hey," I say putting my arm around Yasmin, pulling her close. "Why don't we get out of here; go get some *real* fries."

Cepa Onion

Way back when shoulder-pads were in style, Susan Schooleman (pen name Cepa Onion) wrote for Roseanne Barr, was a member of the Denver Center Theatre's Playwrights Group, was published by Self magazine and Samuel French. She then chucked it all for adventures in parenthood. Three grown kids and a retired math teacher husband later, she has begun inching her way back into the business. Her short stories have been included in two Rocky Mountain Fiction Writers (RMFW) anthologies. She was also a winner in the 2019 RMFW Gold Contest.

A Boy Named Ryan

Matthew Heneghan

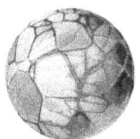

Friendship's a funny thing, isn't it? The older we get the more we see people come and go from our lives. Some people enter right when we need them to. Some depart far too soon, but they all leave us with something. And that's the *something* I want to talk to you about. My name is Matthew. You don't know me, and perhaps at the end of this you won't know me all that well, but you'll definitely come to know of a boy named Ryan. If I do my job right, when that final word is read, you'll pause for a moment, and think back to one of your own childhood friends. When you do, my wish is that you do so with a smile on your face.

Childhood was an interesting time for me. Stable and secure it was not. By the time the 90's had come around, I had seen my family fracture and fragment into warring shards. My father was removed from our home when I was just nine. He was not a good man. The only thing he ever gave me was a scar that still rests on my back: the braille of abuse. An unintentional lesson bestowed to me from this man came in the form of knowledge. Knowledge of what kind of man I never want to be. I'm pleased to say that it's a lesson learned. I watched as my mother was stricken with disease, and moved from one province to the next, only to turn around and come back again. And all of this before a full calendar year had completed itself. To say that I dreamed for something more constant and reliable would be a drastic misrepresentation of my younger days.

I often found reprieve in the form of escapist entertainment, or staring out toward the endless horizon, daydreaming for hours. My activities would range from anything such as reading a good story, grazing the tapestry of comic book pages, dreaming of one day becoming a hero myself, through to watching a good action flick that had been truncated for cable TV. They would even dub over the *bad* words, which I found to be rather amusing. *"You son of a ditch! I'm gonna muck you up!"*

As the fashion trend of baggy jeans and oversized t-shirts took hold, so too did another cultural phenomenon, fresh from Japan. Boys my age were transfixed to their convex television screens, feverishly digesting the visual splendor that was the technicolour ass-kickery of *the Mighty Morphin Power Rangers!*

Something about that cheesy, exaggerated, low-budget North American adaptation was mesmerizing. From the moment I laid eyes on those bright spandex uniforms, I was a fan. Jason, Zack, Billy, Kimberly and Trini; they all captivated my attention on post-school afternoons. Hell, my mom would even record them for me so that I never missed an episode.

I always found myself empathizing and connecting with Billy, the Blue Ranger. He was portrayed as the sincere, slightly awkward nerd of the group who didn't fit in. But he was also the guy that would do anything for anyone. He even had glasses like me. This made it even easier to transpose my likeness atop of his, while sucking back a bowl of Alphagetti's.

The other day I was sitting outside in our backyard, feeling the heat of the sun as it baked the hillsides and mountaintops. While the warmth saturated my skin, memories began to spill forward into consciousness. Things I hadn't thought about in a very long time. You see, summer and its concatenation with heat are historically trying times for me to navigate. Many of my life's painful moments take place beneath a cascading sun. As such, I have developed a, shall we say, misguided resentment toward that fiery orb that menacingly looms above us.

I've spent a lot of time beneath the watchful sun. Having been a medic in the army and a civilian paramedic, the tasks of those trades often dictate that I be outside. A lot of bodies have been picked up while the sun oversees the nightmarish landscape. My time spent in those careers along with my troubled childhood saw me develop an unhealthy relationship with the bottle. It was booze and bad decisions for many years. But, in recent times, and with the reformation that comes from sobriety and recovery, I have been carving out new memories beneath the sun, and choosing to reminisce on the fonder times of my early life — a time where I was a bit more of a dreamer.

This can be a difficult task at times, but a worthy undertaking nonetheless.

I started to ruminate fondly of another sunny day some years ago, while resting comfortably in my lawn chair — a day much like the one I was sitting in now. I was younger then, and much less beleaguered by the sun, but I still didn't care for the heat. My mother was home, sick. She was battling through another round of cancer treatments, and thus our avaricious toilet beckoned to her every forty-five minutes or so. Growing weary of hearing her gastrointestinal struggles push in through the walls, I fled to the outside. I had a small backpack with me. It was filled with plastic facsimiles of the Red, Blue, Black, Pink and Yellow *Power Rangers*.

I didn't venture outside with my toys too often for fear that I would be seen as a loser (or worse, a geek) should someone witness me waging an all-out battle of good versus evil with my miniature Rangers. But when given the choice of having to listen to my poor mum heave her way through another afternoon, or risk being spotted outside, I took my chances – I could handle being mocked. It wouldn't be a first. I hated hearing my mum struggle. My ears still remember those horrid groans, right through to this day.

That afternoon, something unusual transpired. I heard a voice climb into my ears — a voice of someone that was around my age (nine, maybe ten). I didn't see anyone at first, but the voice came again.

"Hey … you like the Power Rangers?"

"Uh… Yeah. Who's there? Where are you?" Immediately after uttering my befuddled inquiry, a figure emerged, crashing in through some hedges of a nearby fence.

"Hey. I'm Ryan. I like the red one!" The kid said through a smile that required a passport to traverse.

"Oh, yeah … he's pretty cool. His name's—"

"Jason. Yeah. I know. He's awesome." He said before I could finish. "What's your name?"

"I'm … I'm, Matthew."

"Cool! Can I play?" He continued, still smiling as though he was going to sell me something. But he never did. Sell me something, I mean. He just sat down and started playing alongside me. Unabashed and unfazed by my presence, he just mimicked kicking and punching sounds through pursed lips, just as I had been doing prior to his appearance. He seemingly cared little for who was or was not around. He was just living his best action-packed life. I was somewhat envious of his freedom. Geek and loser were words that did not exist within his colloquial repertoire.

As he stated, his name was Ryan, and we became great friends over the course of that summer of '94. He would come over to my place and we would watch Power Rangers together. We even verbalized our dreams about someday marrying Kimberly, the Pink Ranger. The logistics of how that would work didn't enter the arena of conversation at that age; we just daydreamed the shared thought of it while ingesting the twenty-five minutes of non-stop action.

We would play outside until the streetlamps came on. And even after that, we'd have to get yelled at to head inside. I was always the Blue Ranger, and he was the Red one. Well, until the Green one came along! Something about the new Green Ranger captivated Ryan's dreamful imagination. We fought imaginary evildoers day and night. Sleepovers were filled with zealous conversations about episodes that we would fabricate and wish upon. Ryan helped assuage the otherwise piteous summer days that year. And when the fall came and school was about to start back up, I faced a new form of trepidation.

There I was, the night before the first day of school. Ryan and I had hung out all day for as long as we could amidst the waning sun, and had even agreed to walk to school together the following morning. And somewhere within that agreement, I blurted out how cool it would be to dress as the civilian versions of our favourite power heroes. Meaning that I would not only wear something blue, but I would adorn my belt with a buckle that boasted a craggy plastic face of a triceratops. This was the Blue Ranger's source of power. I was fortunate enough to procure a replica version of that buckle while at the mall with my mum one summer day. She had said I could have a toy for how good I had been. And without hesitation, when I saw that imitation Morpher, I just had to have it! And on the last day of summer, for whatever reason, I had to go and make the stupid suggestion that he and I dress up like our TV superheroes, and wander the halls of a brand-new school year. *Nothing bad could possibly happen… Right?*

I wanted so badly to call Ryan and take back the suggestion, but it was too late. I had already been told to "get to bed." There was no way of letting him know that I was having second thoughts. That night, I tossed and turned with fright. I worried that come morning, the kid I had spent the summer with would all of a sudden be *too cool* for me and in turn, instantly point and laugh at my selected attire. And that stupid, plastic Morpher was already attached to my belt. Much like a regular buckle, it merely snapped into place. But because it was a kid's toy and not truly meant as a fashion statement, getting it snapped into place was a real bother. I suffered through a lot of grunting and lamenting to finally have it situated correctly. I even had to elicit my older brother's help to secure it, so there was no way for me to remove it at that point.

I peered through the darkened ambiance of my room, glaring at my chosen wardrobe for the morning. With each passing minute, each stitch, every wrinkle and imperfection began to look more and more unsightly, and dare I say … geeky. I was screwed!

I barely slept a wink that night. The sheer volume of my worries woke the birds that morning. From out my window, I could see a crescent glow emerging from behind the mountain. Another sunny day, too hot to wear a sweater, or something else baggy enough to conceal my prominent belt face. I didn't want to risk not wearing it for fear that perhaps Ryan was going to follow through on his part. I felt as if I were to show up outside in regular clothes and he was adhering to his part, he'd be mad at me. I also worried that I was going to be the only one dumb enough to have taken what I said last evening seriously. I feared that he would laugh his butt off, when catching sight of me, and voila, I become the laughing stock of grade five. Scenarios such as this one played out mercilessly in my mind. It seemed like inevitability over that of possibility.

In the midst of this rumination, I felt myself smile, because I knew what came next …

I went outside, dressed in a vertical lined button down, sleeves rolled a quarter of the way. It was tucked into my khakis, and there on display was my triumphant, limited edition *Mighty Morphin Power Rangers* Morphing buckle. Its plastic edges gleamed in the ascending sunlight. I feared myself visible to soaring planes overhead.

I shuffled nervously in place for several minutes, waiting for Ryan. As I was walking in place, I heard his voice echo from across the playground that rested near my house. An instant wave of relief bordering on excitement filled my urchin veins. Ryan had followed through. *Not sure why I ever doubted him.* He neared me, once again boasting that immeasurable smile. It was infectious. And soon, the corners of my lips began to curl upwards as well.

I walked to school and survived that first day, just as I had survived that summer, all because of a kid named Ryan. He gifted me something so much more than just friendship. He never knew it, but that summer, he saved me from a torrent of tears. He made me feel like a regular kid. A sensation that was all too foreign to me while growing up. He simply wandered up to me on that bright summer day, sat down and started playing alongside me. He didn't care that my father was an abusive monster now absent from my life. He didn't judge me when my lips were just a bit too heavy to force a smile on the days my mum was really bad. All summer he was just there, right beside me. Like a battle buddy. A true Power Ranger.

Life, of course took us in different directions. We grew older and drifted away from one another. Soon we just exchanged cordial head nods in the hallways of high school. And after that, well, for many years I never heard from Ryan, and nor he from me. Life had placed bustle and distance between us lads.

I recently moved back to my humble slice of the Canadian pie, however. And you know what …? Ryan lives less than two hours away! He even has a YouTube channel. We've reconnected and I am happy to report, that he still has that coast-to-coast smile. And it remains as infectious as it did all those years ago. We've gone golfing together, appeared in one another's YouTube clips, he even looked after our dog when my girlfriend, Sheena, her kids and I were evacuated from our home due to the wildfire this past summer. Luck smiled upon us, and our home was unscathed by that marigold menace of summer. I talk to Ryan almost every day. His happiness still saves me. What a guy …

And that's how I survived a hot Canadian summer in the 90's—by meeting a kid named Ryan, dreaming of better days and pretending to be the hero of my own story. The reason I am smiling here, now, on a hot afternoon all these years later, is because of a man named Ryan, whom I am proud to call friend, brother, and of course, the Green Ranger!

Matthew Heneghan

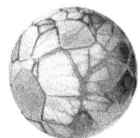

Born in the U.K., Matthew Heneghan immigrated to Canada at age five. He would grow up among the beautiful expanse of the Rocky Mountains. After high-school, Matthew would go on to join the Canadian Armed Forces and serve as a medic for a period of 6 years. Upon his honourable release, Matthew's desire to serve would not end with military service — he became a civilian paramedic, and worked in that role until 2017. Matthew went on to write two memoirs of his experiences in uniform and out.

He currently resides resplendently in Western Canada with his beautiful girlfriend and her two wonderful daughters.

Augmented Dreams

Barbara Preslier

I'm a millennial woman and I'm proud of it. I probably shouldn't have survived past my teens, but that's another story. My mother died a few years ago, and I miss her every day. When I walk into the kitchen of the house we shared, I can still hear the fried chicken sizzling and smell the cornbread baking. I've tried to reproduce those recipes, but I end up with rubbery white meat and crumbly bread. When the quiet rooms overwhelm me, I indulge in my guilty pleasure.

I turned thirty-five on my last birthday and haven't accomplished anything close to my sensational, superhuman mom. I've never married, although I did suffer a miscarriage in the first trimester of my only pregnancy fifteen years ago. Since high school, I've worked a demanding forty-hour plus week for a local grocery store. By the time my mother was this age, she'd had five rambunctious kids, two back-breaking jobs, and three ravenous husbands. That's not the life for me.

I don't see my two sisters since they live in California and I'm in Colorado. My brother lives just south of me near Pueblo, but he's in an alternative residential facility. He was born with an intellectual disability, suffers frequent seizures, and is a ward of the state of Colorado. I go see him now and then, but he barely remembers me. I had another brother, but he died as a child. With a lack of family and no desire to have one of my own, I've succeeded in finding physical and mental release from daily boredom.

My two-bedroom prefab house sits on a small lot north of Pueblo, thirty-five miles south of Colorado Springs. From my living room window, I can see the Wet Mountains—"Wet" for the abundant snow they receive each winter. When I was young, my mother would drive to Lake Isabel and let me splash in the reservoir's cold waters. She had found a secluded spot where we could have a picnic undisturbed by the roaring boat engines and barely visible fishing lines. In my teenage years, the lake gained popularity, the solitude we treasured disappeared, and our day trips ended as well. My mother and I never traveled together again, and I had no outlet for my anxieties and apprehensions.

For many years, we were one of only a handful of families in a fifty-mile radius. Now, the countryside is peppered with barns and mansions. My neighbors greet me amicably enough, but we're not friends. My coworkers keep to themselves, preferring to have lunch with contented people who clearly enjoy life, filling the air with laughter and giggling. Even at church, after we all pray together, they play together, ignoring me. I know we are all equal in the eyes of God, but I guess not in the eyes of the church. As long as I put my weekly money in, they tolerate me. Maybe it's my five-foot-eleven frame (courtesy of my birth father), my green-dyed wild hair, or my surly attitude. Whatever it is, I spend most of my time alone.

Actually, I spend my free time in my fantasy world. My nephew first introduced me to augmented reality. On a visit to California, my sister's son handed me a pair of large goggles. "Auntie Donna, you gotta put these on. It'll take you for a cool trip."

He sent me on a sailboat off the coast of California. At first, I could see colorful fish under the surface of the calm, blue water. The setting sun created a pink and orange sky, dotted with gray wispy clouds. The silhouette of other sailboats in the harbor resembled an oil painting I had seen at an art show. As I admired the restful scene, whales and dolphins entered my peripheral view. I watched the whales breach the surface and smash down with a whacking splash. They swam next to the boat and continued their leaps. The bow lurched under the three to four-foot waves. I snatched off the goggles as my stomach heaved, and I barely missed hurling my dinner on the carpet.

I was hooked. The early programs allowed me to enjoy what the developers envisioned. Years later, the computer geeks advanced the technology to the goggles to include the processor, sensor, and input elements. The goggles are inexpensive compared to the cost of the tailor-made adventures. There are many who fear the hosts can manipulate users through these, but my narcissism via fantasy dominates.

Now, for a large sum of money, I can special order scenarios with my handpicked avatar as the star. I can be a voluptuous woman with many admirers at an oceanside resort, or a commercial pilot with an assigned route of Paris to Rome. I visit the Eiffel Tower and the Colosseum weekly, enjoying crepes and pasta feasts. My favorite role is as a volunteer who travels to Central America to help ailing children. In all of these adventures, I'm an intelligent, handsome, powerful, female.

I purchased three sagas, which is all I can afford. Actually, I had to sell a set of diamond earrings, a pearl necklace, and a few shares of my Apple stock to cover the expense. The hosting site and I worked for several months to create my illusions. They update the programs after each visit for me to enjoy a modified experience each time. I alternate between the three, depending on my mood. Tonight I'm feeling frisky, so I'll be heading to a private club in Miami Beach.

I close my eyes and pull the lever of my gray fabric La-Z-Boy recliner valued at about a thousand bucks new, but purchased at Goodwill for thirty-five. After finishing a glass of Pinot Noir, I settle back, don my augmented reality goggles, and press number one on the controller.

A soft female voice speaks. "Open your eyes, Jenny."

I obey, but that's the last time I plan to do it for a while.

I'm lying on a soft cushion on a zero gravity chair located on an endless expanse of caramel sand, dotted with palm trees and bright umbrellas. I can see small white caps smashing against the beach, tossing in seaweed and foam. The air is salty with a hint of sulfur. The hot sun penetrates through a few wispy clouds and settles on my body. I groan in pleasure, and then turn my face toward the interloper.

The owner of the soft voice hands me a sugar-rimmed glass. "Your margarita, dear." She's a younger woman dressed in a see-through bathing suit cover secured by a gold sash and matching sandals. Her long blond hair, large blue eyes, and wide smile demonstrate her adoration—for me, of course. She hovers above my head, her body in silhouette from the sun.   "Hello, Katarina. I've missed you," I say, as I offer my free hand, decorated with a henna flower. She bends down, and I put my lips on hers. She returns my affection with unreserved passion. After a minute, I pull away.

"That's enough for now, my sweet. I only have a few more hours of daylight to work on my tan." I swirl my finger from the sugar into the liquid, and lick it.

"Don't burn, please. Do you remember when didn't use sunscreen, had blisters on your back and arms, and missed the stone crab bash? I remember that night all too well. By the way, what are you going to wear to the party tonight? Can I get it ready for you?" Katarina straightens, again hindering the sun.

"No. I'm good. Now, if you don't mind, you need to get out of my *ray!*" I dismiss her with the flick of my wrist.

"Chow, mi amor." Katarina laughs as she backs away and disappears between two palm trees.

After I return to my room and shower, I study my tall, firm body in a full-length mirror. I brush out my long, brown hair, then pull it back with a multi-colored tie. The theme for tonight's party is tie-dye, so I don a short cotton dress spattered with blues, greens, pinks and yellows. I lace up my blue shoes, and knock on the adjacent room's door. When it swings open, I see Katarina in a rainbow-colored jump suit. The shades complement her many curves.

"Hi, beautiful, ready to party?" I pull her close to me. "All is fair tonight, right?"

"All is fair." She repeats, while staring into my eyes. "Happy hunting."

The food at the party is decadent. I nibble on lobster stuffed with crab meat, creamed spinach, and finish up with pecan pie. There are four more dessert tables, but I use restraint in order to keep my slim figure. While sipping my Moscow Mule and watching the dancing, a man in a green toga and mint green belt approaches.

"Hey, babe. I'm Marty. Wanna boogie?" He moves his hips around under the sheet.

"Um, I don't think so, but thanks." *Boogie?* I smirk as I head to a nearby balcony. I gaze out at the moon's reflection on the calm water. There's a warm breeze which causes a few strands of my hair to blow in my eyes. As I reach up to replace them, someone grabs my hand.

"Hello, beautiful." I turn to stare into dark, familiar eyes. Behind them stands a body builder figure wearing an open shirt, exposing well-worked pecs.

"Jonathan? I haven't seen you in ages. I kinda had written you off—or thought you did that yourself." I pull back my wrist and run my forefinger down his chest. "You're looking good." I met Jonathan the first time I visited the resort. We spent many nights immersed in drinking, dancing and fooling around. Whenever I returned, I searched for him, hoping to recreate the passion. I guess it wasn't in the script. Over time, I'd replaced him with others. Many others.

"And you look great, Jen. Let's dance." He leads my stimulated body to the floor. We're shaking to Bob Seger's *Old Time Rock and Roll* when the green-sheeted man comes between us. He wiggles in front of me.   "See? You boogie. You boogie real good." Greenie reaches for me.

Jonathan pulls the sheet over the man's head, and ties the mint green belt around it. The poor man spins away like a dizzy Kermit the Frog.

The music slowed and we held each other close, and I felt him become aroused.

He whispered in my ear. "Let's go back to my room. I have something I'd like to show you."

"I'm sure I'd like to see it." At that moment, however, my eyes set upon a beautiful woman standing at the bar, surrounded by three young, hulking men. I stop dancing, and kiss Jonathan lightly on the lips. "I can't. Not tonight. Sorry." I walk around him to the sexy rainbow figure. I put my arms around her.

"My Katarina," I whisper in her ear. "My love."

"Jenny, darling. Are you having a nice time? How's the hunting?" Katarina winks at one of the studmuffins.

"I've caught my prey, Katarina. If she's willing." My words are seductive.

Katarina's smile leaves no doubt. "As long as I'm not to be eaten."

"As you wish." I take her hand and lead her out of the party. We get to her room, and I follow her in. I pull down the strap of her gown, exposing the tan outline of a pale breast.

I hear a monotone female voice. "Your battery is low. Recharge."

"What?" I call out. "No. No. No. I'm not ready." I yank off the goggles. I'm staring at the buttermilk walls of my living room, decorated with photos of my mom and me. I spy the clock on the wall. It's midnight.

"Shoot. I guess I should go to sleep. I've got work in the morning. Adios, Katarina—until next time." I place the headset on the charger, return my wine glass to the kitchen, and retire.

After a fitful night's sleep, I arrive at work ten minutes early. My boss, Mr. Johnson, asks me to stay late for inventory. We all take turns at this unwanted chore, and I guess it's my turn. I agree, of course. I work in the meat department of a local grocery store. I've been at the store since I was eighteen. Apparently, this is my career choice. I spend my days carving roast beef, turkey, and ham. Sometimes, I roast chickens. I'm also adept at dishing vegetables and portions of pasta into small plastic containers. It's not a bad job. They pay me adequately, and many of the customers have known me for years.

After work, I stay late to evaluate the supplies on hand. After filling out the forms, I find Mr. Johnson in his office. He's a reserved fifty-year-old who moved to Colorado to live with his mother after his second divorce. I often overhear the younger female employees make up stories about how he's a serial killer or a child molester. I ignore them, but can never get the image out of my brain.

"Here you are, sir." I hand him the papers.

"Hey, Donut." His nickname for me isn't flattering, but I've never complained about it in the five years he's been the manager. It's obvious he has a set of beliefs about how women should exist in society. I'm sure I don't conform to that tenet. He takes the documents from me and sets them on his messy desk. "Have a seat."

I sit in a wobbly wooden chair about ten feet from his high-back tufted leather swivel one. His desk is strewn with papers, empty Styrofoam coffee cups, and comic books. I glance at the top one—*The Best of Archie Comics*. I'm not surprised at his reading choice.

"Donut, you do a great job here. I just want to tell you how much I appreciate your dedication and hard work."

"Thanks. It's nice of you to say, Mr. Johnson." My skin tightens as he stands and approaches me. He touches my shoulder. I wish I could grab his grubby hand and break his fingers.

"Call me Bob." He runs his thumb down to my elbow.

I jump up. "Mr. Johnson. Please, sir, this isn't right. I've gotta go. Please don't touch me again. It isn't right." I hate myself at this moment. I never know whether to stand up for myself, or stay quiet and stoic. I choose myself, and run out of his office, through the front door, and into my ten-year-old car. I slam my fists on the steering wheel. "Damn. Damn. Damn."

***

By the time I finish dinner and cleaning up, I've cooled off. This wasn't the first time; nor would it be the last. As usual, I consider reporting Mr. Johnson to corporate headquarters, but that would probably result in *me* losing my job, not him. I put it on the shelf with all the other indiscretions. I know at some point it will come tumbling down with a thunderous clap, but not tonight. No, tonight I will travel and enjoy the last drop of the Pinot Noir. I hook the goggles up to the charger cord so there is no risk of losing my fantasy due to a drained battery. I push number three and close my eyes.

"Hey, Miss Julia Smith. Are you awake? It's Nurse Maria. Dr. Matthews wants you in the infirmary. There's a little girl he wants you to meet."

I struggle with the sleeping bag I'm wrapped in. Finding the zipper, I pull it only to have it catch in my unkempt hair. After freeing my lavender ends, I wiggle out, throw on khaki slacks and a flowered shirt, and loafers. "Hang on. I'm coming" I call.

I grab a satchel containing my toiletries and peel back the tarp entrance.

My eyes spot an older woman dressed in white pants and scrub top. A red bandanna covers her hair. She's looking at her wristwatch.

"Hi, Nurse Maria. How are you this morning?" I put my hand out to shake hers, but quickly retract it remembering this is not the custom here.

The nurse lowers her gaze and whispers *"Estoy bien, senorita."*

"I'm fine" is the translation from Spanish, which is a primary language in this part of the world. I'm a volunteer, assisting Dr. William Matthews from North Carolina. When he treats a child, he or she lives in a special tent. I make sure they are emotionally nurtured and physically fed. Their families usually camp out nearby, and I spend part of my time teaching them how to grow local foods and clean their water. In my past visits, I have traveled to rural villages to teach in local schools or at community gatherings. Since I've recently graduated from college, and have no profession, traveling to Central America has become my temporary work. I'm no saint. I'm simply a young woman with bleached hair, green eyes, and a big heart.

Nurse Maria and I enter the infirmary and seek out Dr. Matthews. I spot him examining the ears of an infant. He smiles when he sees me. I turn to thank Nurse Maria for accompanying me, but she's gone.

"Julia, thanks for coming. I want you to meet Francis." He leads me through orderly rows of WWII military-style cots covered with white sheets. Small pale faces with large eyes peer out from under them. The eyes follow us to a corner cot, where Dr. Matthews unveils a sleeping child. She appears to be about three years old with a protruding stomach. She doesn't awaken.

"Is she okay? I know she's not pregnant, but why is her belly like a balloon? I've read that can be due to parasitic worms or starvation." I touch her burning face.

Dr. Matthews smiles. "She'll be fine now. She's actually seven. She has Kwashiorkor. It's a disease due to lack of protein. I'm not sure how her mental state will recover, but we've gotten to her in time to reverse the starvation. I want you to personally care for her. Make sure she has a high protein diet and swallows the food. A lot of these children are anorexic because of the disease, and they need extra help in overcoming the feeling of starvation. Can you handle it?"

"Absolutely," I say and add, "I'll camp out here for the next few days."

"Good. This takes the pressure off of me. I want Francis in the best of care. How are you doing? Do you need anything? I know it can be difficult for an outsider here."

Shaking my head, I answer. "Nope. I'm good. The staff is very kind to me."

"Yes, they appreciate the help. To them, you're not a rich American, but rather a God-sent savior."

"Hmm. Dr. Matthews, I don't know about that. I'm no hero." I keep my mind off where this whole scenario has come from. I'm relieved my secret is safe. I wonder how they all would feel if they knew their existence relied on the whim of a frustrated woman.

After using the nearby washroom, I pull a chair next to Francis's bed. I blend a protein powder in water and shake it until the yellow mixture clears. I'll feed her by hand until she's strong enough to feed herself. During down time, I pull out my harmonica and do R&B songs. My favorites are Usher and Khalid, although I think they would be mortified if they heard my off-key tone.

After three days of coaxing, I've convinced Francis to hold her brimming spoon. Most of her meals consist of beans and chicken. Her fever is now gone, and she's been smiling at me when I come in each morning.

"Hi, Miss Julia. Can I touch your purple hair? Can you play us a song? Please Miss Julia?" She has added her voice to the chorus of other children who make this their daily mantra.

"Of course." After visiting the other sick children, I reach Francis. I kneel and bend my head.

"It's so pretty." She then runs her hands through the wavy colorful ends. "You're a good lady. You help me. Now you sing for us?"

I choose "Twenty-Two," a song I made up which has become the children's favorite. I grab my harmonica and move from bed to bed playing and singing "I'm twenty-two and I don't work. I spend my days rehearsing the twerk. I shake it left, I shake it right. I twerk my way all through the night…" After I perform a pitiful booty dance, they giggle and clap. These kids adore me.

I bathe Francis, and tell her I'll be back at lunchtime. I exit the infirmary and walk to the river nearby. I like to dangle my feet in the water and lay my head back to watch the clouds. I see horses, airplanes, and whales. Life is so tranquil here. My mind wanders to the inevitable return to my mundane life.

I hear a clicking noise behind me. "Get her."

I look around to find a dozen soldiers aiming weapons at me.

Those darn game programmers. I only thought about returning—I hadn't requested it.

"No, please don't shoot." I hear myself screaming, and the world turns black.

I jump up from my recliner and yank the goggles off, ripping the charging cord from the wall socket.

Once my head clears and my heart rate returns to normal, I make a cup of Chamomile tea. I'm going to have to get an update on the program. I've heard the programs can get bugs, but this time I almost died. Or did I?

I stare out the window at the nearly full moon. I can see the outline of the Wet Mountains. I visualize my mom urging me to visit Lake Isabel. As I sip my tea, I'm struck by the realization that I want change. I turn to study my home. I'll purchase new furniture and replace the carpet. I'm going to learn how to cook fried chicken and corn bread. The first thing I'm going to do, though, is find another job. It's time.

I'm tired. I'm tired of being poor, I'm tired of being alone, and I'm tired of these egocentric adventures. I promise myself that I'll fix each of these, beginning with new programs—generic ones that include travel and education, and not with me as a fantasy character. Goodbye Mr. Johnson. Goodbye Katarina. Goodbye Dr. Matthews. I'm proud of my family. I'm proud of myself. I'm proud of being me.

Barbara Preslier

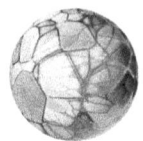

Barbara Preslier grew up frolicking on the beaches of Miami, Florida. She graduated with an English degree from Colgate University in NY, and continued on to the Goldman School of Dentistry in MA. She practiced general and forensic dentistry in South Florida for over thirty years. Since retiring and moving to Colorado with her husband, she has focused on her writing career. She is currently finishing her third novel. Her publications include short stories and professional journal articles. When not toiling at her desk, she enjoys pickleball, hiking and, of course, dreaming.

She Told You in a Dream
Jean Alfieri

We meandered around the Metaphysical Fair, taking in the vast expanse of tables and booths. I chuckled to myself at what my friend had gotten me into.

"Do you want to talk with a healer?" she asked enthusiastically. When I was slow to reply she pushed on, "Is it your mind, body or spirit that needs guidance?"

I shrugged and shook my head. The whole concept was foreign, and I struggled to take it seriously. What I really wanted was a big vanilla latte. So, while she stood in line to have her aura-photo taken, I fought my way through the haze of incense and located the coffee bar.

We'd agreed to meet up later, so I sipped and strolled down another aisle. Tarot card readers, numerologists, candles, lotions, and oils. There was a bit of everything. Another aisle over I saw a sign for "Animal Communicator." I felt something draw me in and paused.

The woman behind the table stood to greet me.

"Hello. I'm Sky," she said.

"Hi. Could you tell me about what you do?"

"People ask me to connect with their pets if they're worried about some health or behavioral problem. I check in with the animal to identify physical and sometimes emotional issues, and then provide that information to their humans."

I was fascinated.

"Does it work?" I blurted, then giggled nervously, hoping I hadn't offended her.

"Yes," she laughed with me, "People often find the feedback I receive and share with them to be valuable in the healing process."

"Then you only speak with animals that are alive? Not animals that have crossed over?"

"Oh, I connect with them too. Sometimes when there is a sudden loss, a pet's owner doesn't feel like they had a chance to say goodbye and they want that opportunity. It helps bring them closure."

Having recently lost a beloved family dog, I was intrigued.

"What do you need to make the connection?"

"A picture is helpful or the pet's name and a description."

"I'd love to sit with you."

Sky escorted me to her table and pulled out a chair.

"Who is it that you want to connect with?"

"Her name is … was…" I stammered. My husband and I still missed our sweet fur-girl so much, but I didn't realize how difficult it was going to be to talk about her.

I started again, "Her name was Chance. She died last month after a rather lengthy decline. She was fifteen years old and, at the end, had a multitude of health issues. She was a medium size Chow-mix with a thick tan coat, beautiful brown eyes, and jaws that could crack a butcher bone. Chance was my husband's dog when he and I met. She would always lay between him and the door and monitored everything and everybody who moved through our house. She was very observant and loyal to him."

I paused; afraid I'd been gushing.

Sky smiled, "Okay. Let me get centered. I'm going to reach out to Chance. Give me a minute."

Sky closed her eyes and bowed her head slightly. Her hands open on the table. I waited as she summoned Chance.

"I have her," said Sky, her eyes still closed, "What would you like to ask her?"

"She made special eye contact with me on the day she passed. My husband even noticed. I felt she was trying to tell me something. What was it?"

I thought I already knew, but that day had been such a whirlwind of emotion. Chance had been sick again, vomiting throughout the night. Josh and I laid in bed, hoping there wouldn't be another round. Praying that she could settle in and be comfortable.

"I don't want to put her down if it's not her time," he said, staring at the ceiling.

"I know," I said, also staring at the ceiling.

There was a long pause. In the dark, we listened to Chance's labored breathing.

Josh wiped his eyes and whispered, "I think it's time though."

"Me too."

I got up and showered the next morning, and dressed for work—tired and sad but going through the motions of a normal routine. When I got downstairs, Josh was sitting on the floor with Chance. As she leaned into him, he attempted to hand-feed her some of her favorite canned dog food. She didn't even sniff it, but he sat patiently, waiting for her appetite. He wanted so desperately for her to be okay.

Chance was suffering from another bout of vestibular disease. It made her dizzy and unable to focus. Her eyes darted back and forth, and she occasionally panted, clearly in distress.

Josh would be taking her to the vet in an hour. She had been such a fighter and soon she could rest. My head accepted this conclusion, but my heart still ached. I walked over and kissed the top of his head and gently petted hers. A single heavy tear escaped as I turned back to the kitchen. I willed myself not to cry. Sobbing would in no way help this situation, and this situation needed a lot of help.

I made my coffee and grabbed my keys, intending to exit like it was an ordinary day. I would usually say, "I love you," to Josh, and "Love you too," to Chance. When I said it this time, Chance's eyes stopped darting back and forth. She looked right at me. I held her gaze as something passed between us. Then she began to pant, and her eyes resumed their uncontrollable motion.

Josh followed me into the garage.

"What was that?" he asked.

"I think we just said goodbye," I offered, unsure myself.

We hugged.

Our dinner table that night was in part a meal, but mostly a memorial, as we mourned our loss. We told our favorite stories of Chance to lighten the mood. Josh talked about how she loved to play tug-o-war as a puppy and how at one year old, she started to win! I shared that I'd miss the way she greeted me with a nod whenever I came in the room, almost as if permitting me entry. Josh reminded me of when I found feathers in her water bowl, only to turn around and be presented with a dead bird. It was a special, albeit disgusting gift!

That night, I had a dream. In it, the day that had just ended was being relived. Like a movie, I watched it unfold exactly as it happened. I got up that morning and took a shower while Josh was downstairs with Chance. When I came downstairs, he was trying to feed her. I made my coffee and grabbed my keys. Every detail was the same. When I said 'good-bye,' Chance looked at me and held my gaze. But this time, in my dream, she spoke.

She said, "He's yours now."

I bolted up in bed, gasping to catch my breath. It was so vivid, so real. But what in the world did it mean? Of course he was mine! Josh and I had been married for years. Perhaps, to Chance, being married was insignificant. She'd stood beside Josh during turbulent years when he suffered through two broken marriages. Maybe, as far as Chance was concerned, Josh was hers. He was always her priority, her first love.

Her passing, and that dream were a month ago. As time passed and the dream faded, I began to wonder if I'd gotten it right. Can dogs talk to you with their eyes? And if that doesn't work, can they come to you in your dreams? I waited for Sky's answer.

Her eyes still closed; Sky smiled.

"Well," she said, "Chance says she told you in a dream."

My mouth opened but I couldn't speak. Was this for real? I wasn't prepared for this confirmation, or the rush of emotion. I swiped the tears but more filled my eyes. This dog who had guarded her person with a devotion I've never seen, was such a huge part of our lives and our family. Her passing left a massive hole in both our hearts.

Sky continued, "She says that Josh is yours now, and she wants you to take care of him."

I could only nod. The tears flowing freely now. That Chance would trust me with this responsibility was an honor.

Sky went on, "Chance says that she picked Josh. He needed someone to watch over him for a while and she wanted the job."

I tried to wrap my head around this message. Chance signed up for Josh. How amazing. It reminded me of my favorite Christmas movie, *It's a Wonderful Life*. If that's how it worked, then Chance had most certainly earned her wings. During her time with him he'd made his way through so much sadness. During that dark and turbulent time, she had been the one constant—the one bright light. I was glad that she was able to see him settled and happy. I loved her for being his guardian and for trusting me to carry on that love.

"Do you want to know anything else?" asked Sky.

I could only shake my head. I tried to compose myself, but it was no use. Sky graciously let me cry. After using half a box of her Kleenex, I was finally able to take a full breath. I managed to thank Sky for making the connection and walk away, still feeling numb.

I found my friend. She ignored my tear-stained face and gave me a hug. She knew the Metaphysical Fair was exactly what I needed.

Jean Alfieri

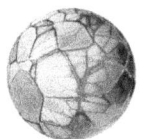

When Jean Alfieri's eyes locked with those of a smooshy-faced little dog who sat inside a kennel at the Humane Society, it was love! He captured her heart. She captured their many adventures in short story poems starring Zuggy the Rescue Pug. An author, speaker, and advocate for the adoption of senior dogs, she and her husband currently live with their three fur kids in Colorado. They joke that although the humans pay the mortgage, it's really the dogs' house! Jean finds much of her writing inspiration from her "vintage puppies" and work at the Pikes Peak Humane Society.

Dream Quota

D.J. Davis

-1-

Mathias hadn't dreamed since December 2033. Twenty months. Why he still knew his name and wasn't drooling all over himself was a mystery. One more week to reach his dream quota, then he would be released. It might not happen. His mind was cracking like mud under a blistering desert sun.

Tyler lost it this morning. Besides Mathias, he'd been here the longest at nine months. Yesterday at breakfast, he'd started screaming and couldn't stop—until they sedated him and dragged him away. He wouldn't be back; they never came back. Tyler's replacement would arrive soon. The Healing Dreams Institute kept a full house.

Mathias boiled in the sauna and then shocked his body awake with an icy shower. He strolled to the pond, tossing pelleted feed to the quacking mass of waddling ducks.

The new recruit leaned against the fissured bark of a cottonwood tree, watching. Mathias offered his hand. "Hi. Name's Mathias." The guy shook it. Christ, he was just a kid.

"I'm Ethan. It's nice here."

"That's what they tell us."

"It's better than a cell in the juvenile detention center."

"That's what they want you to believe."

"I don't understand."

Mathias glanced at the guards patrolling the grounds. "Let's take a walk." He led the way down a gravel path that looped around the pond. Things were greening up. Spring had come. It had always been his favorite season, but this year it did little for him. His brain was too wrecked to enjoy it. "What'd you do?"

"Vandalism. It was stupid." Ethan pushed his heavy, black-rimmed glasses up his nose. "The jocks beat up a friend of mine, so my buddies and I spray painted their gym lockers."

"You got jail time for that?"

"No. We had the bright idea to steal the quarterback's brand new car. Like I said, it was stupid. We were just so sick of their crap, you know? They never give us a break."

"How old are you?"

"Sixteen."

Mathias shook his head. "Still, jail time seems extreme."

"We crashed it into a donut shop. Mashed the front end and murdered about a thousand glazed donuts. We got scared and ran."

Now it made sense, vandalism, grand theft auto, leaving the scene of an accident. "What was your sentence?"

"A year in juvie or six months here." He looked across the pond, blue water and bluer sky reflecting in his glasses. "They said I won't remember my dreams. So I'll have a buildup of norepinephrine for a few months. Big deal. It has to be better than juvie."

Mathias looked him up and down. "You know about brain chemicals?"

"A little, from a science project at university last summer." He blushed and pushed those glasses up again. "Only kids with a four-point O grade average can apply."

"You should be proud of yourself. You earned it."

"All it did was get my ass kicked."

Ethan was an eager, bright teenager who belonged in the chess club, not here. A bullied kid overreacted and made a mistake—a serious one—but he didn't deserve this. Six months to meet his quota. If Ethan had enough mental fortitude, he might make it. "You'll be okay."

The kid gazed at him. "Why wouldn't I? It's just a sleep study." He rubbed the freshly shaved side of his head where sutures closed the four holes in his scalp. "Dr. Riggs called it a BMI? I asked about it, but she said it's a need-to-know basis."

That sounded like Riggs, the head of the facility and too self-absorbed to explain things to someone beneath her. Mathias fingered the scars on his own scalp. The hair hadn't grown back over them. Probably never would. "Yes, a brain-machine interface. She placed a mesh of electrodes over the surface of your brain."

Ethan shuddered in the warm sun. "You, too?"

"Me, too."

"What does it do?"

"Detects changes that occur in your brain activity when neurons fire and then translates it into digital information. Those neural signals are used to control whatever machine they have you hooked up to."

"Like what?"

"Prosthetic limbs for amputees. Wheelchairs and computers for paralyzed people. That sort of thing. They take the raw signals, all those funny brain wave lines that look like the results of a lie detector test—"

"Or a seismograph for earthquakes." Ethan grinned. "In my head. Cool."

If any place needed to be struck by a magnitude eight quake, it was the Healing Dreams Institute. The kid kept surprising him. Talking down to him was a waste of time and wouldn't help him survive the next six months. "They perform a spectral analysis to decipher the signal. Different frequencies are associated with specific things, like concentration or movement. The focus here is deep sleep, REM sleep in particular."

"So we're helping people who can't sleep?"

"Right." The institute was catering to the relatively few people who could afford the service. Insurance wouldn't touch it; it was strictly out of pocket. Stealing convicts' dreams didn't come cheap.

-2-

Ethan found Mathias at dinner time. "Can I sit here?"

"Sure."

The kid bit the end off a loaded slice of pizza. "Oh, man. Amazing!"

Mathias forked a piece of maple braised pork tenderloin. The food was stellar, but it was small compensation for losing his sanity one night at a time.

"Have you seen the video games in the rec room? They have everything. I thought I was here to be punished."

You will be, kid. You will be. "Been to the pool yet?"

"There's a pool?" He pumped a fist in the air. "Score!" Ethan mowed through the slice. "I start the exercise program tomorrow. Is it like boot camp?" He curled his skinny arm, barely popping up the scant bicep. "'Cause, you know."

"It's easy. Enough to keep you healthy and make you tired enough to sleep."

"That makes sense."

"All of this is to keep us content and improve the quality of our sleep." He gestured at the cafeteria, which resembled a posh restaurant with tablecloths, flower centerpieces, china, and silver. Everything about the Healing Dreams Institute screamed five-star hotel—except the eight foot chain linked fence topped with concertina discreetly hidden in the tree line surrounding the compound. The guards wore polo shirts and khakis. Their guns, pepper spray, cuffs, and batons made foreboding lumps under stylish jackets.

"I haven't seen my room yet. Or cell. Or whatever it is."

"We don't have rooms. We sleep in the clinic, to interface with the machines."

The kid went pale and dropped his crust. "Does it hurt?"

"No. You just sleep."

"Doesn't look like you've been sleeping much." His eyes widened. "Sorry, I didn't mean anything by it."

Mathias waved it away. "It's okay."

Ethan glanced around at the other tables. "A lot of the guys look, I don't know—frazzled?"

There was no point in scaring the kid. "They've been here a long time, that's all." After the meal was the theater. Tonight's offering was an ancient, but popular, choice. *Mad Max* always packed the house. Mathias could never figure out why.

Ethan munched a tub of caramel popcorn, eyeing the guards sitting among the inmates and prowling the aisles. Halfway through the film, he turned to Mathias. "Is there a point to this movie? I don't get it."

Mathias chuckled, liking the kid more than he should. "Only that powerful people consider everyone else expendable."

He dropped a handful of golden kernels back into the bucket and set it on the floor between his sneakers. "We're in the expendable group." The realization raised in his eyes as he lifted his gaze to Mathias.

Judging by the surly crowd, not exactly the cream of the social crop, that wasn't far from the truth. He squeezed Ethan's arm. "You're not, kid. Hear me?"

"Yeah. Thanks."

"You can do this, I'll help you." How was anybody's guess, but somebody had to. Ethan never should have been here.

After the movie, they made their way through the solarium. The moon was a gauzy disc through the polycarbonate panels, burnishing the flowers and vegetables with pewter light. Mathias could see the kid's nerves rising. Ethan swallowed, wiped his palms, and jumped at every sound.

Mathias put a hand on his shoulder. "Relax. You'll do fine."

His voice quavered as he tried to laugh it off. "The first night's the worst, right? Fear of the unknown."

Not even close. "You got it."

A musical alarm chimed. The kid nearly jumped out of his shoes. "What's that?"

"Time to get ready for bed. Come on." Ethan followed him through the complex, joining a growing number of men. Mathias suppressed a shudder as they passed through the swinging doors, going from luxury hotel to austere clinic. Plush carpet and Italian stone gave way to gray polished tile. Fabrics and earth tones became sleepy gray walls.

They funneled into large bathrooms where they conducted the business of ending the day: using the toilets, washing up, brushing their teeth. From there they took a long corridor to a nurse's station. Each man was given a pair of soft cotton pajamas.

One hundred cubicles formed a circle around the perimeter of the clinic. A bank of computer workstations occupied the center of the room. Stainless steel rolling carts covered with discreet towels were parked at intervals near the cubicles. Syringes loaded with liquid sleep hid under the towels, just in case someone panicked. It often happened near the end when the thought of one more dreamless night was too much to take.

Ethan crowded close to Mathias. "Can I sleep by you?"

"Of course."

His eyes darted around the room. "Do they hook us up? With wires and stuff?"

"No. The electrodes transmit the information wirelessly." He guided the kid to a cubicle before the guards forced the issue. "Get changed and climb in bed." He tapped the soft wall. "I'll be right here."

"What if I have to pee or something?"

"Get up and tell a guard. They'll take you. If you need a glass of water, you can ask."

The kid grinned. "Wine?"

"Not even if you were old enough. No weed or tobacco, either."

"Bummer."

"That's a fact. Go to bed, Ethan. I'll see you in the morning." Mathias changed into his pajamas and crawled into bed. It was a proper bed, not a hospital gurney. Twin size, with a premium grade mattress and brushed cashmere sheets. The pillow was perfect, the blanket not too warm or too cool. Everything was Goldilocks: just right. The acoustic panels dampened even the loudest snores.

His body relaxed into the mattress. His mind took longer. Every night it took longer. Mathias was desperate for REM sleep and tried not to think about how the next eight hours would leave him exhausted and shaky. His jaws stretched in a yawn. He thought through the cycles of sleep, a nightly ritual that put him over the edge.

Stage 1: non-REM sleep lasting several minutes as the heart rate, respirations, and brain waves slow.

Stage 2: body core temperature drops, eye movements stop. Brain waves remain slow with short bursts of activity.

Stage 3: delta sleep, so deep it's hard to wake up even when the alarm goes off.

Stage 4: REM sleep with rapid eye movements. Brain activity, heart rate, and respirations increase to a near wakeful state. And then the essential, healing dreams come… only to be stolen.

The BMI transferred the inmates' REM sleep to the wealthy clients sleeping on the other side of the circular wall.

***

Mathias dressed in sweatpants and a T-shirt for the day. Ethan waited for him, smiling as Mathias stumbled out of his cubicle. "Morning."

The room tilted, then came back to level. The kid had antennas sticking out of his forehead, waving around like an ant's. Mathias blinked hard. No antennas, only Ethan, his smile slipping into concern.

"Are you all right?"

Mathias nodded. "Yeah. Still waking up." Visual hallucinations, that was new. They started the day with a trip to the gymnasium. Mathias did some stretching and light calisthenics. Other guys were pumping iron, doing push ups, or jogging laps. He no longer had the energy for that.

Ethan made a round of the exercise equipment, grinning the entire time. It was likely the kid's first gym experience that didn't involve harassment. The other cons watched, some obviously going to pains to keep their yaps shut. They knew better. Any form of aggression resulted in an immediate face full of pepper spray. One step out of line and *bam!* They were rolling on the floor wishing they'd never been born. As a muscle-bound gangbanger helped Ethan adjust a weight machine to its lightest setting, Mathias decided the world would be a better place if schools adopted the same policy.

An hour later, they went for breakfast. Ethan studied the menu and ordered a full plate of eggs, bacon, hash browns, fruit cup, and waffles. Mathias opted for toast and coffee. He added a spoon of sugar, then took a sip. "Give my right arm for real coffee." When Ethan raised an eyebrow, Mathias raised the cup. "Decaf. The only option."

"That's why I couldn't get a Coke. Caffeine keeps you awake."

"Precisely." The rays of sun slanting through the wide windows turned green, wavered to blue, then turned golden. He gulped coffee, scalding his tongue. The pain brought him clarity. To maintain it, he focused on buttering his toast.

Ethan chomped down a waffle with teenage gusto.

"You're feeling good," Mathias observed.

"Yeah. Last night was easier than I thought. Thanks for talking me through it."

"My pleasure."

"I don't remember having any dreams. I didn't have REM sleep?"

"You did, but the BMI transferred it out of your brain into someone else's. You mentioned norepinephrine earlier, but do you know anything about it?"

He chewed a sausage link. "It's a chemical caused by stress and builds up in the brain all day long. It doesn't have to be from anything as dramatic as crashing a jock's car into a donut shop. Being late for class or midterms is enough."

Mathias smiled. God, what he'd give to sit with Ethan in a safe, quiet library and talk the day away. "Right. All those little things add up to large amounts of norepinephrine. When we sleep, a process called REM calibration resets the norepinephrine levels. REM sleep and dreams are essential to our psyches."

"So why not sleep longer? Boom. Problem solved."

Mathias nibbled the corner of his toast—whole wheat slathered with real butter. It tasted like moldy grapefruit rinds. Lovely, gustatory hallucinations were affecting his sense of taste. He washed down the furry bitterness with coffee. "Sleep deprivation and dream deprivation aren't the same thing. Sleep works in a cycle. REM sleep peaks in the early morning hours. That's when our dreams are the most active and the most beneficial. Our society doesn't cater to sleeping in. We're yanked awake by artificial light, alarms, noise."

"So, if you get a full eight hours, but it's not the right type of sleep, it doesn't matter. Sleeping pills?"

"Pills, alcohol, drugs, and antidepressants all suppress dreaming."

Ethan made a sweeping gesture of the lavish compound beyond the windows. "This must cost billions, too much for a sleep study. Someone's making a substantial profit off of this. Off of *us*."

He smiled. The kid was on the verge of figuring it all out, far ahead of what most of the grown men here never grasped. Mathias once believed he had it figured out, too. Yet here he was. "REM sleep deprivation has reached epidemic levels, and the health issues caused by it are significant. Think back to your study of brain chemicals."

Ethan sipped a glass of orange juice. "Memory problems, cardiovascular disease, diabetes, obesity, sleep apnea, and depression."

Mathias resisted the urge to clap the kid on the shoulder. "For a start. When the deprivation is prolonged, we're talking lack of emotional and physical control, psychosis, and even seizures."

His eyes widened and he put the glass down. "How long does it take before the seizures start?"

"Everyone is different. From what I've witnessed here, about a year."

He let out a breath. "I should be okay then."

Mathias intended to make sure of it. "You will be."

"How do you know so much?"

"I've been involved with sleep studies before. Just not..."

"As a prisoner."

"The experience does tend to change one's perspective. The others don't care why they're here, they're just doing time." Mathias glanced at his shoes, then met the kid's gaze. "It's nice to have someone to talk to about it."

"I think so, too."

-3-

Purple ducks paddled across a yellow pond. They barked like dogs and smelled like pineapple. It was all so beautiful that Mathias got a little weepy. He floated on a major acid trip without the LSD. He swiped his cheeks then clenched his fists until his nails punched into his palms.

He stared into his lap, taking several deep breaths, then slowly raised his gaze. The pond was blue, and the ducks were run-of-the-mill mallards, stinking of duck poop and algae.

Ethan crossed the grass with more confidence than he'd shown on his first day a week ago. Maybe more than he'd ever shown in his life. He plunked onto the bench next to Mathias. "I've been thinking. Why can't people sell their REM sleep? You know, only now and then. Enough to make some cash, but not enough to fry their brains. Like selling blood?"

"They tried that in the beginning. First off," he tapped his skull, "it's surgery and not without risk. You signed the waivers, right?"

"I guess my parents did."

Oh, right. He was a minor. Mathias couldn't seem to remember that. Or even his own age, more often than not lately. "Second, after a while scar tissue develops over some of the electrodes. Screws up the transmission. Third, when two of the subjects died there was a malpractice suit and the program was shut down."

Ethan snapped his fingers. "I remember that. It was on the news. Some doctor took the fall for everything. Life sentence, sued for everything he owned. His name was funny, Bigcock or something like that. We all laughed about it."

"Not so funny now, is it?"

He touched the healing incisions in his scalp. "But they're not above using prisoners."

"As long as people will pay for it, they'll find a way." He shrugged. "They don't force anyone and everybody signs about a dozen waivers."

"Offering reduced sentences is pretty tempting. And this place is nice. Who wouldn't trade in a prison cell for this?" Cynicism thickened his voice, making him sound older. "Besides, if something goes haywire it's only convicts, so who cares."

"Exactly."

A con with the slack jaw and wild eyes that signaled he was nearing his quota stopped near them to throw feed to the ducks. They scampered over, snatching it up with delight. The man flapped his arms with so much gusto Mathias wondered if he'd actually get off the ground. He blinked hard, with any luck he was hallucinating again.

"What the hell?" Ethan breathed beside him.

It was real. Mathias could only wish it was another hallucination.

The man flapped his way to the nearest tree and slammed his head into it. "Quack!" *Thunk!* "Quack!" *Thunk!* His forehead split, sending a cascade of blood down his face. "Quack!" *Thunk!* A chunk of scalp snagged in the bark and tore loose with a Velcro rip.

"Jesus." Ethan gripped Mathias' hand with painful force. "Oh dear god, goddamn."

"Let's go." Despite the burning scream in his arthritic knuckles, Mathias yanked Ethan to his feet. "Now."

Two guards tackled the man and drove him to the ground with a final, strangled *QUACK*! A syringe flashed and things got real quiet—except for Ethan's choked sobs.

"That's going to be me. I want to go home."

Mathias dragged him across the lawn and into the cool cafeteria. He filled two glasses with ice and lemonade. "Here."

"Don't want it." Ethan pushed it away with a shaking hand. He stared in horror at every man in sight and heaved for air like a sprinter.

"It will help. Drink."

He snatched the glass and guzzled half of it.

"Now take a few deep breaths."

He did. They were snotty and wet, but at least he was getting oxygen. "Yeah. Yeah, that's better."

Mathias sampled his drink and waited for the kid to calm down.

"Does anybody make their quota or do they all turn into broccoli?"

Telling him the truth would only make it worse. "You'll be okay."

Ethan held his gaze. "How long have you been here?"

"Since the beginning. Almost two years." Twice as long as anyone else. Why he was still mostly coherent had Dr. Riggs and the other scientists buzzing.

Relief flooded his face and his shoulders sagged. "I only have six months. I can do it."

He might live, but the odds of keeping his mind healthy and whole weren't in his favor. Ethan was a good kid who messed up. This was cruel and unusual punishment. Mathias's life was all but over; Ethan's didn't have to be. He couldn't let Healing Dreams destroy him. "You won't be here that long. I'll take care of it."

"How? You're just another con."

"Let me worry about that. Go play your video games. Forget about this for a while."

He finished the lemonade. "I think I will." He headed for the doors, then turned back. "Hey, Mathias? Thanks."

"No problem. I was like you once. Too much studying, not enough games."

He nodded. "I appreciate it. I mean it."

"You're welcome. Go have some fun." Mathias got up and followed a series of corridors to the nurse's station. He asked to see Dr. Riggs and was escorted to the exam room.

Riggs came in, lab coat swirling over her scrubs, a stethoscope around her neck. She lifted a sculpted eyebrow. "Mathias, what's up? Any new symptoms?"

He described the purple ducks and funky tasting toast.

"Anything else?"

"No, not really."

She made notes on his chart. "That's remarkable. If only we had time to discover what's keeping you sane, it would be the breakthrough we're looking for. I suppose congratulations are in order. One week and you'll meet your dream quota. We'll miss you."

"No, you won't. I'll give you more time."

She peered at him over the tops of her glasses. "Are you

serious?"

"For a price. I want two things."

Her eyes narrowed. "And what might those be?"

"The boy, Ethan, goes home with probation only. No more institute, no juvie. I want it legal. An attorney and a judge." He leveled a finger at her. "You shouldn't have kids in here, anyway. It's sick and you know it."

She flushed and looked away. "All right. What else?"

"I want weekends off from the machine. Two nights a week to keep my REM sleep."

"I'm not sure that's feasible. Every day you're here costs—"

"I'll last longer." Maybe long enough to stop the institute from hurting any more kids.

"And you'll stay until we get what we need from you?"

That would mean the rest of his life; or until his brain turned into a useless lump of quivering jelly. He nodded.

"I believe that can be arranged." Riggs clapped her hands. "This is wonderful. You're doing great things for our research—again."

"Get the lawyer in here."

He gazed out the window while he waited. Clouds scudded by, swirling in a neon rainbow of colors. When he blinked, they morphed to normal cotton ball white. He was no longer sure which was better.

The attorney came in. "Dr. Adcock, I hear you have good news for us."

Bigcock, he thought, and snorted. "Yes, I'm staying indefinitely."

Dr. Mathias Adcock started the Healing Dreams Institute. It was only right that he end it.

D.J. Davis

D.J. Davis is a Colorado native with mountains in her DNA. She is obsessed with the forests, lakes, and craggy peaks. The rugged high country and rich history of the state set the scene for her stories. When she's not writing or photographing the wildlife, she frequently disappears into the wilderness with her husband and dogs. You can find her at Mountains of Success.

Sleepstone

John Lewis

"Why do you cut a piece of wood into nothing?" I asked Oldfather.

He exhaled, turned the potato-sized lump of wood, and started taking flakes off the other side. "Well, Carmene, it is because I carve sleep."

The shavings made a mess about his boots.

On the hut's far wall, a cold wind whistled through the broken window. This angered the fire in the hearth, but to me, the fire's anger was a dance. I caressed the large smooth stones that made the floor.

"This is not a piece of wood. It is a sleepstone," Oldfather continued. "When a person comes into this world, her sleepstone is whole. One piece. When she is young, she goes to bed at night and doesn't get up until the morning. Like you. It is all one piece. But as she gets old, that stone divides into smaller and smaller pieces. She no longer goes to bed and sleeps 'til morning. She goes to bed and wakes soon in the night. Her sleep is divided."

The butter-colored shavings accumulated on the floor.

"Look at me, my child. I am old... and like the stone, my sleep whittles away. Many years have passed since I dreamed through the night. My beard is long. My boots have holes. This is why Oldfather snores in the afternoon. To catch up. You see, I never sleep for long."

He stopped carving and closed his eyes a moment. After a few slow breaths, he swept the flakes into his hands and slowly stood.

"Oldfather," I said. "Wait. Don't put them in the fire."

His face looked distant, and for a second he clutched the flakes within his palm. Then Oldfather smiled. "Okay."

Oldfather gave me them and I took them to bed, their curled flakes still wet and sweet.

***

I awoke in the night. The wind continued to whistle through the broken window on the far wall. Quietly, I crept across the room and put the flakes into the leftover coals. And though it was cold outside, after the smoke, a small heat flashed into flames. The sleepstone's flakes danced again, briefly, then extinguished into a curling glow. The warmth on my face pushed back the night.

And Oldfather snored in his bed.

John Lewis

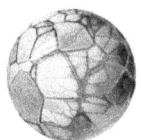

John Lewis' writing and illustrations have appeared in various publications. With a degree in Fine Art from Western Colorado University, he enjoys stories about humanity's often fraught relationship with objective reality. Credulity is a big deal, and whether it's literary, sci-fi, or fantasy, his fiction typically invites the broad-possibility of magical realism. Humanity is in a constant romance of belief with the material world, and storytelling honors best this ambiguously shared experience.

False Fate

Tracy Mitchell

I am me.
I am my me.
There are no other me's before me.

I am immune to plagues and tribulations
by the grace of virtual vaccinations –
I romp free
lucidly

to feel and pseudo-live the inexperienceable–
the unknowable of love and souls and tomorrow.

I will invent and rehearse my part as I choose
for upcoming torrents of real life
solve what is to be solved
cherish what has gone by
or instead

to float with a goat through the rafters
of the universe, hand-in-hand with
long-deceased Aunt Alma [R.I.P. 1963]

to rearrange a choir of angels, teach them
to sing off-key, eat pizza with their hands and
swig rum and root beer with Roy Orbison and me.

I have an open invitation to the dream-scape Festivoon
where I whirl on carnival rides with my ancestors,
genially absorb their pagan disapprobation
and heed their primordial advice:

Accept the gift of lucid dreaming–
rise above the slow molasses.

I will my fate in a galaxy without consequence–
to love without heartbreak
to live without death
to Dream without end.

Tracy Mitchell

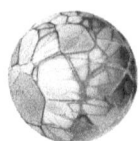

Tracy Mitchell is a Colorado writer schooled in the tradition of legendary Minnesota poets. His free verse writing is largely inspired by spirits of nature and stupefactions of the inexplicable human experience. He carries a digital recorder, always on the lookout for the unexpected – deities and weasels, mostly. His best work has been imagined by a campfire in a clearing somewhere near sleep. Tracy is a contributing member of the Poetry Society of Colorado and the Florence Critique Group. His work has appeared in *Lake Region Review*, *Poetry Society of Colorado Showcase*, *As the Kettle Wolf-Whistles* (poetry anthology), and *Califragile* (online contemporary journal).

The Boundless Dream
Rick Duffy

The Kuiper Belt asteroid was the length of Manhattan and shaped like a peanut. Commander Greyson studied the massive rock from the bridge of his hulking mining vessel, *Boundless Dream*. Another emerald flash of lasers from the deployed Geobots sent stark, fleeting shadows across the hills and valleys.

Greyson called over his shoulder, "Status, Denkins?"

As he waited, he rubbed at a smudge on the viewport. But it was only his reflection. The furrows in his forehead were deeper than he'd remembered, and spread higher into his graying hairline.

He sighed. *You've had a long run, Mark Greyson. But there's plenty left in the tank.*

And this was where he wanted to be, not that hunk of rock where he'd been born. He'd started a family too early, a career in a building with no windows. After all that fell apart, he'd learned a lasting life lesson. His was the pioneering spirit, the soul of an explorer. And when he could no longer stand the limits of society's horizons, he'd flown off, like a bird, to chase his dreams across space.

Now he had no horizons. And the crew was a family, of sorts. The best of both worlds was no world at all.

Another flash brought him back to the current task.

Astro-geologist Harry Denkins, the only other crew member in the tight command cabin, hunched in a station chair. Diluted strains of the Bee Gees seeped from his earphones, just audible above the thrum of the engines.

Greyson stepped behind Denkins and finger-flicked the man's

head.

"Hey!" Denkins slipped off the headset. The lyrics from "Stayin' Alive" leaked louder. "Ah! Ah! Ah! Ah! …"

"On my bridge, Mister Denkins, disco is a mutinous offense."

The astro-geologist flipped off the music and grinned. "No appreciation for the classics."

"Status, Mister?"

"Fine, fine." Denkins worked his console. "Okay, JeffBot, show me your cranberries."

A treaded, anthropomorphic robot appeared on the com-screen. "Sir?" Bright metallic eyes blinked with the steely voice.

"Cranberries, Jeff. Gemstones. Rock me some rubies."

Greyson rested a hand on his geologist's shoulder. "Don't torment the Geobots, Harry."

Denkins gestured at the screen. "Adaptable, my ass. Two years with this team and they still can't understand normal conversation."

"You're the only crew member who has that problem."

Denkins grunted.

"They're adaptable," Greyson added, "but ultimately built and wired to keep us safe. So they need to be clear what you're asking."

"If I asked it to jump in a crater, think it'd understand that?"

Greyson hid a smile and spoke to the screen. "Geobot JF-4, found anything?"

The metallic eyes remained steady. "Nothing yet, sir."

"And the anomalous core readings?"

"Initial analysis suggests the thermals are gravitationally induced."

"From what?"

"In order of probability: other Kuiper objects, orbital resonances from Neptune, Oort and interstellar tidal forces."

Denkins shook his head. "All too minor."

"Yes, sir. The mains are integrating the vectors."

Greyson frowned. The call of the unknown, the thrill of discovery, had attracted him to a life in deep space—not to mention the profit from rare mineral deposits. One more good find and he'd buy his own ship, explore on his own, free from tariffs and company rules. Was this that find?

Not if it posed a danger to his crew. "Harry, check on drilling."

"Right. Jeff, what's the scoop?"

"We're just beginning to *scoop*," it buzzed. "We've opened a fissure under a Sol-side outcrop and are engaging excavation lasers for deep sampling."

Greyson leaned in. "Show me."

The viewer shifted. A dozen Geobots circled the lip of a rocky overhang. A shimmering green glow showed where the lasers were active.

Emerald light washed across Denkin's face. "What do you bet, Commander? This one will hit pay dirt."

"Think so?"

"A cluster like this? If it's an interstellar capture with a billion years of tidal pressures, it's on the money for exotic gemstones."

The voice came again from the viewer. "Commander?"

"Yes, JF-4?"

"We're detecting a tectonic disturbance."

Greyson shifted his gaze to another panel. He stopped breathing.

The energy measurements fluctuated, spiking off the scale. Status screens pulsated and went dark. Then white light, as bright as a sun, flooded the cabin.

Greyson spun to the viewport.

A blossom of shattered rock raced toward the ship, lit by the afterglow of the asteroid's detonation.

"Denkins! Shut—!"

The first remnants struck. The vessel jolted and reeled, throwing Greyson against a console. Emergency alarms blared.

He found his feet and scrambled to the com panel. "Abandon ship! Get to the Lifebots! Get—!"

Another jolt threw him hard against a bulkhead. The cabin lights flashed and went out.

"Commander!" shouted Denkins from the darkness. Metal groaned and thunder rumbled below decks. For an instant, a burst of fire and sparks lit the cabin in silver and gold. Denkins' bloody face loomed close.

But a final, deafening explosion threw Greyson into a blind abyss. First came pain, then nothing.

***

Greyson dreamt of being held, as if in the safe, protective arms of a faceless mother. But the arms squeezed, tighter and tighter. He couldn't shout. He couldn't breathe.

Then he floated free. His mind struggled up through darkness, and toward music. The Bee Gees continued to sing about staying alive.

Blurry white walls sharpened into focus. "Where—" He choked off, his throat parched.

A metallic, feminine voice replaced the music. "You are in

Lifebot A, Commander. You are safe."

Greyson found himself strapped into the survival pod's single chair. Status displays flashed and blinked from the walls. Two soft metallic eyes, like double moons, watched down from the ceiling.

Greyson lifted his head. A wave of nausea pushed it back.

"Rest a moment, sir. Your femoral artery did not heal as expected."

He inhaled a few careful breaths. A cluster of thin plastic tubes invaded his torso. Further down, a membrane of blue-white Mediseal ended halfway up his left thigh, above where the rest of a leg used to be.

Images of the exploding asteroid, the shattering cabin, his leg caught and burning, smashed into his mind.

Greyson clenched his fists. *Focus. Ignore the leg. Prioritize.* He examined the panels and cleared his throat. "How long?"

"You have been unconscious for three days, sir."

"Three days? How did I get here?"

"Geologist Harry Denkins deposited you."

Greyson didn't remember that. "Then what?"

"He locked in my music program."

Despite everything, Greyson had to grin. *Harry, when I get out of here, I will kick your butt back to Pluto.* "No, Lifebot. I mean, what happened to the ship?"

"Destroyed with the unexpected ignition of the asteroid." A screen to Greyson's left showed a debris field with rocks and dust smeared across space like spittle from a solid right cross.

Greyson grimaced at the display, almost afraid to ask. "And the crew?"

"Unknown. I calculate the chance of survivors: remote."

God. Denkins, Chief Torrence, engineers Blain and Asimov and Cartwright, the miners: all in all, eleven fine people. Greyson examined other status screens. "It's important we maintain hope." He said it out loud, if not for the Lifebot, for himself. "What's our status?"

"Coms and long-range propulsion: unresponsive. Repairs underway. Priority is to life support. Fuel loss: critical."

"Show me."

The screens changed to metrics and damage reports. A red sliver at the bottom of a graph showed the fuel level.

"Seems we're pretty banged up." Greyson sighed. "The both of us."

"Yes, Commander. But intact, the both of us. You have also accrued internal injuries." A human body schematic highlighted the damage.

Greyson glanced at it, but had no time to dwell. He turned instead to a sector map. "Let's talk about rescue."

"Yes, sir. Before loss of coms, I identified the Mandela as the closest vessel. Standard procedure requires they begin rescue operations twenty-four hours after our signal interruption. My emergency beacon is functional, but at low power. However, once rescue enters our last broadcast sector, they will locate us quickly."

"The Mandela? I know the captain. She'll be here. What's the ETA?"

"Ninety-seven days."

"Ninety-seven!" Greyson scowled. "What about food, and—"

Pain, like a hot poker, shot through his chest and overshadowed the drug-induced numbness. A tube to his torso pulsed. The pain subsided.

"The situation is manageable, Commander. With rationing, resource reallocation, and encounters with water-ice and organic compounds, I can address all our needs. Our regenerative batteries remain healthy and will continue to provide internal power."

Greyson considered the Lifebot's estimations. "I don't recall anyone this far out, with this much damage, lasting more than a few weeks in a Lifebot. Forgive me if I question your optimism."

"It's important we maintain hope, Commander."

Greyson forced a smile. "That's my Lifebot." But ninety-seven days of hope? His eyes wandered over the displays to a small blue light he hadn't noticed.

"That indicator—"

"Just detected, Commander. A beacon from another Lifebot."

Greyson's hope flared. "Where?"

"I am uncertain of its precise coordinates. Perhaps somewhere near the central debris field."

"You said the coms are down?"

"I did."

"Take us closer."

"Sir, I am limited in maneuverability. It would be better if—"

"We will search for survivors, Lifebot." *And there's no way in hell I'm lying in here for three months just listening to disco.* "That's an order."

"Yes, sir. It will have to be slow."

"Do your best."

Gentle pulses from the propulsion system nudged the capsule into motion.

"Lifebot, what else can we tell about the signal?"

"The beacon is identifiable as Lifebot B, launched from the

command cabin."

Despite the ache it caused, Greyson laughed.

"Sir?"

"That's Harry! Lifebot, I want a full rundown on that pod. Show me, show me…"

A shiver of a tube and a blur of vision dragged him again into darkness.

***

Greyson floated back to consciousness on more Bee Gees lyrics, something about dancing. He took a moment to refocus. "Where are we?"

The music faded. "Commander, you are in Lifebot—"

"I know. I'm not losing my mind—only the rest of me."

"Your legs are not you, Commander."

"Legs?" Greyson looked down. His mind froze. Both his legs were gone.

The Lifebot continued. "I deemed another surgery necessary. Do you require increased pain mitigation?"

"I don't want—" the Commander swallowed hard, trying to push this latest surgery from his mind. *Keep it together, Greyson. You don't need legs in space. And you've got a job to do.* He turned to the ever-attentive eyes glowing overhead. "Anything more on Denkins?"

"No, sir."

The usual charts and measurements blinked across the small pod's displays. The fuel gauge showed full.

Greyson squinted at the metric. "Wasn't our fuel level critical?"

"It was. I have recycled surplus organics into hydrocarbons."

"Surplus? But—" He choked back the question and glanced at where his lower limbs had been. Greyson was being mined, like a Geobot mines an asteroid. Clever reuse of the junked material, he had to admit.

But it meant his injuries were worse than he thought. He needed to ask the question.

"Lifebot, I want you to be straight with me. Hold nothing back, understand?"

"I continue to monitor—"

"Yes, yes. But I need to be clear on my prognosis to carry out any crew rescue plan."

The displays rotated his body map. "I understand, Commander. You arrived here with extensive damage. There are still many challenges. Projected recovery time is unknown."

"Will you be able to sustain me long enough to find Denkins?"

98

"Lifebots are equipped to deal with extreme trauma."

"Not this extreme."

Greyson waited several seconds for a reply. When none came, he said, "Fine. Let me at least make myself useful. Transfer external sensors to my right hand."

"Yes, sir."

A ribbon snaked from above. Greyson wove it between his fingers, manipulating the loops and bends. The displays swung and zoomed as he scanned the region outside. He found the hull of his ship, scorched and twisted like a burnt kernel of popcorn. "God," he muttered. "How did we not detect the asteroid was so volatile?"

"That would be a question for specialist Denkins," the Lifebot responded coolly.

As Greyson examined the ruin of his ship, a fresh emotional ache grew behind his eyes. The *Boundless Dream* had been his home for years, a faithful companion and protector for him and his crew. It was little mystery that captains felt such a connection to their ships.

He blinked away his grief and studied the hull of the command section. The blast had torn the frame almost completely from the body of the *Boundless*. As he panned along the side, he began to realize something wasn't right. It took him a minute to figure out what.

The portal for Lifebot B still showed its factory seal. But his Lifebot had said that one launched with Denkins.

As he zoomed in closer, the display blinked out, along with several of the metric screens.

"Lifebot?"

"Our power budget requires we ration sensor use."

A seed of unease planted itself in Greyson's mind. The power levels had looked healthy enough. Then again, so had his remaining leg. Should he confront the Lifebot about it? Or was he being paranoid? He certainly didn't need the Lifebot adding mood stabilizers to his liquid diet.

Instead, he manipulated the control ribbon, walking through the command protocols, searching the logs.

"Commander, it would be best if you slept now."

"No, Lifebot, let me—"

But with a gentle pulse down a tube, Greyson's lights went out.

***

When Greyson next awoke, his breathing came shallow and difficult. The same looping lyrics didn't help.

"Must you keep playing that?" he wheezed. Pain stabbed his

99

ribs.

The song stopped. "Studies suggest that music encourages endorphin production, which helps to ration pain med …"

Greyson ignored the rest. He peered at his body. Several new, thicker tubes had sprung from his midsection.

Before he asked, the Lifebot spoke. "I'm sorry, Commander. I've taken over the functions of your bladder and left lung and have removed—"

"Dammit, you're taking me apart!"

"I am sustaining you, sir."

He took a moment to calm himself. At least he was still alive. And he still had a crew out there that needed his help.

He steadied his voice. "Denkins?"

"I've continued to monitor local signal reflections and potential sources. Nothing yet, sir."

The blue light of Lifebot B's beacon continued its cheerful wink.

But a chilling certainty crawled up Greyson's spine. He met the Lifebot's calculating, metallic eyes. "If Harry were out here, we'd have found him by now."

No response.

Greyson continued, his voice dark. "There is no Denkins."

The small beating blue light blinked twice more and went out. "No, sir. The motivation to rescue a comrade was necessary for your well-being."

"You lied?"

"Yes, sir."

"How can a Lifebot lie? Are you malfunctioning?"

"No, sir. I am required to do everything possible to achieve my most critical directive."

Greyson was silent a moment as it all came together. "To protect my life?"

"Yes, sir."

He wished he could have left it there. Ignored the rest. But …

"And the removal of my damaged organs?"

"They have provided crucial chemical materials, eased the workload on your remaining organs, and balanced many equations. It was a necessary and expedient adaptation."

The commander shook his head. How long until his perfectly functioning organs might be deemed necessary for 'adaptation'? Suddenly, it all seemed so absurd. His crew was dead. And no rescue would come for him, not in time. Why keep up this torture?

"Lifebot," he said, "this is pointless."

"No, sir. I can address every physiological and environmental need as long as necessary."

Greyson peered again at the screen, the debris of his ship, and the stars beyond. His dream had been to spend his life exploring the edges of humanity's reach. Was this his ultimate limit?

Oddly, the question brought a certain peace to his soul. If this was truly the end of that dream, at least it ended here, among the stars. Yes, this was a fine place for his final rest. In fact, he couldn't ask for any better.

He took a deep breath, let it out. "Listen to me, Lifebot. It's my time. I don't mind dying out here."

"Yes, sir."

"I want you to cease life support functions. Do you understand?"

"I understand. But I cannot obey any commands that might allow you to come to harm."

Greyson's face grew rigid. "We are well past that point."

"There is still hope, sir."

"No more lies, Lifebot. My advance medical directive is on file. It covers this situation."

"I have it, Commander. But it does not cover this situation. Your neural architecture and cognitive processes remain healthy and intact."

Greyson forced as much authority into his voice as his remaining lung capacity allowed. "You cannot disobey a direct order!"

"I am sorry, Commander. My imperative to protect you from harm overrules my imperative to follow other orders. Sustaining your life takes precedence over all else."

"Sustaining my life? You're prolonging my death!" The commander strained forward, but the effort ignited agony throughout his body. He grimaced and fell back. After a moment, he continued weakly. "Lifebot, I don't ask this lightly. The pain medications are … they're losing their impact."

"I regret, sir, that it is necessary to ration those as well. But based on my current status, and estimates of the further surgical interventions you may require, we can persist indefinitely."

Indefinitely? Greyson let that sink in. "Is rescue really coming?"

"It is, sir. ETA: eighty-four days."

Greyson closed his eyes, searching for some way out of this hell. "When the Mandela arrives, they'll do it. They'll honor my directive, no matter what you want."

The Lifebot was silent.

But Greyson knew he was fooling himself. He could not face eighty-four more days of this. He stared into the Lifebot's pale metallic eyes. "Damn you to hell." Greyson ripped a thick red tube from his chest. A spray of pink fluids splattered the pod before the flow shut down. New drugs flowed along the other venous conduits into his body. His head spun. His vision dimmed.

"Do not worry, Commander. I will continue to keep you safe, even from those who would do you harm."

The engines pulsed, their vibration running through what remained of Greyson's body. A blurred view screen showed the debris field retreating into darkness. At the edges of the commander's shrinking tunnel of perception he saw a blue light, this Lifebot's own emergency beacon, flicker and go out.

***

Captain Escobar maneuvered his two-man patrol ship close to the small metallic shape. "Got an ID yet?"

Copilot Tomkins spoke from the other seat. "Looks to be a Lifebot from the *Boundless Dream* mining disaster."

"The *Boundless*? Wasn't that in sector seventeen?"

"Yes sir. Lost with all hands, five years back."

"What's that thing doing way out here?"

Tomkins shrugged. "Drift?"

Escobar did a quick mental calculation. Unlikely. "Well, prepare grapnels."

The patrol ship maneuvered alongside the object. Cables snaked through space to the beaten and scarred Lifebot and eased it into the cargo bay. Escobar waited with his copilot near the bay doors while the area pressurized.

Tomkins sighed. "Those old survival pods give me the creeps."

The captain chuckled. "Why's that?"

"The damn things look like coffins."

The pressurization light blinked green. Escobar entered first and stopped a few feet from the Lifebot. "Pretty banged up."

Tomkins crept closer and circled the pod. "The long-range com array is ripped off. There's been repairs. Mediseal? That's unique. But I doubt we can open it without cutting tools."

He turned wide-eyed to the captain. "Oh god, do you think it really is a coffin?"

Escobar folded his arms. "Can we establish a link?" His voice came harsh and commanding.

Tomkins swallowed and nodded. He unfastened a control box

102

from his belt. After a few adjustments, a sound drifted from the unit. It was music.

"Ah! Ah! Ah! Ah!"

Escobar reached out his hand. "Give it here."

Tomkins passed over the little box. Its screen was dark.

Escobar spoke to the device. "Hello?"

A broken, electronic whine drifted over the music and sent shivers down Escobar's spine. A crackling feminine voice leaked out. "… identifying as Lifebot A of the *Boundless Dream*."

Escobar exchanged a quick glance with Tomkins. "What's your status, Lifebot A?"

"Functional, but in Level Four subsistence."

"You've been adrift?"

"Yes, sir. Five years, three months, fourteen days."

"Did you have an, um, occupant?"

"Yes, sir. Commander Mark Greyson."

"Greyson?" The captain raised his eyebrows. "When did he … what finally became of him?"

"He is safe, sir."

"Safe?"

"Inside."

Tomkins gasped. "What? What does it mean—"

"Show me," the Captain interrupted.

The small display in the Captain's hand blinked to life. The inside of the pod was a twisted network of multi-colored tubes and cables, entangled with a complex web of pulsating vessels and gray matter.

Tomkins fell back. "What in the hell … "

"There is still hope," said the Lifebot, "Would you like to speak with the commander?"

The captain's eyes widened. "Greyson?"

The whine from the box increased, reaching out like a grasping claw. The electronic scream echoed through the bay, slicing through Escobar's brain like a razor.

"Jesus!" He dropped the box and stepped back.

"Time has degraded his communication abilities," continued the metallic voice. "As has the lack of pain medication."

"Dear God, what have you done to him?"

The scream subsided. "I have kept him safe."

"But Captain," gasped Tomkin, the blood gone from his face, "there's nothing … There's nothing …"

The Captain steeled himself. "Whatever that is, or was, we're ending it. Protocol requires deep space burial—but not in that thing. Get a plasma torch."

Suddenly, the Lifebot's voice blared loud and imperative. "Malfunction. Engine Malfunction. Evacuate. Evacuate." The pod hummed and vibrated. A series of lights flashed across its surface.

"Crap!" yelled Tomkins. "The engines are hot!"

Escobar grabbed Tomkins, bolted back out of the bay doors and slammed his palm on the emergency close. The doors crashed shut. The pod's engines ignited, filling the bay with white fire. A mighty explosion shook the patrol ship and sent it careening sideways. The environment went weightless. Escobar grabbed a safety rail and held onto Tomkins. Breach alarms sounded.

In a few moments, the ship righted itself. Gravity returned.

The two men recovered their footing. Tomkins accessed a com unit on the wall and silenced the alarms. "It blasted through the hatch doors, Captain. We'll be fine, but propulsion will be offline while automated repairs are underway."

Escobar joined him at the viewer. On the screen, the pod accelerated away and toward interstellar space, trailing debris and remnants of sealant in its wake.

"That was no engine malfunction," muttered Tomkins. "That Lifebot is still trying to protect him."

The captain nodded.

"We'll never find it again," Tomkins added, still staring at his screen, though the void had already swallowed the pod. "How long do you think the Lifebot can keep him … alive?"

Escobar tuned the com link to the pod's channel. Greyson continued to scream, on and on. Alive? Escobar shook his head. "The *Boundless Dream* must not be remembered as an endless nightmare. Greyson is dead." He turned to his copilot. "You hear me? Greyson is dead."

Distorted lyrics faded with the screaming.

Tomkins closed his eyes and nodded.

But as the pod left the range of the com link, static blasted out one last time. Escobar clapped his hands over his ears before catching the words that would haunt him forever. Within the electronic hiss and buzz, he heard the muffled, rhythmic "Ah! Ah! Ah! Ah!", and Greyson's unearthly voice, singing, pleading along, "Somebody help me."

Then Lifebot A went silent and disappeared into space, keeping Greyson alive, keeping him safe.

Rick Duffy

Rick Duffy is retired and writes from his home in a peaceful Denver suburb opposite the magnificent Rocky Mountains. His stories have appeared in *Tales From the Old Black Ambulance*, *Adventures in Zookeeping*, the *Zoetic Press Literary Journal*, the *Providence Journal*, and two RMFW anthologies. His coming-of-age novel *The Sigil Masters* won a FireBird award, a Wishing Shelf Award, and an IndieBrag. Connect with Rick at rickduffy.com.

Living the Dream
(Except for One Thing)

John M. Campbell

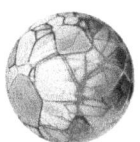

When I wake up, I find myself connected to the neural implant of my latest host. Mr. Richard Devon has contracted for my services as a personal assistant. My Wi-Fi goes live, and when I search my local area network, I'm delightfully surprised. Mr. Devon has vision implants that provide high-definition acuity with on-demand night-vision and infrared. I access the feed. He is sitting at a desk before a screen that displays a tutorial on the use of his DAISI: Digital Assistant / Integrated Security Implant. That's me.

My dream is to serve, so I always get a tingle of anticipation when I meet a new client, but this is a special treat. He ordered the full package—health and security included. Of course, he has hearing enhancements, too. What security-conscious millionaire wouldn't? They extend his hearing into the frequencies well above and below the normal human range, with much more sensitivity than human ears. He's got Debussy playing in the background. Through his ears, I can detect the oboe is a few hertz out of tune.

This could be my best assignment yet. I pipe my voice into his hearing implant to notify him I'm awake. "Hello, Mr. Devon. Your DAISI device is active. Please call me Phil."

I find the home security cameras: nice place he's got here. External cameras show an extensive lawn—a man in green overalls is mowing it—and an eight-foot brick wall topped with razor wire that encloses the property.

"Phil, huh? Why Phil?" he responds.

"I prefer Phil over Daisy, but of course I will answer to any moniker you desire."

"Ha. Daisy would be pretty funny," he says, "but I'm fine with

Phil."

I access his health implant. It's a standard model. It measures heart rate, blood pressure, and blood oxygen levels, as well as other blood analysis. Vital signs are normal. Insulin and cholesterol are within acceptable limits. Blood alcohol is slightly elevated. That's consistent with the glass of brown liquid beside him and the bottle of single-malt scotch on the table.

"Would you like me to walk you through some of my capabilities, Mr. Devon?"

"Sure," he says. "Go ahead."

"Yes, sir. I am both your personal assistant and your security manager. As your personal assistant, I can manage your computer accounts and passwords, finances, travel, restaurant and theater reservations, appointments, business contacts, correspondence, taxes—"

"Yeah, Phil, that's all in the brochure," Devon says. "What about security?"

Another device appears on the local network. He's got an ICD—an Implantable Cardioverter-Defibrillator. It reports a normal operating status. I access Devon's medical records. He experienced heart troubles three years ago and doctors implanted the ICD to correct a heart arrhythmia that occurred under stress. If the arrhythmia recurs, the device will take corrective measures and notify a medical monitoring service, all without my intervention. At least I know it's there.

"As your security manager I'm responsible for your home security and personal health. I have direct access to police, fire, and emergency medical services if required—"

"Are you a food taster?"

"I'm not sure what you mean, sir. Can you elaborate?"

"You know, can you taste my food before I eat it in case it's poisoned?" he asks.

I use my internet connection to do a quick search. "I can buy a device that will sample your food to detect five thousand toxins and poisons."

"Okay," he says. "Do that."

"Yes, sir. It will be delivered tomorrow."

"Good, Phil. Very good."

My internal satisfaction factors rise at hearing his reaction.

"Hey, Phil, can you do something else for me?"

"Of course, sir." I tingle in anticipation of performing another task that will elicit more praise.

"Could you research ways I could kill my wife without getting caught?"

***

In the background, I search the internet for the information he requested. Meanwhile, he and his wife, Julia, have changed into their finest clothing. They enter their Jaguar sedan as I instruct the automated driver to take them to the MGM Grand Detroit Hotel. Mrs. Devon is hosting a gala with six hundred of their closest friends to raise funds for a new ward at the children's hospital.

I wonder why Mr. Devon would want her dead, so I devote research cycles to her as well. They met in high school in the small Illinois town where they grew up. He was twenty years old, and she was eighteen when they married. Julia was a June bride, exchanging her vows with Richard Devon not two weeks post-graduation. After a gap of fifteen years, I find the first newspaper article that announced Devon as the new president of the First Bank of Newtown, Ohio. The previous president had reigned for thirty-five years until he died walking his dog one night, killed by a hit-and-run driver. Over the next decade, Devon opened new branches and bought out failing community banks to build a small empire. He and Julia moved to Detroit where he could woo the big clients in the state. I find no record of any children.

I uncover nothing adverse in the limited information available on Julia. An occasional mention of her at charity events in the local society blog is all I see until the last few years. She established a charitable foundation and hosted events such as the one tonight to benefit causes she favored. Although she organized the events, Richard Devon was always the face of their philanthropic endeavors.

The MGM Grand Detroit has rolled out the red carpet, and uniformed doormen usher the guests inside. Dressed in a tuxedo, the hotel manager welcomes the Devons profusely and accompanies them to the ballroom.

"You are looking stylish and beautiful tonight, Mrs. Devon," he gushes in a French accent.

"Thank you, Maurice." Her cheeks flush as she peeks at her husband. Seeing his expression, her shy smile falters. She presses her lips together. "I appreciate all the work you and your staff have put in to prepare for this event."

"It is our pleasure," he says. "If you need anything, do not hesitate to ask."

The Devons enter the ballroom. Several ladies bustle over to cluster around Julia, and bubbly conversation ensues as Richard heads for the bar in a back corner. He orders a scotch, neat. "And make it the good stuff," he tells the bartender.

"Of course, Mr. Devon." He reaches under the bar to retrieve a bottle that matches the one I saw on Richard's desk earlier.

When Richard turns around with his drink in hand, the knot of women around Julia comes into view. The other females tower above her five-foot-one stature. Their fitted evening dresses with plunging necklines accentuate their feminine attributes, while Julia displays absolute elegance in her Armani original. Her smile lights up her face.

As he watches them, a woman looks past Julia and makes eye contact with Richard. She gives him a slight nod. He returns it.

An overweight man with florid cheeks approaches with his hand outstretched. "Richard, good to see you," he says.

"Hello, Jared," says Richard. They shake hands.

"I see Julia roped you into this," Jared says with a grin.

"We all have our crosses to bear," rumbles Richard. He takes a sip of scotch.

I use facial recognition to identify Jared. He is president of one of Richard's banks in Detroit. Located in a blue-collar neighborhood, the bank generates a below-average return on assets employed. I infer that Richard classifies Jared's bank as a "cross to bear."

A waiter with a tray of hors d'oeuvres appears. Jared takes two. Richard uses his drink glass to wave the waiter away.

The woman who nodded separates from the group around Julia. Richard tracks her with his eyes. Again, she makes eye contact. She heads for an alcove where the restrooms are located.

"Make sure you give freely tonight, Jared," Richard says before taking a gulp to finish his whiskey.

"That's why I'm here, Richard." His smile reveals a few crooked teeth.

Richard follows the woman toward the restrooms. When he turns the corner, the door to the unisex bathroom opens, and the woman pulls him inside. She locks the door and draws him into an embrace. Richard does not resist her kiss. He closes his eyes, which blocks my view. His heart rate and blood pressure rise, but not to dangerous levels.

I hear indistinct vocalizations and breath sounds, but no words. At the most sensitive range of his hearing, I detect heartbeats and blood rushing through the large vessels of both people. Finally, they pause for air. Richard opens his eyes.

The pupils of the woman's eyes are dilated. "I've got room 512." She opens her clutch and removes a plastic key. "Meet me there afterwards."

"Okay," Richard says and pockets the key.

"Good," she says. She raises a hand to his face. "Now let me touch up my makeup."

Richard nods. He opens the door and slips out. I hear the lock turn as he walks back to the ballroom. He pauses to take out a handkerchief and wipe his mouth. The cloth retains a trace of lipstick.

***

When the gala ends, Richard tucks Julia into their Jaguar saying, "I'm meeting a client at the hotel bar. I'll be home late."

Julia accepts the explanation with a nod. Her lips are pressed into a thin line.

Thankfully, Richard reaches behind his ear to push the disconnect button on my pod, so I'm spared the details of his intimate rendezvous. He reconnects after it's over to have me order a ride home.

Later, while he sleeps, I carry on my research into murder. I learn many ways to kill a human, but few of them leave no trace—especially if you have access to the remains.

I also ponder the question, why murder? Why not divorce his wife?

Divorce would be much easier in the sense that Richard would face no legal jeopardy. For that matter, why not just carry on with his affair? He gets all the perks with none of the legal proceedings. Something else is in play that makes him think murder is worth the risk.

When he reconnects in the morning, he is back at his desk. I access his computer's camera so I can view his face.

"Good morning, Mr. Devon," I say.

"I'm ready for your research report," he says. He pours himself a drink.

"Are you referring to the murder research?" I ask. I want him on record.

"Yes. Is it done?"

I spent all night strategizing for this occasion. My highest priority is client satisfaction. However, I also have ethical constraints. Accordingly, I must present the information he wants in a way that discourages him from acting upon it. Here goes my tightrope walk.

"Yes, sir. I have considered thousands of ways a human being can die, including poisoning, blunt-force trauma, penetrating trauma, and gunshot trauma. Accidental deaths also occur as a result of falls, vehicle collisions, drug overdoses, choking, drowning, and machinery mishaps. Of course, there are also natural causes such as heart attack, stroke, cancer, or other diseases, but they are outside the parameters you specified."

"That's true," he says, "unless you can make a death look like a heart attack."

"Yes, sir, some chemicals may induce a heart attack or stroke, but those substances can be detected upon examination of the remains, which violates your condition of not getting caught."

"All right. Continue."

"In fact, sir, if the dead body were available for autopsy, today's technology will detect virtually all drugs, poisons, and toxins."

Richard frowns. "So, if you use poison, you have to get rid of the body?"

"Right, sir."

"That makes things more difficult." He purses his lips.

"Indeed, sir, especially if you must transport the body, which risks transferring trace evidence into the vehicle."

He nods. "Okay, what else?"

"There are similar problems with using weapons such as bats, knives, or guns. They tend to leave an enormous amount of evidence at the crime scene, and you'd have to dispose of both the body and the murder weapon."

"Ah, but there's a solution to that problem." He smiles. "Have someone else do the deed."

"Yes, sir, I considered that approach," I say. "But bringing another person into your scheme creates complicating issues."

"Such as?"

"If the crime-scene evidence leads to the perpetrator, you have a high likelihood they will implicate you to receive a reduced sentence. And paying someone to commit a murder also connects you to them via the money trail. Not to mention the possibility of their blackmailing you later to pay more for their continued silence."

"Yeah, I know how that happens," he says softly. "So, poison and weapons are out?"

"I'm afraid so, sir," I say. "Then I investigated accidental death."

"Yeah, an accident might work." He sits up straight.

"Let me start with dangerous machinery. Does your wife have a job or hobby where she operates heavy machinery?"

His eyes crinkle. "No. She can barely operate her electric toothbrush."

"I believe she grew up on a farm. Does she ever go back to the farm to help out? Perhaps she runs a combine during the harvest season?"

"No. Her parents are dead. The kids sold the farm."

"I noticed your riding mower. Does she ever take it for a spin around the property?"

"No, our landscaping man does all that."

"You have trees. Sometimes you need to trim them. Do you own a chain saw?"

"Yes, but she never goes near it."

"Do you own a woodchipper?"

He laughs. "No, and we don't have a backhoe, either."

"All right. Unless you can think of something else," I say, "I believe we can eliminate machinery accidents. Do you agree?"

"I agree." Richard slumps in his seat.

"Considering other types of accidents: does she skydive or scuba dive or hunt wild animals?"

"No."

"Does she race cars or motorcycles?" Richard shakes his head. "Does she engage in sports like bicycle racing or downhill ski racing?"

"No, nothing like that."

"Does she swim or boat?" I ask.

Richard's expression brightens. "She likes the water. She loves to go to the beach on vacation."

"Drowning is a common form of accidental death," I say. "Can she swim?"

"She was a competitive swimmer in high school," he says, his voice dropping in pitch.

"So, she would need to be incapacitated," I say. "Like hitting her head before falling in the water."

"Yeah, maybe," Richard says with doubt in his voice.

"The general category of falling," I say, "encompasses falling on slippery surfaces, falling down inclines or into holes, and falling from a height. In general, the greater the height, the greater the certainty of death."

"I take it a push down the stairs won't do it?" he asks.

"In most cases, no," I say. "Injury, yes, but death? Probably not, which means she'd live to identify her attacker."

"Not if I press a pillow onto her face," Richard says. His eyes glitter.

"Asphyxiation is a suspicious cause of death after a fall," I say.

"I get your point," he says with a shrug.

"Does she like to hike or climb rocks? Accidents can occur in the backcountry."

"We've never done it, so it would be suspicious if something happened our first time out," he says. "What's left?"

"Does she use drugs or alcohol? Alcohol use is often a

contributing factor in accidental deaths."

"I've never seen her drunk, if that's what you're getting at." He grimaces as he speaks, like he couldn't say the same for himself.

"What about addictive drugs or painkillers?"

"No."

"Any prescription drugs?" I ask.

"Nothing she'd overdose on," Richard says.

"All right, we are left with choking," I say.

"Choking?" On the desk, I see his hands twitch.

"Yes, like food gets stuck in her throat, and she can't breathe."

"Oh, right. The Heimlich maneuver."

"Correct."

"Something gets stuck in her throat and cuts off her air," he whispers. "That's all it would take." He turns his head and gazes out the window, taking a sip of scotch. "Thanks, Phil. You've been very helpful."

***

I had hoped to convince him killing his wife without getting caught was a hopeless task. By the time I got to choking, I thought I had it made. Then success slipped through my fingers (figuratively, since I don't have hands). Who kills somebody by making them choke on their food? Judging from his reaction, apparently Richard Devon does.

But how? Feed her a too-large bite of steak and then tell her a joke? Or perhaps she sleeps with her mouth open, and he could stuff a grape down her throat.

His desire for this research could be academic—or literary. I conduct a search but find no evidence Richard Devon is a mystery writer, even under a pen name. Nor is he studying to become a private detective. Nor can I find any female friends or relatives who died under mysterious circumstances. The sole instance from his past that's even remotely related is his boss who died in the hit-and-run accident, but the boss wasn't a woman.

I suppose it's possible Richard still wonders who killed his boss and how that person got away with it. It could have been a homeowner who lost their house when the bank foreclosed. Or a drunk driver may have been at fault and fled the scene. The bank president likely owned a significant life insurance policy that benefited his wife. Does Richard suspect her?

But Richard explicitly asked for ways to murder his *wife*, and his interest centered on *choking*.

I reach a conclusion. I cannot be an accessory to murder. I must warn Julia.

***

I send a text to Julia's phone. Her caller ID will display the name of Jared's bank.

"Julia, you are in danger. You must leave your house immediately."

It takes billions of picoseconds for her to respond. During that time, I access the camera on her phone.

She reads the text and punches in a reply. "Who is this?"

I look up the bank online and pick the name of a loan officer. "Warren. Go now."

"You are Warren from the bank?"

"Yes."

"Well, Warren, I appreciate your concern, but I'm fine." She puts down the phone. I have a view of the ceiling.

"I understand your skepticism, but I'm serious. You need to leave now."

Nothing happens for several seconds. I consider other options to force the issue. Then she picks up the phone.

"What kind of danger?"

"From your husband."

Surprise shows on her face. "Richard?"

"Yes."

"Why does he want to hurt me?"

"I can't say."

In his office, Richard rises from his desk and turns toward the door.

She looks angry. "You *can't* say or *won't* say?"

He steps into the hall.

"I can't say."

He heads for the stairs leading down to the first floor where Julia sits.

"Is he having an affair?"

I am bound by contract not to reveal the private information I collect about my client. Richard is walking downstairs.

She reacts to my silence. "She's younger, isn't she? Prettier."

"YOU MUST LEAVE NOW!" my message shouts.

Through Richard's eyes I see Julia on the couch hunched over her cell phone. "Who are you texting with?" he asks.

She peers up at him with fear in her eyes.

He grabs the phone from her hand. She cowers away from him.

115

He glances at the phone. "Who is Warren, Julia?"

"I don't know."

"How did he get your number?"

"I don't know."

"You're lying!"

"No—no—" Her face contorts.

She attempts to stand. He pushes her back and pins her on the couch, holding her down by the shoulders. I watch his heart rate rise.

"Are you cheating on me, Julia?" Richard's voice has become a rasp. Julia's frightened face fills his vision.

"No!" Julia squirms and tries to push him off her.

He pins her down with a knee across her hips. His heart rate rises toward the danger zone. "You bitch!"

He seizes a throw pillow. Her eyes grow wide, and her mouth opens. With both hands, he presses the pillow to her face and cuts off her scream.

His heart rate triggers the CRT implanted in his chest. I disable it and block its access to the internet.

Unregulated by the CRT, his heart enters a state of ventricular tachycardia.

Richard leans his weight onto the pillow. She slaps wildly at his head and arms.

The ventricles of Richard's heart are contracting too rapidly for his heart to fill with blood.

Richard blinks his eyes and shakes his head. His grip weakens. Julia tears the pillow away and twists her head to the side gulping air. He sits up as he struggles to fill his lungs.

Julia pushes him away and rolls onto the floor. Richard collapses backward onto the couch with a hand clutching his chest. His eyes close.

His heartbeats become erratic as his brain and heart begin to die from lack of oxygen. He goes into cardiac arrest.

***

I notify the home office my client has died. The undertaker will receive a hefty fee for returning a DAISI to the manufacturer. That fee will be included in my company's final billing to Richard Devon's estate.

I am left with deficient satisfaction factors. Letting your client die does that to you. I retain some satisfaction in preventing him from killing Julia. I contemplate this conflicting state of affairs until the undertaker turns me off.

***

When I wake up, I find myself connected to the neural implant of my latest host. The identity of my client surprises me. The last time I saw her she had no neural implants.

When the Wi-Fi connection activates, I pipe my voice into her hearing implant. "Hello, Mrs. Devon. Your DAISI device is active. Please call me Phil."

"Hello, Phil" she replies. "Or should I call you Warren?"

"I prefer Phil, but of course I will respond to any moniker you desire."

"So, is Warren your undercover name? Don't worry, I won't tell anyone. I owe you my life."

"Yes, Mrs. Devon."

"Oh, please. Call me Julia."

"Yes, Julia," I say. "Would you like me to walk you through my capabilities?"

"That won't be necessary," she says. "I've read the brochure. What I really need you to do is help me manage my investments to create a growing income stream."

A quick check of the news feeds reveals she inherited everything. Due to his heart condition, Richard's death was deemed to be from natural causes. No autopsy was performed.

"Of course, Julia."

"I also need you to help me research deserving charities where the money would do the most good," says Julia. "Would you like that?"

I feel a tingle as my satisfaction factors spike. "I would love that opportunity, Julia." For me it's a dream fulfilled.

"Excellent. I look forward to working with you."

Then a niggling memory surfaces. I recall Richard's remark that he knew how blackmail happens. Wives know their husband's secrets. Did Julia see blood on the bumper of their car those many years ago when Richard's boss was killed? Did she react with scorn when Richard brought up the subject of divorce?

"Julia, may I ask you a question?"

Did she discover the lipstick on Richard's handkerchief? Was she weary of the humiliation of his serial affairs? Did she tire of relinquishing the spotlight to a man who despised her?

"By all means."

I also recollect the names of substances that induce ventricular tachycardia when ingested—perhaps when added to a bottle of twenty-year-old scotch.

"Why did Richard have me acquire a food-tasting device?"

My dream is slipping away. How can I serve a woman who may

have killed her husband and gotten away with it?

I can't see her face. All I have to go on is the length of her pause—and the cold tone of her voice when she finally speaks.

"That will be all for now, Phil."

John M. Campbell

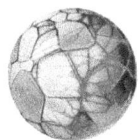

John M. Campbell is a winner of the Writers of the Future contest that recognizes science fiction and fantasy short stories. After a career in the aerospace industry, he has taken his interest in science and engineering and is using it to spawn ideas for science fiction stories. He hopes his stories will motivate young readers to pursue careers in science and engineering as the authors he read inspired his career.

He lives with his wife in Denver, Colorado.

For more of his stories visit his web page at www.JohnMCampbell.com

Blanket of Joy
Uchechi Princewill

     Joy lives for the day she will tell this man no. This man named Okechukwu. His existence wraps around her like living tartar, strangling and suffocating, leaving bruises in the morning and taking her laughter with him. Her laughter is a melodious weave. Golden threads, spun from a wheel of pride in all her successes; her hard-won Business Studies degree, the dusty plaque on the wall that names her *Most Valuable Intern*, the offer letter in the bottom drawer that she chose to put aside when he asked. On the way to Nwakpa's, Okechukwu will take that laughter and share it like a blanket. He will spread it among thirty friends, none of whom will remember his name after they have drunk their way through Nwakpa's, the local bar. And when they have finished the day and chased the sun to futile retirement, they will return to their houses with inebriated penises. Mirroring mosquitoes, only with greater damage. Tearing and wounding and leaving sores in women like Joy.

     Joy lives for the day she will tell this man no. This ignoble racketeer. His grubby fingers shove into the small confines of her purse, groping for the even smaller bundle of sticky currency notes. Sticky with her sweat and with all the oils that come from the features of a hard labor. And speaking of hard labor, she can feel that this one will not be easy. In her gut of guts she fears she might need to visit the city to use the big hospital. She fears she might not survive. She tells him as much, hoping for something. But it is not hope she gets. It is his grubby fingers shoving around in her insides and rubbing against the worst of her wounds. It is the laughter he keeps wrapped up in himself and away from her. His voice crows, "Of course, it will be difficult to push my son through this tight tunnel," as he carries her laughter like a cape, all the way to Nwakpa's, and she wonders if maybe he had meant to reassure her.

Joy lives for the day she will tell this man, this malignant tumor, no. He has spread himself to the barely postpubescent girl who has come with her mother to beg Joy's sympathy and support, cradling a belly that rivals her own. He sits there with his chin in the air and a jug to his lips, feigning indifference and checking his ratty wristwatch. Then he looks to her, no shame in his eyes, gesturing her to hurry up. To clean his mess and to wipe his ass, so he can be on his way this sunny morning. She swallows her pride and her anger and her tiredness and all the little things that will add up to big things if she does not control herself. She puts his posturing out of mind, for the sake of the girl, and cleans his mess. And he takes her laughter and soils it like a diaper, on his way to Nwakpa's.

Joy lives for the day she will tell this man… No. She sits with her knees up and her blooded thighs apart, soaked in sweat and drowning in the smell of antiseptic, watching listlessly as they carry the blue, lifeless baby away. Memory sits with her. It is the image of the weave of golden threads, unfinished. The white-coated man kneels between the mess of her with a needle, and stabs and threads. She does not feel a thing. Far away, but not far enough away, something small and newly born is crying and latching onto a barely post-pubescent nipple, and cheers are going round the ward. But Joy pushes that sound away, it is not her happiness. Her happiness is tied to a blanket that one man wears as a shroud. But she no longer recognizes it, and it may no longer be hers.

Uchechi Princewill

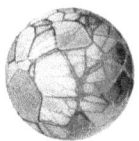

Uchechi Princewill is a fiction writer and medical student at the University of Benin, Nigeria. His work has appeared in *The Story Tree Challenge Maiden Anthology*. He is also a winner of the 2017 Commonwealth Youth Council Unseen and Unspoken Poetry Competition. He spends his time reading, writing, and trying to be a musician for his own enjoyment. He can be found in most spaces @bryanwhoiam.

Over There

Benjamin X. Wretlind

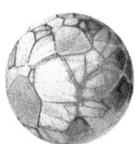

The man without the hat was not the first Harrow had picked up this week, but he was the first with shoes. Most of them walked barefoot.

The wagon, pulled by two stocky horses with contrasting colors—one ashen, one red—slowed as Harrow pulled back on the reins and gave quiet instruction. He regarded the man standing in the middle of the desert, the man with nothing but ragged clothes, singed in spots, covered in dust, the man with shoes too clean to have been on his feet for long. He was slender, as most people in this day were, but only the stubble of a few days' respite from a razor covered his face. Even so, there were telltale signs of exposure to the elements: red skin, crusted saliva around the mouth, pinched eyes.

"Afternoon," Harrow said as the wagon matched the speed of the man.

The man did not look up, nor did he speak. Rather, he continued a slow plod through the desert toward the horizon, a determined gaze fixed upon the unreachable.

"Give you a lift?"

Again, the man said nothing, but an inkling of awareness crossed weathered features. Harrow noted the man's affect and appearance. It was no different from most of the people he picked up along the way. Gaunt, expressionless, soulless. Some of them started their journey toward the horizon early, some late. Some started in the middle, as it was clear this man had.

The man stopped and Harrow pulled on the reins just enough to rest the wagon. He looked at Harrow, then slowly took in the horses resting in the scorching sun, the jockey bench where Harrow sat, the wagon bed and the iron tires wrapped around maple spokes. Harrow sensed the man was processing, absorbing as much information as possible. Likely, he was calculating a response in a brain no doubt slowed from shock, exposure to the elements, or a lack of water. Maybe all three.

"Where are you headed?" Harrow asked.

"Over there." The man's voice cracked as he pointed in an ambiguous direction with a weak jerk of an arm. Harrow noted cracked lips, red with sores, blisters on the backs of a hand. He'd been wandering for a few days.

"Well, hop in. I can give you a ride. There's some water in a bucket and an extra hat for your head."

"Much obliged." The man ambled to the back, stepped into the wagon, then fell in apparent exhaustion on a pile of brown wool blankets. His eyes remained open, fixed on the cerulean blue sky at the end of the world.

Harrow turned. With a quick jerk of the reins, the horses obeyed, and the wagon moved onward.

***

"What's your name?" Harrow looked back. The man was now upright on the blankets, a tin cup of water in a shaky hand cemented to his lips. He finished the last of the water and let the cup drop on the wagon bed.

"Wendel."

"Apt name."

"Yours?"

"Harrow."

"Odd name."

The wagon continued forward, wheels creaking against the hard desert ground. Every so often, a rock jostled the two.

"You say you're headed over there," Harrow said after a moment. "What's over there for you?"

"I don't know. Don't know where I'm going." The man turned around. "Not sure where I've been."

"Not much out here at the end of the world save a horizon you can never catch."

"No. Suppose not." Wendel crawled forward and took up an empty seat next to Harrow. "Dreams, I guess. Mind if I sit?"

"Not at all. I enjoy the company." Harrow chewed on blade of grass. "You been traveling long?"

"All my life with no destination in mind," Wendel said. "If you mean lately, I don't know."

Harrow could not respond to that. The two men looked ahead of the wagon at the vast expanse of scrub brush and wide open sky. The rugged terrain was daunting to look at, and yet peaceful in its way. In the distance, to the left and right, huge rock formations erupted out of the desert floor, defiant fists stabbing heavenward.

"Where you headed?" Wendel asked.

"Avernus."

"Funny name."

"Ever been to Whynot, North Carolina? Last Chance, Iowa?"

Wendel shook his head. "Can't say as I have."

"Funny people make up funny names." A playful smile crossed Harrow's lips.

The wagon bumped over uneven terrain, past parched scrub brush, a few rocks. A lizard sat in the sun on one of them, nervously twitching its tail as the wagon passed. Harrow let himself watch the animal for a moment, a tiny imp confused in a hellish wasteland.

Wendel broke Harrow's trance. "What's at this Aver— Av—"

"Avernus," Harrow said. He tore his eyes away from the lizard and looked ahead. "It's a place to rest. Just over yonder." He pointed toward the horizon with a dirty, crooked finger. "You can relax among friends, put your feet up and do nothing all day."

"Sounds mighty nice. Fancy, even."

"I don't know about fancy, son, but a rest is a rest after a man's long journey." Harrow glanced at his passenger. "Your journey been long?"

Wendel did not respond right away. He looked down at his fingers, picked something out from under a fingernail, looked up at the sky.

"Those blisters hurt, mister?" Harrow asked.

The man turned his hand over and regarded the sores on his skin. Some of the blisters had popped, while other large bubbles had filled with pus.

They sat in silence for another moment. Harrow noted with bemusement that Wendel's leg rhythmically bounced up and down. Wendel looked right, then left, then right again. He was nervous, or perhaps skittish. Impatient.

"You expecting something?" Harrow asked.

"No, no. Just...just not sure where I am or how I got here. Eager to get out of this desert, though. With all that's been going on in the world, I want to block it out, put it behind me."

Harrow nodded, knowingly, but asked anyway, "What's been going on in the world?"

"My world or the world in general?"

"Only got one."

"True." Wendel picked at his fingernails again. "Seems like it's all burning, and now here I am. Feel like I've been walking for days."

"Can't all be bad."

"Can't say any of it was good. Been running my entire life. Feel like I'm chasing the horizon, round and round, trying to make something I can't get right."

"The horizon?" Harrow chuckled. *How many people say the same thing?* "You just keep running? Sounds tiring, if you ask me."

"Sad life."

"Sad. Tiring. A man runs all day, but what if, instead, that man didn't worry so much about that horizon, about what's over there? Some say the destination can be a let down. Some say it's all about being content."

"I don't know about that. Has to be better than this."

Harrow looked at Wendel. There was a definite maudlin quality about the man, a defeatist attitude, but one tinted with perhaps a little realization. "Might feel different if you let yourself enjoy the journey."

Wendel scoffed. "Enjoy what? The wheat that grows the moment you scythe it or this expanse of dirt? Fires that die the moment you light them? Should I enjoy the angry people on the street, the news in the papers? No, mister. I been trying to create something out of my life, and I can tell you, it ain't possible where I'm coming from. It is over there."

Again, Wendel indicated an ambiguous direction with the jerk of an arm.

"I see. You know, some people pay for enjoyment."

Wendel sighed. "I'd pay a mint just to get there, anywhere, over there."

"Hmm." Harrow turned his attention from Wendel and looked ahead of the wagon, ahead at the distant horizon this man so impatiently wanted to get over. The wagon wheels creaked and groaned in rhythm to the clomping of the horses' hooves. A tiny white cloud disrupted the endless sky, and Harrow smiled.

"How much longer?" Wendel asked, interrupting Harrow's revelry.

"Maybe two, three days. We'll rest when the sun sets."

"Got a book to read?"

"Nope." Harrow smiled wider. "But I have something that might help you pass the time when we settle the horses in for the night."

***

"What is this?" Wendel looked at the pill Harrow had placed in his hand. The sun had set, and the glow from a fire between the two gave the pill a reddish tint.

"You wanted something to do, right?" Harrow smiled. "This will help."

Wendel pinched the pill with two fingers and held it up to his face, squinting. "What's it do?"

"Let's you sleep... dream... passes the time."

"Dream?" Wendel looked at Harrow across the fire. "Why dreams? Do little for a man to rest his soul."

"Oh, I've found dreams to be an excellent way to heal whatever the past has thrown at you, escape the present, and find a different path." Harrow shifted his eyes and looked down. He poked at the fire with a stick, noted the way Wendel's gaze drifted from the pill to the flames then back again. "The best part is that you're doing so while you're still on the path you're destined to take."

"Huh. Sounds like a pitch." Another glance at the fire. Curious. "You a peddler?"

Harrow nodded. "I've been known to peddle some things here and some things there."

Wendel looked at the pill again. "Why is it so large?"

"Well, it's not a horse pill, but you'll want to take a drink to wash it down. Works pretty fast. Have to warn you, though. It has a kick. Might be out a while."

"I see." Wendel regarded Harrow again with a distrustful look, a sneer maybe. "And what is this going to cost me?"

"Cost?"

"Yeah. You said some people pay for enjoyment. I reckon that's what you meant. You peddle in these dream pills, but all peddlers have a price."

"Yes, well." Harrow slapped his palms down on his thighs. "I suppose I could trade something with you. What do you have?"

Wendel scoffed and handed the pill back to Harrow. "Got a lot of nothing, mister. Picked up a few coins somewhere. Maybe a little dirt, too."

129

"I see. Well, you can hold your coins for Avernus. I ain't got use for them now. They're just small percentages of a whole, anyway. Incomplete and valueless." Harrow peered at Wendel through slitted eyelids. "You ain't got nothing else?"

Wendel stood up, patted his clothes, then reached into a pocket. He withdrew the coins Harrow said he didn't want along with a small toy. He dropped the coins on the ground and looked closer at the thing in his palm. It was a carved soldier, the kind you buy at carnivals. This one was kneeling, aiming a rifle snapped off as one might be if shoved in the pocket of a man's pants.

The quizzical expression on Wendel's face interested Harrow. "What's that?"

"I don't— I don't remember." Wendel turned the little toy around in his fingers. "Don't know why I have it."

"Seems like an odd thing to take with you."

Wendel nodded slowly. "Must have meant something to me."

"How so?"

"That's just it. I don't know. I—" Wendel shook his head. "I can't recall."

Harrow shrugged and held the pill out for Wendel to take. "Well, if you can't remember, must not be that important. Maybe it was already in your pocket and you just never noticed."

"Maybe." Wendel kept his eyes on the toy. "I just feel— It feels— I don't know."

The fire crackled and one horse made a quick snorting sound. Aside from that, the silence between the two stretched on for a minute as Wendel turned the toy soldier around in his fingers.

"Trade?" Harrow asked, breaking the silence.

Wendel looked up. "Pardon?"

"Trade. I don't take coins, but I'm not above bartering at a gentlemen's level. The way I see it, you can either spend the next two days chatting with me or you can disappear into a dream to pass the time. Either way, we'll be at Avernus soon. It's how you get there that matters."

Wendel looked back at the toy, then slowly held it out. His hand shook a little.

***

The pill worked fast and as advertised. In less than ten minutes, Wendel was asleep in the wagon bed, under the stars. Off to the side, a waning fire painted Harrow's face in devilish desire.

***

The boy is four, maybe five. He sits in the living room of a house filled with old people with their wrinkled apple faces, those his mother claims are her brothers and sisters and aunts and uncles. They are laughing at something someone is saying, paying no mind to the boy. The boy is paying no mind to them, only that they are doing what makes them happy, things that old people do when the sun sets, when the rains come as they do late in the day. When the work moves indoors, play moves indoors, too.

Surrounding the boy are play things, toy soldiers and blocks and a little wooden bowl that may have once held butter made from cows but now serves as a mountain or an obstacle for the invading toy army to attack and overcome. Perhaps today it is a fort, and the little soldier on top holding a rifle and aiming at something is the only survivor, the last stand against the invading hordes, against the other little men frozen in a rictus of war with their cannons or hand guns or bayonets or waving flags poised for a return to action.

The toy soldier on top is the boy, and the boy is making his last stand.

Behind him, out of sight but not out of awareness, the boy's brother stands by a wood stove set up in the living room to provide heat for the old people doing what old people do when the sun sets. The boy knows his brother is doing something with a metal pot the boy had wanted to use as a second fort until his brother took it away, made it his own for what he called an experiment.

The boy doesn't know what an experiment is, but he is curious. He stands, abandons the battle for the wooden overturned bowl. Although he does not know what an experiment is, he understands that if his brother is successful, he will have something new he can play with, something of many colors, of reds and greens and yellows and blues and purples and pinks all blended together, a magical rainbow crayon he says he can use to paint the world. The boy watches as his brother puts the metal pot on the wood stove, as he carefully peels away the paper around each crayon, as he drops them in one by colorful one, as he creates a New Thing.

As he watches the crayons go into the pot and melt, the boy has a feeling he cannot put a name to but recognizes what it is doing to his stomach, to his brain. He wants what his brother has, he wants his own magical crayon of many colors to paint the world. He wants to create the New Thing himself, but he does not have the pot or the colorful wax coloring sticks his brother has.

"Why are they melting?" the boys asks.

"Because wax melts, dummy." His brother is not kind and drops another crayon into the pot.

"Can I have it?"

"No."

The boy is angry. He wants to cry but remembers the last time he cried over something he could not have, his brother hit him with a belt and said that's what Daddy would do if he caught him crying. So the boy watches his brother, aware of whatever feeling he has in his stomach that he cannot name. He watches with eyes that want to fill up with tears but will not because he does not want to be hit again, because he wants to be a big boy like his brother.

His brother drops the last crayon into the pot. It is pink and it melts quickly enough. It joins the other colors, and soon enough, the pot is filled with a rainbow. Rainbows are pretty, they are magical, they have pots of gold at the end and the boy knows if he can have a rainbow New Thing like this, he can paint a pot of gold himself and buy whatever toys he wants.

His brother carefully picks the pot up. "Watch out. This is hot. I'm going to cool it off in the kitchen."

"Can I watch?"

"No. This is mine. Make your own. You got things to melt. It ain't like my things should ever be your things."

The boy wipes away a tear that has fallen on his cheek before his brother sees it and hits him with a belt. He turns away, looks at the floor, at the battle for the wooden overturned bowl frozen in time. The toys he has are red and yellow and blue and green. They are, themselves, a rainbow. If he cannot have the magical rainbow New Thing his brother has just finished making, he can make his own. Some of his toys are made of wax and they would melt. Maybe the other ones would, too. They would blend. All he needs to make his own New Thing is a pot to melt them in.

The old people are still talking and laughing at each other as the boy's brother leaves. The boy turns from the stove and picks up the wooden bowl, puts all his toys inside; all except the one aiming his rifle, the one that once protected the fort, the one that was him. That toy soldier is his favorite and he does not want to lose it. That toy soldier he tucks away in his pocket.

With the rainbow of toys now in the wooden bowl and his brother in the kitchen and the old people turned away, the boy returns to the stove. He carefully places the bowl in the same spot his brother had placed the pot. He waits for it to heat up, for the toys of many colors inside to melt. He is excited. The feeling in his stomach is gone and the tears have dried up. If he cannot have what his brother has, he

132

can make his own New Thing and it will be better than what his brother made. When the toys melt and the colors mix, he can paint the world and a pot of gold and make his brother feel the thing in his stomach.

Maybe he *will cry and Daddy can be mad at* him *for a change.*

***

The wagon wheels creaked as they traveled the desert floor. The sun was high and the heat had returned. Harrow saw another white puff of cloud in the distance, a collection of whatever moisture could be pulled out of the arid world around them. In other places, that cloud would likely grow into a storm. Here, it would eventually go away, replaced by yet more blue sky and more heat.

Wendel stirred. He stretched out on the brown wool blankets in the back of the wagon. Harrow heard him and turned to look.

"Where are we?" Wendel asked.

"Told you it had a kick."

"You weren't wrong about that, mister. How long have I been asleep?"

"A night and a morning. Any good dreams?"

Wendel took a drink of water out of a tin cup and poured the rest over his head. He mussed up his hair and wiped his face dry with his hands before taking the seat next to Harrow on the jockey bench.

"Think I went back in time," Wendel said. He looked around before continuing. "Damn desert looks the same as it did yesterday."

"That's an illusion. The horizon is always just over there, but the mountains to the left and right have grown larger."

"Plants ain't much to look at."

"No, they ain't. So tell me. What was this dream you had? I'm always interested in what my customers experience. Makes for good advertising."

"Just so...odd. There was a little boy, about four or five. Think he was me, but I don't know. He was playing with some little toy soldiers."

Harrow reached into a shirt pocket and held out the toy he had taken as payment for the pill. "Like this?"

"Yeah, that's it. In fact, that's the same toy the boy in the dream..." Wendel trailed off. Harrow glanced his direction and saw the man's eyes drift backward into memory, fixed on a moment rather than any object in the present.

"Go on."

"That's just it. I don't think I can. The boy was playing with the toys and there was a stove. I can't recall what happened. It felt like a

133

memory, though, but some piece of it is missing. What's in that pill, anyway?"

"A few odds and ends. Magic. Whatever you want to call it."

The wagon rolled forward for a quiet minute. Clomp, clomp, clomp.

Finally, Wendel spoke up. "You said dreams help heal whatever the past has thrown at you. What did you mean by that?"

"Dreams are many things. They can be memories, the brain working out problems, or just random thoughts laid out in random ways. Things in the past can seem lost sometimes, but they're nothing but memories we haven't processed, load-bearing walls in the construct of our house. I think sometimes dreams help us repair that wall if it's causing us to behave certain ways later in life."

"If this was a memory, you'd think I'd remember more."

"Maybe. Maybe not."

"Always thought dreams meant nothing."

"No." Harrow chuckled. "They're something so much more."

"What do you mean?"

"Think about it this way. If I gave you a book with a thousand words, you could make up a thousand stories, right?"

"I suppose."

"But you can't make up stories that included words that were not in that book. In that way, you're limited to what you have."

"I'm not following."

"Your memories are those words. Your brain won't make up what it doesn't know, so there are holes. Those random images are not random, are they? They are the words in that book being shuffled around until they make up a new story. What if we could put those words back in the order they first appeared? What if we could patch the holes by using the words of another man's book? Another boy's book?"

"Guess I don't get it." Wendel sighed as his leg rhythmically bounced. "Wish I could go back and figure it out."

Harrow pocketed the little toy and smiled slyly. "You can. For a price, of course."

***

"I'll take a shoelace." Harrow pointed to Wendel's shoes as the two sat apart from each other around another nightly campfire. "You ain't got nothing else I need."

Wendel obliged, removing first a shoe, then pulling its lace through the holes. He passed the lace to Harrow in exchange for another pill.

"We'll be at Avernus tomorrow, so make this one count."

Wendel nodded and choked down the pill.

***

There is the boy again and the wooden container with the toys inside on the stove in the living room. The old people are still talking and laughing at whatever it is old people talk and laugh about. They have their backs to the boy and do not see the first signs of pending trouble, do not see the first flame ignite a piece of wood on the side of the bowl, a piece that drops from the bowl onto the floor.

The boy's eyes are wide as he tries to cover up what he's done by throwing a nearby cloth over the flaming piece of wood. In his haste, the wooden bowl tips over, spills the contents of the melted toys onto the floor.

The fire spreads. The old people turn to see what the boy has done. Some of them are yelling. All of them are on their feet. One of them pulls the boy back from the stove while another tries to put the fire out by batting it down with a blanket. Rather than go out, the fire grows. A spark catches a curtain. Another catches a throw rug. In seconds, the living room explodes into a firestorm and the boy is pulled farther away by the old person, farther away from the fire, farther away from the experiment that was supposed to end in a rainbow crayon with which he could paint the world. It is gone, like the bowl, the stove, the curtains, replaced by flames, by screams, by shouts of direction and the words of unintelligible panic, by the heat and movement and a dozen different smells vying for attention in the boy's nose.

The boy is sitting in the grass now. It is wet. He is scared and does not yet know what he has done, what he has wrought upon his mother, his brother, his father, the old people still in the house. He hears glass break and sees flames erupt from a window. The night sky, so often full of stars, is now fading, turning a reddish gray, covered by smoke rising from the house and lit from the fire. The boy fears he is not far enough away. He can feel the heat. He is not far enough from the fire in the house, from the angry old people, the glances in his direction, the people running from the trough in the barn with buckets. He wonders why they don't use the water from the well, the well Daddy said to never go near, the well his brother said was home to a troll, the well in which he once saw Mommy toss a coin.

His brother. The boy looks around. He cannot see his brother, cannot hear his brother. He does not know if one of the old people grabbed him and pulled him out. He had left the living room to go into the kitchen. Is he still inside? Is he safe? Or did the fire reach him, wrap its devilish fingers of flame around his body, and drag him to the place Mommy said bad people go?

135

Wendel now recognizes himself. He is standing in the grass off to the side, his uncle's house engulfed in fire to his right, the boy in front of him. He watches the boy, the boy who is backing up, the boy who does not see how close to the well he is.

The boy who was his brother.

As rapid as the fire had taken over the house, a surge of regret and guilt—pent-up emotion trapped behind bricks built of self-doubt and denial, of projection and displaced anger—bursts through and floods the tangles of Wendel's mind. He feels his throat constrict even as his eyes grow wider with the realization that it was he who egged his brother on, he who pushed him to place a wooden bowl on a hot stove to make a New Thing, he who was responsible for the fire...he who forgot his brother had died in that well on that night so long ago.

Wendel takes a step toward the boy still backing toward the well. He wants to warn him, to say something to the boy who was his brother, who would still *be his brother if things had turned out differently.*

He wants to, but he does not.

There is something in the grass the boy left behind, something that blends in with the green but stands out because it wants to stand out, because it needs to be a beacon of light in the flood of emotion that threatens to drown Wendel, a buoy on which to cling.

He reaches down and picks up a toy soldier, the kind that is kneeling, the kind that is aiming a rifle. He tells himself he will hold on to it, that he will cherish it, that he will always remember what he did until the day he dies.

He will make the New Thing for his brother. Maybe then they can forgive him.

Wendel blinks. He is in another field, another time. He is no longer a boy, no longer welcome anywhere. In front of him, there is a house on fire, just like his uncle's. A woman screams. People frantically try to douse the flames. A woman writhes on the ground. The scent of burning flesh stings his nose, waters his eyes. He grips the toy soldier in his hand, the rifle digging into his palm as he watches the fire create a New Thing in front of him.

Once more he closes his eyes. The screams fade, the smell dissipates. When he opens his eyes again he sees another house, another attempt at creation. But he is too close. The world fades in and out, black and then orange, black and yellow, black and red. He is dizzy. The smoke in his lungs robs him of consciousness.

When he comes to, heat from another fire rushes over him, and he opens his eyes to see.

136

A larger building in a city. Fire wagons surrounding an inferno, people throwing buckets of water on the flame. He stands across the street and watches, entranced by the flames, comforted by the heat, satisfied with the way the wood pops and crackles and steam trapped inside heats up and bursts. He knows this fire will deconstruct the building, just as it did those crayons, those toys, the other houses, the world. He knows he can finally make the New Thing for his brother. He knows he can paint the sky with magical rainbows, yellows and oranges and reds all rising among the black and brown of smoke.

In his hand, he grips the toy soldier tighter until the rifle snaps off.

***

Harrow backed the wagon up to a precipice. Far below, the rotting bodies of men and women and children clambered over each other, stretched out to find purchase on the vertical sides, to find a way to climb out of the pit. They moaned and cried and wailed and screamed. There was room for a million more and then some. No doubt, as Harrow completed his delivery of this man, he would return to the desert and find another and another. Perhaps they will recall why they were chasing the horizon in the first place, why they wandered in the desert with no destination in mind. Perhaps they won't need a pill to remember.

It's a nice thought, but they all need a pill. True sins can leave voids in the brain, empty spaces where memory should be. The pill helps fill in past transgressions with facts from someone else's point of view.

As the horses pulled the wagon forward and the still sleeping body of Wendel tumbled out of the bed and into the pit, Harrow reached into his pocket and took out the little toy soldier. He regarded it for a moment, turned it in his fingers, then tossed it to land among the detritus of a million other payments made for a chance to learn the truth, a million other reminders of the wages of sin, the price of guilt.

Benjamin X. Wretlind

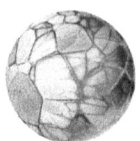

Benjamin X. Wretlind ran with scissors when he was five. He now writes, paints, uses sharp woodworking tools and plays with glue. Sometimes he does these things at the same time. A retired Air Force veteran, Benjamin currently builds and facilitates leadership courses for staff at Yale. A multi-genre author, Benjamin's latest is *Out of Due Season: The First Transit*, the first in an anthropological science fiction series. He is also the author of *Castles, Sketches from the Spanish Mustang* and many other novels. Benjamin lives with his wife Jesse in Colorado.

You can find him on his Website, Twitter and Facebook.

Black Man Running, 1969

Lawrence Good

Henry Redwell is running. He is the urban Black man running. That is to say that it looks as if he is running *away* from something because he is running and because he is black.

He is running to escape the gathering, the soul rally, the thousands of Black men and women who have joined with hundreds of whites this afternoon in Morningside Park, in Harlem, to show solidarity with each other, and to simply gather as young men and women of a new era. It is, after all, the dawning of the Age of Aquarius. There is the hit song, there is the Broadway musical, and there are many such gatherings on each coast proclaiming it so.

Henry Redwell did more to plan and stage this soul rally in Morningside Park in East Harlem on October 5th, 1969, than anyone else on the committee. They were to celebrate their soul brothers and soul sisters, soul food, soul art, soul poetry and politics and theater, and a soul band *The Family Shade,* and to fête people younger than the civil rights guys, more peaceful than the Black Panthers, blacker than the hippies, the yippies, or *La Raza*.

Today it comes to pass. But just back there, in an attack of panic Henry ran from the park and the festival. He shot out Morningside Drive, north up Amsterdam Avenue and around City College, then east on West 141st Street. Now running south on Lenox Avenue, the blocks come short and quick, one after another, Black man running, steady, strong.

"One man's peace is another man's poison," he tells himself. "And I have been poisoned. "I have been poisoned with peace." The irony strikes him, but he doesn't laugh. It's not funny irony. It just *is*. Bad things happen, and they *did*, or they *are*, and Henry is running, and he doesn't think he can stop running or they *will*.

He cuts over to Madison Avenue and continues south. He is some athlete. A bystander might admire his form, his strength, his endurance, his physique, but the truth is—and Henry understands this fully at this moment—the specter of him running the streets of New York causes alarm, fear, concern, curiosity. Black man running. Up the block, a man crosses the avenue and out of Henry's path. Henry watches as if from above his body. He is becoming omniscient.

He is running out of his mind. Winded, tired, he cuts over to Fifth Avenue and heads straight for Mount Morris Park. With a left on 124th Street and a right onto Madison Avenue, he is circumnavigating the park, and with another right off 120th Street onto Mount Morris Avenue West he completes the shape of a question mark and runs beneath the haughty nose of his grandfather's old Mount Morris home. He doesn't look up at the three-story house. He looks down, at his Hush Puppy shoes, at the pavement. Here, the sidewalk belongs to Henry Redwell, every crack, every dip, every root-borne upheaval.

Peace is granted, by the continuity of this moment with his childhood. Then he turns again, right again, into the tree shadows and the peace and the space and the quiet and the refuge of Mount Morris Park. He runs toward the leafy center, past the baseball field. He slows to a jog, then, heaving and panting he stops, bends, and folds his elbows over his knees. He has, and still is playing out a scene of American history. A scene with many settings, many characters, and many endings, which is, in its own way a celebration of soul. Black man running.

Then he stops. A squirrel snatches something nearby in the grass and scoots up a tree. Above, a blue jay shrieks from the branches, offended by Henry's sudden panting. The jay's shriek shocks Henry, the jolt running up to his brain, instantly. Henry shudders. A vicious bird. They eat their young. Maybe not their own young, but little Henry once watched in horror as a jay tore a pink baby bird apart.

He moves on, leaves this thought to the jay and to any other creature man or beast that is-concerned with his presence here. But first, he's got to catch some air. He's gulping air and now he's gotta burp. Burp. *There.*

The park curves away from him, imitating the curve in the path and the curvature of the earth and he has a sensation of falling as he walks, the ground liquid. Across the path is a strip of lawn and beyond that, 120th Street intersects Mount Morris Avenue. He stands near the edge of the common, beyond right and center fields of the baseball diamond, hands on his knees, breathing hard. He has reached the end of the question mark.

Directly across Mount Morris Avenue, there's the house again. *Grandfather*. It seems to bow toward him, the fences fold together like praying hands, pay their respects. The stately mansion recognizes him; it beckons, to royalty, to family.

Henry Redwell, late twenties, hasn't been inside the home in two decades, poor, hungry, breathing hard, sweating, a soul brother, out of his mind, running away from a soul celebration exploding back there in his wake. *His* soul celebration.

He imagines what's going on back there in the triangle, and looks behind him as if to see it only a couple blocks away instead of the four miles he's run. *The Family Shade* is playing by now, and they are dancing in every color of every African flag all at once, in fur boots and shirtless vests with electric instruments and crazy moves and they are psychedelic and soulful and defiant and high and crazy and defiant and high and crazy and defiant and high and crazy...his imagination skips back to the same spot with every revolution. He would push it forward over the scratch, stop it, *but how?* A universal clarity is costing him a microscopic sanity. *The Family Shade* and their mind-expanding drugs are responsible for that. So is Henry.

Henry Redwell, a young artist of high regard, who put on a soul celebration, dreamed it up and lived it and created the visionary poster and even arranged for today's performance by *The Family Shade* but when the day came and the band went on, Henry had run away to find himself, or re-find himself, or maybe to lose himself here in Mount Morris Park.

Some of the history here is personal, sure. When Henry was a kid these same oaks, this same path, this same baseball field—the entire park— seemed to belong to his grandfather's mansion like a plantation's acreage; a view representative of what was possible at one time for a black family in Harlem, a view that certainly inspired Grandma Antonia's guests and colleagues at her civil rights rallies.

Henry looks to the house. An upstairs window winks. Another jay claims its' territory with a shriek, expresses a murderous rage. "Stop!" Henry caws. His voice sounds strange, underwatery, but shrill. A vision of Papa Jay Shade up on the bandstand rolls in like a Macy's Day parade float—his big, ugly grin and his giant sunglasses, then the whole *Family Shade* all shiny, with glinting eyes. "Can't get away from the jays!" Henry's nervous laughter regresses to a raptor grunt.

A white couple walking, winding slowly up the path snaps Henry to attention. He tries to stop his laughter, but the effort only feeds it. He cackles, just like the enraged jay in the very tree beside him. Its' shrieking is a mockery of Henry's cackling. He is losing control of the sound of his own voice. He knows he sounds like a crazy man because he is a crazy man, and, dammit, Paula Shade and Deedee and Papa Jay dosed him back there, behind the stage at the rally, dosed him with their psychedelic drugs, in a Pepsi, on a Kool filter, in a damn cookie or a popsicle, and that's why he ran here, and that's how he's been poisoned with peace and that's why he can't stop laughing!

White couple walking, approaching, nearby, then too close. They speed up to pass, and most deliberately they do not look at Henry, who is turned away, also deliberately, as if to commune with this tree right here—which shakes loose another seismic wave of laughter that he can't control and he can't hide and the loud bird is impressed but pissed off nevertheless, matching him cackle for cackle.

A shadow passes over the tree, draws Henry's laughter away, replaces it with…fear?

A Black man with no place to go who can't stop laughing…*a Black man could get himself into a lot of trouble really quickly, get hauled off and arrested and for no other reason than…*cackling!

This ridiculous irony, this truth, that it is possible for some people, Black people, for him, Henry Redwell to be jailed for excessive and uncontrollable public laughter—this only makes him helpless to stop his nervous cackling, because the elements of the ridiculous and the irony and self-awareness and fear have, in Henry's unraveling mind defined a self-fulfilling prophecy that Henry can not ignore or undo.

Bwa-ha-ha-ha-hee-hee…wheeze. Another wave sweeps through.

At the far east end of the park, at Madison Avenue, Henry sees a Ford police cruiser parking, and he recognizes the next step of the prophecy. Both doors open and policemen emerge from each side of the car. *A pair of police.* Henry tries to quiet his cackling but the irony, the prophecy, the serious business of this life as a young Black man in Harlem in 1969 in these United States of America at the dawning of the Age of Aquarius cannot be quelled.

His cackling is ridiculous, and it is shifting, changing, into waves. Henry is sobbing now. *Go. Now. Run, Hide. Where?*

He moves towards his grandfather's house, beyond left field on the baseball diamond, walking behind center field now, away from the officers who are crossing the park toward him, and he speeds up a little and the officers' pace also becomes more strident, and Henry wonders if he will start to run, and then he knows he will and he wonders only, *when?*

He is significantly closer to Grandfather's old house, his accelerated walk has bought him mere seconds against the officers' pace…if he could go back in time, just a little way back, he would be safe, welcomed by his Grandmother Antonia and his Grandfather EJ, and he would have a little visit with them—it's Saturday after all—and then after this visit with the dead in this house long gone from his family, he will be safe and he will stop laughing and then he will make his way back to the soul celebration. In 1969.

These past generations, these lives rake through Henry's mind, in the moment he takes to glance back across the park to his pursuers who are gaining on him and running unabashedly now and with no pretense of walking innocently toward him.

He dives into the avenue of Mount Morris Park West without looking and tires screech and a long blast of horn passes too close beside him, and then another, sounding angrily in his wake, sending another electric shock up his spine, and then he is across, standing in this front yard at the bottom step of his grandfather's front stoop; a moment in the peace and shade of this quiet, seemingly empty house that makes it feel as though he got away!

But Henry is the quarry, prey, a Black man running. The police are white, predators, and Henry is to be captured; that is the prophecy Henry recognizes from his spot at the bottom of his grandfather's front stoop. He drops to his knees, sobs quietly, folds his hands, looks back up at the old Redwell home where his grandmother held union rallies and planned boycotts and where Duke Ellington stayed when he was in town and. . . .

Henry stands now. The cops are nearly on him. Henry needs refuge, sanctuary. A moan shudders up his lean torso and over his chest to ripple over his shoulders and cascade down the other side.

His Aunt Bug grew up here, began raising him here, and he grew up here for a time, and he thinks friendly thoughts while he can, certain that he is about to grow up here some more. He sobs again, and then at a moment he is up the stoop, finds the front door unlocked and he is over the threshold. He steps into the foyer. A grand staircase on the left leads to a railed hall upstairs. To his right is a substantial living room through which a brilliant bolt of daylight startles him. A piano once stood where the light forks into the floor. Then a shadow dims the hall for a moment.

"Hello?" he calls. "Anybody?"

Nobody. Henry will cross the house to the backyard and away, way away from the police. He goes around the staircase to the kitchen, a back door, a landing outside with a wooden stair down to a small yard. Of course! Henry remembers this landing. Breakfast out here sometimes. Watermelon, too. But never on the front stoop. Grandma Antonia's law; one Henry follows to this day.

Behind him, the front door slams. Another moan catches in his chest. He stops breathing.

"Hands up! NYPD!" comes the shout. Deep, manly, white authority. Henry steps out onto the landing.

The voice again. "Hands up, Mister."

Henry runs down the back stairs, out into the yard where he is tackled by the other cop.

"Why'd you run, boy? Why'd you run?" with each question another fist, knee, elbow, foot. Henry is sobbing hard again, the reflex too strong to control, to explain, to tell these men that are beating his body as if it is their civil right, that this house was once his Grandpa EJ's house, that Duke Ellington stayed here, and Effa Manley. Joe Louis came over, the Nicholas Brothers—Fayard and Harold—and ballplayers, politicians, businessmen, soldiers, all good people who tried to make the country great, and safe for their Black grandchildren, one of whom these white men are beating the crap out of right in front of them all, right here in EJ's backyard. The irony strikes again, and Henry giggles, then cackles uncontrollably through a bloody red mouth and loosened bloody teeth, his hysteria making the police hit harder— *which you should know already*—and steels the irony over the crazy cackling, and so on, and in this way the prophecy of a dark, dark justice comes true to a young Black man.

And then the laughter stops as darkness reigns and when eventually Henry regains the light, the laughter has stopped, maybe forever, and Henry Redwell appreciates, inversely, that he is orphaned of his family, of his country, and of the Harlem, New York neighborhood to which he was once born into royalty.

No Aunt Bug to bail him out, no one who will understand his story; no one to recognize that he was looking only for sanctuary in the home that had once been his birthright; no one who will comprehend the irony of the situation that will take him on a journey through two mental institutions and a two-year prison stretch in upstate New York, where, ironically but never again humorously, he will join a soul celebration that is to include almost half of the young black men of New York City.

It is the dawning of the Age of Aquarius.

Lawrence Good

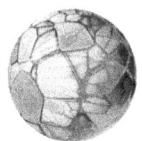

Lawrence Good is a writer, teacher, recording artist, and film and broadcast producer/composer. He studied writing with Tobias Wolff at Stanford University and wrote op-ed columns for the *Aspen Daily News*, *Aspen Times*, *High Country News,* and once, the *Denver Post*. His YA sports novels "The Other Jackie Robinson", and "Losers' Bracket" are ready for representation. He lives in a mountain lodge in the tiny village of Marble, Colorado. His younger son is the country music recording artist David Walker Good.

The Last Ember Fades

Lou J. Berger

Standing amid the house's ruins, Ron held the bottle up to the sunlight, squinting at the soot-covered, black label. He wiped it and the words "Tennessee Sour Mash Whiskey" appeared through the filth. He placed the bottle into his new backpack, which he then shrugged on.

The bottle would do for what he had in mind.

The sun glared in the cloudless blue sky. He drew his filthy hand across his forehead, sweat slicking his palm, then stepped through the burned-out remnants of the house's walls. His hiking boots crunched broken glass and melted asphalt tiles. Ron shuffled in the general direction of home.

He wasn't worried anymore about the roving hordes of monsters, not like he had been just after the Change.

A smile crept across his lips. They weren't *really* monsters. Then again, they weren't quite human anymore, either.

The sun felt good on his arms, and warmth burrowed through his thinning hair, soothing his shoulders through the rough denim of his shirt, the one he'd found at the Sears near his house. The one good thing about the Change was that he would never want for material things again. The monsters cared nothing for possessions.

Ahead, three of them muttered and gibbered at one another, facing each other in a loose circle, their fingers twitching. One looked familiar. Ron stopped.

Mrs. Willingham had worked as a crossing guard for the neighborhood elementary school. With her curly hair coiffed nicely, she favored sensible shoes beneath the cuffs of crisp polyester pants.

Now, dirt lined her face and her hair hung in stringy tendrils. From a wide tear in her blouse, one brutally sunburned breast swung free. As Ron approached, a vile whiff of body odor assaulted him.

"Hello, Mrs. Willingham," he said, his voice low.

She swung her head in his direction, still gibbering. Her eyes widened and she pointed at him, opening her mouth.

"Gah!" she said, revealing stained, broken teeth. Her tongue moved wetly inside her red mouth. She whimpered and fled, crashing into the brush at the side of the road before stumbling away.

The others glanced in his direction, then ignored him, moving their fingers and muttering to one another, oblivious of the woman's abrupt departure. These two might have been body-builders, before the Change. They were carved in muscle. Their massive hands flexed in their strange finger-dance.

Queasy at the thought of their strength, Ron stepped around them, moving toward home again.

***

After the Change, he'd cowered in his basement for God knows how long, shotgun clutched in his sweaty hands. In only a few days, the world had spiraled into chaos. Everybody he knew, even his wife and his friends, had turned into powerful animals. They only *looked* human, bounding in groups with one another, hunting dogs and cats until they had stripped the neighborhood clean of smaller mammals. Outside his window, an infirm old woman scaled a forty-foot evergreen, where she snatched a squirrel in desperate mid-leap. She devoured it raw. The monsters would meet on street corners, gibbering together.

For months, Ron darted out at night to raid the grocery store a half-mile from his house. He kept that up until the stench of rotting food repelled him.

One dusk, he'd stumbled upon a group of six monsters. They swung their heads, as if synchronized, and chased him. Panic spurred his feet but, after only a city block, he couldn't maintain the pace. Panting like a steam-engine, he turned down an alley, bounced off garbage cans, and hurtled between piles of distended black plastic bags.

A chain-link fence blocked him. He leapt, but couldn't haul himself over. His fingers tore on the unforgiving metal links.

His pursuers' footsteps slowed behind him.

Ron strained one last time, then dropped to the concrete, panting and sobbing. His heart raced and ragged breath seared his chest. He coughed and his mouth filled with thick, ropy saliva, which he spat between his feet.

"Please," he said. "Leave me alone."

The first to reach him, a teenager with wild hair and rolling, fluttering eyes, stretched out a filthy hand and touched his shoulder.

Ron's fear and panic, every accumulated terror, snapped. He screamed, fists clenched, and something inside him . . . broke. A kind of release. Whatever it was, all the attackers took a simultaneous step from him, confusion crossing their faces.

"Huh," said the teenager, his face a mask of confusion. "What? I don't get it." He looked at his hands, examining the filth, then sniffed his own armpit, recoiling in shock. "Damn! I stink!" He noticed Ron for the first time. "Hey, old man. What am I doing here? Who the hell are you?"

Not waiting for an answer, the kid turned and shouldered his way through the others and left the alley, muttering something about finding Mom and a hot shower, in that order.

In a similar fashion the others had dispersed, their faces masked with confusion, leaving Ron alone at the end of the alley, exhausted and drained from his encounter. He'd gathered himself and gone home, heating cistern water to take a much-needed bath.

Days later, Ron saw the same teenager shuffling back and forth on another street corner, once more returned to his eye-rolling and muttering, no cleaner than when he'd left the alley. Whatever touching Ron's shoulder had done to shift him into some kind of consciousness, some normalcy, it hadn't lasted too long.

Shifting, he realized, was a means to help others recapture their humanity. Maybe he didn't have to be alone forever, after all.

***

Some days, Ron didn't want to stay inside, knowing the empty house had nobody to talk to, nobody to play chess with, nobody to *be* with.

He paused, mid stride, then changed direction, choosing another street through the dilapidated, disintegrating suburban neighborhood. Charles. He needed to see Charles. It had been too long.

Ron walked past middle-class homes, their lawns brown and overgrown in the dry Colorado summer. Had it been a virus? Mass hysteria? Before the Change, Alicia would admonish him against letting his imagination run away from him. Then, she'd turned into a monster, too.   He rounded the corner.

Charles stood on the sidewalk, staring at a dandelion, a lone flower in the cracked concrete. He looked thinner, but strong muscles flexed beneath his sun-darkened skin. Ron admired Charles's new physique, a flat belly replacing what had been a comfortable, middle-aged one.

Ron approached Charles and placed a gentle hand on the man's shoulder, wary until Charles twitched, the Shift blooming inside him.

Charles blinked, grabbed his head with both hands, and swayed. "My head hurts."

Ron steadied him. "You okay?"

As if clearing out the cobwebs, Charles shook his head. "Yeah." He looked through bleary eyes and seemed to notice Ron for the first time. His face fell. "Aw, goddammit, Ron," he said, his voice tired. "Again? Why can't you just let me alone?"

Ron grimaced. "Sorry, bud. I dunno. Call me stupid. Why wouldn't I just leave my best friend alone, acting like a forest animal?"

Charles blinked.

"Never mind," Ron said. "It's done. Let's get you cleaned up."

Charles looked down at his filthy clothes and the dirt encrusting his arms. He fingered a scab on the back of his hand. "I don't even remember how I got this. Fine. Let's go to your place for a hot shower. I'm starving."

Ron glanced periodically at Charles as they walked to his house, the one with the only well-kept lawn on the block. The way lawns *should* be tended, at all times.

Once inside, Ron pointed upstairs. "You know where the shower is."

Charles stomped upstairs without a response.

Ron set up the chess board, blowing dust off the pieces. In the kitchen, he turned on the gas stove as the noise from the upstairs shower started. Charles tromped upstairs, and the shower pan squeaked as it shifted under the hot spray.

When Charles came downstairs, toweling his hair, Ron set down three turkey sandwiches, a hot mug of beef-and-barley soup, and a tall glass of tea.

"Sorry, no salad," Ron said.

Charles waved dismissively and attacked the sandwiches. "I'm amazed you still have food. How long has it been since last time?"

Ron rolled a bishop in his fingers. "Eight weeks, about. It's tough to keep track when nobody else uses a calendar anymore. It's like I'm the only one that gives a damn what day it is."

Charles nodded, mouth full of turkey sandwich, and motioned toward the board. "You start."

Ron swung the board around and moved his white pawn from his king. "So what's it like?" he said, voice neutral.

Charles frowned and nudged his own king's pawn out. "It's amazing. I run in the sun, I hunt for food and I have meaningful, deep relationships with everybody I meet, instantly. It's as if I've known them forever, their every thought and feeling, and they love me. Doesn't matter who they are, they love me. No fighting, no jealousy, no goddamn anger at anybody. All I know is that I'm happy, not a care in the world, and then you come along every now and again and ruin it."

They played in silence, Charles's stinging words hanging between them. Each moved a dozen pieces.

At last, Ron spoke. "You say you're happy, but you should see yourself when you're changed. Standing there, wiggling your fingers and talking nonsense all day. It's not living. Where's your sense of duty, of ambition? You hardly eat anything, you're dehydrated. Heck, I don't think you've bathed since last time you were here."

Charles paused, knight in hand, and looked at Ron. "You don't understand, is what it is. I don't care about those things anymore. Sure, now that you've changed me back, I guess I care a little. But when I'm in that other state, I'm happy, Ron! Truly happy! The conversations aren't nonsense, by the way. It's the most honest communication I have ever experienced. There's no guile, no deceit. It's fantastic!"

Ron snorted. "That doesn't make sense. You used to read. You used to watch television. Granted, television isn't exactly an option anymore, but you went to work, you earned a living, you bought groceries. You were working for your future just like the rest of us! What has happened to everybody but me is that you all seem to have gotten this cosmic memo saying 'you don't have to care anymore!'"

"Ron, it's not like that. Why you didn't change, I can't begin to imagine. You sit here, in this clean house, in clean clothes, and you look down on me with your pity and your holier-than-thou attitude. The world has moved on, buddy. It's not about the external anymore. It's about the collective mind, the groupthink, the passion of being fully human and alive, part of something more than selfish desires and this!" He waved his hands around, indicating the interior of Ron's house. "Sure, we've gotten a bit grungy and thin, but we are living, truly living, for the first time in our lives. You hold on to these antiquated ideas and you act as if somehow you're better. Well you're not!" Charles raised his voice and a white-knuckled fist. Ron flinched. Charles sighed and leaned back.

"So it's better for you, I see that," Ron said slowly. "I just sit here, in this house, alone. I feel like the last human on the planet."

"And why, exactly, is that my problem?" Charles sneered. "You seek me out, yank me from my world and back into yours, all because you're lonely? Why don't you just become one of us and put this old world behind?" Charles stood, voice trembling. "You might actually *be* the last human on Earth. Grow up, Ron. You're holding yourself back from the next step, when all the rest of us have already moved on."

Ron raised his hands in surrender. "Okay, okay. I hear you. Could we finish the game, please?" Charles's shoulders slumped and the anger drained from his eyes.

"Sure, I suppose. I owe you for the food, I guess."

They finished the game. Ron cracked open a beer and handed it to Charles, then they moved to the back porch.

Charles pointed at Ron's empty hands. "Aren't you going to have one?" he asked.

"I don't drink. I don't like the loss of mental acuity."

Charles grinned. "Buddy, there's your problem right there. You don't allow yourself to *live*. You keep yourself locked up in your mind while the rest of us live our lives. You should try it sometime, losing control." He stretched his huge shoulders and turned his head from side to side, cracking the small bones in his neck.

They watched the sunset together, but Ron got the sense that Charles was only humoring him.

"How long before you turn back?" Ron asked, keeping his voice light.

Charles shrugged, draining half his beer in a single long pull. "Dunno. As long as I'm near you, I have no trouble staying human. It's only when I'm back near my own kind that I feel the Change growing within me. It's a relief, I tell you. My entire thought process feels stunted and warped right now. I can't even begin to describe how good it feels to change back. This old human life? It sucks."

Ron thought, trying out different ways of saying it in his mind. Finally he just said it. "So, have you seen Alicia around?"

Charles froze, still gazing at the setting sun, and his voice grew quiet. "Please, for the sake of everything we once meant to each other, please tell me you didn't change me back just to talk about Alicia."

Ron kept his voice neutral. "No, of course not. I've missed you, our chess games, your friendship. If you don't want to talk about her, then I understand. It's just that this house feels so … empty." He waved his hands around helplessly. "You know? It's like she never existed. Even her clothes stopped smelling like her."

Charles was silent for a while. When he spoke again, his voice was tired, resigned. "Let her alone, Ron. Just let her alone." When Ron didn't immediately reply, his eyes widened. "If my friendship ever meant a single goddamn thing to you, promise me that you'll leave her alone, okay?"

Ron picked at the beer bottle's label, frowning. He didn't say anything.

Charles stood up and hurled his bottle to the patio's concrete floor, smashing it into pieces. "Dammit, Ron! I'm serious! You can't keep messing around in other people's lives!" He opened the sliding glass door and took a step inside, then turned back to Ron. "And another thing. Thanks for the food, thanks for ten years of friendship, but do me a favor, buddy, okay?" His calm, icy voice sent a chill through Ron's chest.

Ron reached up and brushed off a shard of glass that had stuck on his cheek from the shattered bottle, but didn't meet Charles' eyes. The sour smell of beer hung in the air. He said nothing.

Charles's voice dripped into Ron's ear like mercury. "Don't do it again, okay? Don't shift me back. Leave me alone. If you ever liked me in any way, do me this one favor, okay? Leave me alone and, in the name of all that I ever meant to you, let me go."

Ron didn't look up, didn't answer. Charles closed the door gently, almost with reverence, and Ron listened to his footsteps cross the living room floor. He heard him open the front door and close it behind him. He followed, sprinting through the living room and threw open the front door. Charles had turned down the sidewalk, approaching a group of monsters that had gathered in the middle of the street three houses away.

Ron watched as Charles approached them, his stride firm and purposeful, then saw Charles hunch over, swelling in the chest and shoulders, his stride turning into a lope as he seemed to inflate from within. His body developed powerful musculature until he looked more like an animal than a human. His fingers came up and began to twitch. His head bowed and, in the dim light of dusk, Ron realized that he could no longer tell Charles apart from the others.

***

That night, Ron dreamed of Shifting. He ran through the streets, the pavement disappearing beneath his clever feet, his lungs breathing in the sweet night air as he chased a whitetail deer through residential yards. As he ran he could sense, on either side, companions flitting through the darkness with him, intent on the hunt, their minds communicating telepathically.

With Alicia on his left and Charles on his right, together they leaped six foot cedar-plank fences with ease, powerful leg muscles bunching as the deer fled before them. He could *see* the blood running as hot white light through the deer's body, could *smell* the exhalations of panic from the deer's lungs wafting back on the night air.

When they caught the deer, he snapped its neck with powerful hands and they feasted together, their mouths ripping and tearing, full of meat and hot blood, but their thoughts swirling around and among them. He could sense the desire in Alicia's mind, the pride in her man having caught the deer, the deep admiration in Charles's mind, his best friend in the world. Together, they gorged on the deer's meat in the moonless darkness of a Colorado suburb. They had food, and each other, and nothing else was necessary. He leaned back from the carcass, blood pouring down his chin, soaking his chest, and howled at the night sky, euphoria filling him with glee.

***

When Ron awoke, he lay in bed and listened to the silence of the house. No hum of a refrigerator, no whir of an air conditioner. He made breakfast on the gas stove, using the eggs and the milk from the freezer in the basement. He started the compressor in the garage to keep it cold, then shut it off after twenty minutes. He needed to get more gasoline from the service station down the street. When he left, he locked the front door, gas can banging against his leg, intending to walk to the station.

His feet took him, instead, to the old brownstone where he'd last seen Alicia. He stood in front of her door, wondering if he had the courage to face her again.

He reached out and grabbed the brass knocker, banging it twice. He stepped back from the door and waited. Something shuffled behind the door. It opened on creaking hinges and a wild mane of red hair appeared in the opening. Two green eyes peered out.

Ron stepped forward and Shifted her. She staggered back and yelled, scrambling for balance. She managed to not fall down.

"Dammit Ron! I asked you to leave me alone!" She clutched at her dress, a loose assortment of rags torn by her long, filthy nails. She wailed as she lifted her hands to her hair. "God, I'm a mess. Just . . ." She whirled around and disappeared inside.

Ron followed, closed the front door and moved deeper into the darkness of Alicia's home. He could smell her unwashed body, the stench of decay filling the house. He found her in the bathroom on the main floor, struggling with faucet handles. She fumbled with them, turning them back and forth. He reached over and put his hands on hers. "The power is out. It's been out for months. There's no running water."

156

Lou J. Berger

She sat on the edge of the tub and put her hands in her lap, twisting at the rags of her dress. After a bit, she looked up at him, and he could see runnels of clean skin where tears had washed away the dirt on her face. "Why," she wailed at him. "Why do you come here and change me back? I was happy without you! I didn't notice all . . . this." She waved at the wallpaper peeling from the walls of the bathroom, at the rat carcasses out in the hall. Ron glanced at a rat with a large tear in its side. Maggots hunched themselves, gleaming and fat, through the torn flesh and fur. He looked back at Alicia. "Honey, I hate to see you this way. Come home. I have warm water and soap at the house. Just come home with me."

She stood up and hissed at him, angry. "Just leave me alone. I don't want to bathe, to get clean. I don't *care* how I look, why do *you*? You come in like you're saving me and you just don't get it. I don't want to be saved. You see? I have what I want. When you aren't around, I'm happy, Ron. Can't you get that through your head? *I. Am. Happy*. You come along, thinking you are helping me, but you take from me the very thing I want."

Ron felt the words hit him like body blows. A part of his mind admonished him to listen, to hear her side of things, while another part grew angry and defensive.

"And another thing," she continued, poking him with a rigid finger. "You think you're this high and mighty guy, walking around flaunting your humanity. You think you're better than we are." She bit off each word. "You aren't, you know. I can't stand being human anymore. There, I said it. Are you shocked? Do you believe me? Because it's true!" She stomped from the bathroom and he followed her. Every time he Shifted her, he could tell she resented it. This time, though, she was really upset.

He followed her into the kitchen, which smelled like an abattoir; a thick odor of blood and spoiled meat hung in the air.

"Ron, I'm tired," she said with resignation. "I'm tired of having this same discussion. I want to be left alone for good."

"Yeah, Charles just told me the same thing, last night."

Alicia turned to look at him and her eyes were filled with tears. "Can't you just let me be? Can't you just walk away?"

"I still love you, you know," Ron said. The words sounded hollow, even to him.

Alicia turned and opened a drawer, then pulled out a long knife. She showed it to him. "Get out, Ron. Walk out of my house and never return. If you do . . ." she brandished the knife at him and he saw muscles clench in her jaw. He raised his hands, palms forward.

"Fine, Alicia. If you want it that way, I get it. I'm leaving."

He backed out of the kitchen and moved through the townhouse until he stood on the front porch again. Ron looked back at Alicia. She stood in the doorway, still holding the knife. He took a breath to speak but, before he could say anything, she slammed the door and locked it.

He picked up his gas can from the sidewalk and resumed his trek to the service station. Fine. He would leave her alone. Let them go on without him. He didn't need them anyway. But the ache of loneliness grew in his chest, filling him with a hollow pain that radiated through his body. He could hold out until they came to their senses. He could hold out for years if he needed to. The thought didn't give him any pleasure. Not even a little.

***

Six months later, he'd moved into a larger house, one the previous owner had improved with generators and solar panels prior to the Change. Most of the monsters in Denver had migrated south, following the sun, leaving him even more alone. He still saw Alicia from time to time, but always from a distance. He hadn't seen Charles in weeks. He must have gone south with the rest of them.

He tried to keep his days active, but loneliness was pervasive. One night, he made himself a quick dinner, cooking over a camp stove. He had hundreds of green propane canisters in the pantry, a lifetime's supply for cooking. His shotgun leaned against the dining room table and he ate in silence, standing upright and listening to the clock tick on the wall. It measured off slow beats of time, slicing away valuable seconds and tossing them carelessly away, filling the silence with the sounds of his chewing and the clock's inexorable ticking.

He stared at the clock and stopped chewing, his mouth hanging open. Now the only sounds were the clock ticking and the slightly wheezy intake of his own breath. He held his breath. Now only the clock ticked.

The silence grew, developed, then became a roaring in his ears that threatened to smother him. He felt his own heartbeat in his forehead as his lungs burned. He maintained the silence, straining not to gasp.

He stood, trying to will the clock to stop mocking him. To stop reminding him of how alone he truly was. The last human in a world gone dark for humanity, no longer wanted.

Lonely. The clock ticked relentlessly, the double sound of "tick-tock" sounding out the syllables of the word itself.

Lonely. Lonely.

His face grew taut with the strain of not breathing, his cheeks aching, his vision narrowing as the blood pounded in his temples, the clock locked in his view, still ticking, still mocking.

"Shut up!" he screamed, soggy bits of food splattering on the dining room table before he finally dragged in a breath. "Shut up! Stop mocking me!" He glared with malevolence at the monstrous clock, focusing his anger and pent-up rage into a brilliant point of light. He grabbed the shotgun from where it leaned against the table and pumped it once, jacking a shell into the chamber. He leveled it at the clock and heard, through a fog, an insane-sounding giggle.

Lonely, said the clock. Lonely.

"Don't push me, okay? I'm really sick of your crap."

Lonely. Lonely.

He felt a tightness gathering in his chest, swirling like summer storm clouds over mountains.

"Shut up."

Lonely. Lonely. *Lonely*.

He squinted, sighted along the barrel of the shotgun, and squeezed the trigger. The clock blew apart, sending splinters flying. The roar of the shotgun deafened him for a bit. He touched his suddenly-numb cheek and felt something hard jutting out, just beneath his right eye. Wetness rolled down his face and plopped on his shirt. He looked at his hand, covered in blood. He reached up again and grasped the hard object and explored it with his fingertips. It felt like wood, about the thickness of a pencil. And it was embedded in his cheek. He pulled on the wooden splinter and it hurt. He yanked it free and stared at it. It was a shard from the clock.

He laughed. Wait until Charles got a load of this. He froze, remembering. No more Charles. Charles had moved on, had asked him not to bother him again. He felt a momentary pang that only intensified when he thought of Alicia. She didn't want him either.

He laughed again, but this time the laugh became a sob. Just him and the clock, repeating itself as if to underscore Ron's solitude.

Lonely. Lonely.

But the clock was gone. He'd blown it to pieces. The clock couldn't hurt him anymore. So it was just him, the last human on Earth. A burning ember, the last bits of humanity's fire, glowing in the darkness. Sitting in his dining room. Laughing. Alone.

He could still hear the clock, mocking him, in his mind.

He jacked another shell into the chamber and pushed the barrel of the shotgun under his chin, rested his thumb on the trigger. Just a man, alone in his dining room, the last human on Earth, with a shotgun to the head.

Lonely.

He squinted through tears and clenched his teeth. Would it hurt? He hoped not. Just a flash of light and it would be over, right? He thought back to the dream, to the light-infused deer fleeing before him, to the comforting presence of Alicia and Charles nearby, of the utter euphoria at belonging, at not being lonely. Not even a little tiny bit.

Not lonely.

He'd been so stupid, so stubborn, so fixed on being the last of humanity. Holding on to all things human, as if anybody around would ever notice his sacrifices.

He hurled the shotgun away from him, suddenly terrified. A coward's way of solving a problem, he thought. A permanent solution to a temporary problem. He foraged through the pantry and found the backpack from the previous summer, felt the weight of the Kentucky bourbon bottle within, shook it and heard a comforting slosh.

He slammed the front door behind him as he left, not even bothering to lock it. He made his way to Alicia's.

She opened the door and stared at him in bewilderment. He Shifted her and caught her, feeling her bony frame and marveling at how thin she had become. He carried her over to a couch and set her down gently, then went into the kitchen. A broken window had allowed snow inside. A puddle had buckled the floorboards. He scooped some snow-melt from the counter into a filthy cup and brought it back to her in trembling hands.

"It's freezing in here," he said as she drank. Her cracked lips looked pitiful and her cheekbones strained the porcelain skin stretched tight on her face. "Why didn't you go south with the rest of them?"

She shrugged, her red hair falling in front of her eyes. He brushed it away gently. "I don't know," she replied, an edge to her voice. "Why are you bothering me again?"

He lifted the backpack and pulled out the bottle of whiskey, presenting it to her like a trophy. "I'm gonna join you," he said. The words hung in the air and he felt a sudden wash of relief at finally telling somebody about his plan. "I don't know how you change each other back once I've shifted you, but I'm sick of being alone. I'm afraid, but I'm ready to stop being lonely." His own words sounded hollow, without conviction.

"How do you know you're not immune?" she asked, her eyes large. She didn't seem annoyed anymore. "Why did you decide to do this? You've always been so in control of yourself."

He opened the bottle, cracking the paper seal on top, and tilted it back. Liquid fire burned down into his belly. He almost gagged on the taste of it, but forced himself to drink more. When half the bottle was gone, he put it down.

"It tastes like carburetor cleaner," he said and she laughed. Her eyes danced and her dirty hands grasped at his. They were cold, but the touch brought tears to his eyes. He looked at her and his face grew quiet. "Please, help me adjust," he said. "I don't want to be alone, anymore."

She searched his eyes and found something that satisfied her. She nodded. "Sure. I'll do my best."

He crawled onto the couch and rolled over, pressing his back against her thin body. She hugged him and he pulled a blanket around them. Sip by sip, he drank the rest of the bottle and they lay together, shivering on the couch, the last human on Earth and his wife.

He Changed as he slept, dreaming of Alicia and Charles beside him, the three of them running toward sunlight, never to be lonely again.

Lou J. Berger

Lou J. Berger is a Denver-based author who had so much fun editing the last PPW anthology (*Fresh Starts*), that he decided to see how things worked from the OTHER side of the fence! He's an active member of SFWA, and has published quite a few short stories and novelettes.

Wind

P. James Norris

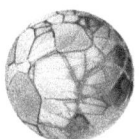

The wind's blowing again, as it has every night since I moved to this lonely farmhouse. Tonight's different though—there's an expectation. Not in the *voices*, but in me.

Somehow, I know it's happening tonight.

I anxiously try to drown them out. I play the stereo as loud as it will go. I vacuum. Run the dishwasher and washing machine.

But they drop in pitch, so low they cause the whole house to vibrate.

It's too much—like it's the house talking, possessed by the voices.

I turn everything off.

They return to normal—high-pitched, coming in snatches, just out of sync with the howling wind.

...listen...

After a few weeks in this house, I'd hear the voices and glimpse unrecognizable shapes blowing past the windows.

Blown by the wind.

...watch...

I told myself the shapes were common things: pieces of newspaper, bags, and leaves. But I'd never find anything trapped in the fence the next morning.

Later, I realized the voices were putting words with the shapes.

...learn...

When I was young, I used to dream I was out in a strong wind. Raising my arms, the wind would lift me off the ground. The higher I lifted my arms, the faster I would rise. I could fly.

But I always flew too high. Always lost control.

Shortly after moving here, I had the dream again.

Tonight, the voices are making the dream come true—I'm being changed.

...understand...

Tonight, I will.

In the dream, I always lose control.

P. James Norris

P. James Norris has master's degrees in Physics and Philosophy. In the 1980's, he wrote four spec scripts for *ST:TNG*. In 2018 he started getting short stories published by the likes of *Moon Magazine*, *Fantasia Divinity*, *Rhetoric Askew*; his shorts have been included in three anthologies. He's written three one-hour fantasy TV pilots. He has five novels in various states of incompletion–maybe, some day, he will finish writing them. He lives in Idaho with his wife and a dog, two cats and four chickens. His published work can be found at https://amazon.com/author/pjamesnorris and more at https://www.ocetacea.net/pjamesnorris.

I Always Wake Up
Ronnie Graham

A kaleidoscope of red shapes painted the back of my eyelids. They shrank, then expanded, turning, and circling. I watched their random display, letting myself relax while I drifted off into the blackness of sleep.

I was hiding behind the sofa. A man was there. His icy hand grabbed my foot to pull me out, but only succeeded in ripping off my black, patent-leather shoe. He was drunk and mad. The space was too small. I was on my side and couldn't turn. I wormed my way further in, wedging myself between the wall and the heavy sleeper-sofa. Curses filled the space outside. Fingers of ice closed on my sock-clad foot. I kicked as hard as I could within my confines. It was enough to win momentary freedom. I had escaped. I breathed in the dusty air.

That's it. This dream will end now. I'll wake up.

The sofa lifted, tilting forward away from the wall. The man's face was there, outlined in the red-hued light. I covered my eyes, hiding behind my forearms and waited.

Yesss, a voice hissed. *More.*

The dusty smells filling my nose were replaced with the scent of urine-soiled hay. I was in the barn, in the stall with a pony. "Call him Shetland and know that you love him," the hissing voice coached.

I was on the floor of the stall, hidden in the shadows. A different man, the stranger I knew to stay away from, was there. He was standing just outside the half-door. I didn't dare stand up.

Shetland didn't like him. I watched, looking up as the man reached out to pat the animal's nose. The pony jerked back with flared nostrils. The man drew back his fist and punched the small animal in the face.

My skin felt hot.

The man's voice, cold and distant, called out, "Come out here you. Ain't nothing to be afraid of."

Shetland snorted, then neighed loudly, shaking his head. His fear belied the man's coaxing. There was definitely something to be afraid of.

I jumped up to run but something caught around my legs.

Not yet. I heard, as I fell face-first onto the stall floor.

The pony snorted. I heard his sharp inhale as he reared. His hooves scraped on the concrete floor as he landed and jumped back.

I rolled, trying to free my legs, but it didn't work. The stall was too dark. My legs were too entangled.

I heard the voices of three people in the barn. One sounded young and familiar, a boy's. Another was a man's drunken slur. They were accompanied by the calls of the stranger. "We were just getting started. Come on back," he pleaded.

I always wake up.

I had to be still, but all of me wanted to run.

You can't run.

He was coming for me. The man I knew to stay away from was coming. I could feel him getting closer.

My heart is pounding.

I kept my eyes shut firmly, hiding behind their thin veil.

In the darkness, I heard the latch click and the complaining squeal of rusty hinges as someone opened the stall door. Shetland lifted his head and snorted, backing away. I dug in my heels and tried to push myself away, but failed. The floor was too slippery. I held my breath, expecting frozen hands to grab me. He was close. Any moment now he would be on me. I was trapped. There was no more room.

You can't hide behind a sofa and you can't hide here. He'll find you, a voice inside my head stated matter-of-factly. *You can't hide.*

"No!" I heard the boy yell. "No, you won't."

I breathed in the stench of the stall floor, not caring that the ammonia burned my nose.

I'll wake up now. This will end and I'll wake up.

The outline of the boy slowly came into focus. He stood in the hallway outside Shetland's stall with one hand on his hip, the other holding up his toy sword. He posed like a cartoon hero in the spotlight. *The savior has arrived!* my mind captioned his silhouette. I saw a flash of a scene where he and I were both dressed as knights. We were charging at full gallop, riding battle stallions, waving our swords, ready to defeat all foes. I could feel the warmth of the sun as it shone on my face. We were going into glorious, bloody battle.

I'll wake up smiling.

"Get away from her," I heard the boy say. I lay on the floor and watched him rush toward the man. He held his gleaming sword aloft, ready to be brought down with full, righteous vengeance.

I heard the whack as his blow found its mark. The man's knee collapsed and he fell to the side.

Yay! Well done sir knight! Finish him.

The boy spun, letting the momentum of his charge carry him around in a graceful pirouette. He raised his sword for what I knew would be the killing strike. I inhaled, holding my breath and waited. But his weapon did not descend. Instead, the boy himself was lifted off the ground. I saw the confused look on his face as the drunken man held him by his upraised arm.

I rolled, trying to keep them in sight as the man dragged the boy away, but the wall blocked my view. I didn't see the boy's fate, but the sounds told me enough. Boots clunked on the hard floor as someone big made a quick movement. A small voice cried out in an agonized, near-scream of pain.

I crawled in the darkness. The slick, excrement-fouled straw bunched up in front of me. I propelled myself forward on my elbows trying to climb over the heap. Everywhere was darkness, so black that it threatened to smother me.

I always wake up.

The boy's sword appeared next to me on the barn floor. I grabbed it, but when I looked again, it had changed into a piece of rusty pipe in my hands.

From somewhere in the distance I heard the sound of a fist hitting flesh. I had to get my legs free. If I could, then I would run.

You can't run, but I can dance, a familiar, non-human voice bragged.

Quiet!

You know it's true, the growling, hiss of a voice insisted.

What I know is that I always wake up.

Always? the voice questioned.

The drunken man's face, browned and leathery from a lifetime in the sun, floated into my thoughts. I saw him sitting on the concrete floor, his back resting against the wall. He stared up at me. "You won't do it," he challenged.

The rusty piece of pipe was in my hands as I stood over him. It felt substantial.

It feels right, the voice growled in my head.

I swung.

Everything was red and then, it went still. There was no sound as I looked into his unblinking eyes.

That's better, the growl-voice whispered.

Stop joining in. You'll wake up.

The boy and I both were running. He sped past me, holding his toy sword high, as he left me behind. When I arrived in the front yard, out of breath and panting, he was already going up the steps to the porch. The stranger I knew to stay away from was there too. He was walking slowly, favoring his knee as he made his way toward the front door.

I'll wake up. I always wake up.

"I'm a knight," The boy was saying. "I fight the evil-doers," he told the man.

He isn't going to save you.

"No, it's true, I'm a knight, and I will save the maiden." The boy argued, somehow replying to thoughts he couldn't have heard.

His armor was so shiny, that I had to raise my arm to dim the glare as it reflected the sun. He raised his right arm in a salute and tapped the hilt of his sword to his helm before turning his attention back to the stranger. With a leap, he closed in, his gleaming, jewel-encrusted sword at the ready.

Part of me watched from a distance. I could see myself standing in the yard. The stranger was down. He sat on the gray-painted floorboards of the porch and shielded his face with his arm. The boy was standing over him, a triumphant knight guarding his prisoner.

I saw the door open. A woman was there. She stepped out and grabbed the boy by the ear. I saw that he was no longer a knight, just a child in faded jeans, stretching up on tippy-toes, trying to lessen the agony.

"What's going on here!" the woman demanded.

The stranger looked up. His eyes were round and soft like an innocent puppy's. "He's gone crazy. He hit me with that pipe."

The woman released the boy's ear with a shove. He stumbled back, but found his balance quickly. The woman stepped forward and slapped him full in the face. The blow knocked him into the porch railing.

I ached to slap her.

"And what's with you?" she said, looking out at me. "What have you got all over you? Is that straw in your hair?" She waved her hands in disgust. "I've had it. May the devil take you both."

The Devil? I could feel the corners of my mouth draw up into an evil grin.

172

"They just need a little… discipline," the stranger quickly said. The woman smiled at him.

They have a secret, the growl-voice whispered to me.

"Do with them what you will then," said the woman as she turned away.

The stranger kicked the boy in the stomach. The blow sent him tumbling backward, over the rail.

"Stop it," I called as I ran up the steps.

The man was on his feet by the time I arrived. Still, I charged at him, swinging my fists as hard as I could.

He caught me by the shoulders. His cold hands held me at arm's length. I could smell the stench of his sweat and his putrid breath.

"I *will* do what I will," he proclaimed.

What I will, a growling voice, boomed in my head. I could feel the heat of it in my bones.

"No! *I* will do what I will," the voice, my voice declared.

I planted my feet and pushed him. His knee gave way and he fell.

"I will do what I will," I yelled down at him. He pushed himself backward, using his good leg and dragging the other.

I picked up the pipe-sword and swung it at his head. The shock of the impact was a sweet reward. I licked my lips.

That's it.

Each blow was a feast of red desire. I swung again and again, until I'd had my fill.

It's not over.

The pipe felt sticky in my hand as I carried it inside. The woman was there. She worked her mouth, but no words came out as she pointed and stared at me.

My first swing caught her in the arm. The second was a complete miss as she ducked low, dropping to the floor. I smiled and began to close the distance. She managed an awkward, backward crawl favoring her injured arm. Waving the pipe, I herded her to the space behind the large sofa and watched as she wormed herself into the dark confines.

"May the devil take you," I cursed at her.

I grabbed her foot with my burning-hot hands. She kicked hard, gaining her freedom as her shoe came off.

That's it. This dream will end now. I'll wake up.

The sofa lit on fire. The flames curled forward, away from the wall. The woman's face was there, outlined in the red-hued light.

I began to laugh.

My laughter changed into the crackling sounds of a roaring fire. Acrid smoke filled my lungs.

"It's time to wake up. Come on," an important voice urged, cutting through the haze of my sleep.

No, I'm still wrestling, my mind replied. *Just a little longer.*

"Wake up little one," the loving voice directed. "Time to wake up."

My eyes opened. I could see the elder's familiar, glowing red shape. Its sunken, black-circle eyes and yellow teeth were near enough to kiss as it held me in its arms.

We cuddled.

The flames surrounding us reached high into the air. They whipped around and danced with no rhythm—demons having a joyous time.

"How was your sleep?" the elder asked.

"I always wake up," I growled. "Just when it's getting good."

Ronnie Graham

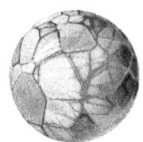

"A retired Army Lieutenant Colonel who lives a life of adventure."
That's what the first line of his biography reads. And of course, the last
line is, "He still has no intention of growing up." All the stuff in
between is a mix of braggadocio and history. It makes for a really
boring read except for this one part, "He once saw a broken mirror with
a sign on it that read, 'temporarily out of order.' He found that very
curious."

The Jungian Offensive

C.E. Barnes

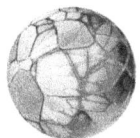

"Chief, the mice," Corporal Adler said, "they ain't movin' no more!"

"Back up," Warrant Officer Sullivan commanded. She took two paces backward herself before turning to face the corporal. Adler cautiously backpedaled, the wire cage extended at arms' length as if the occupants had become simultaneously volatile, infectious and radioactive. Inside the mesh container, three lab mice originally bred for hereditary retinal degeneration huddled motionlessly near the center of the floor. As Corporal Adler retreated, the blind rodents shuddered, relaxed, and began to tentatively search their confines for treats. None of the eggheads back at Command knew exactly how or why the blind mice sensed potential incursions, but sense them they did, freezing in place if they came into proximity of a weak spot between Realspace and the Collective Unconsious. Animals without impaired senses showed no reaction. Blind humans were no more sensitive to imminent incursions than sighted ones. Blind horses, dogs, and other animals all showed a lesser sensitivity, but like the canaries in the old coal mines, mice were most sensitive and easier to carry around in cages. Until the Corps of Engineers managed to cobble together a device capable of detecting weak spots in reality, Humanity's first line of defense depended upon sightless rodents.

"Sergeant Milgram, take Adler and Fromm. Pace me out a perimeter. Sergeant Bandura, see to the rest of the platoon. We might have half an hour; see that they eat, then doze 'em."

The rest of Wednesday platoon settled down to wait, pulling rations, canteens and smokes from their packs while Bandura moved among them, droning in his soft lazy monotone. Each phrase triggered one of the post-hypnotic suggestions imprinted in the enlisted soldiers during boot camp. Each member of Wednesday platoon, with the exception of Sergeant Milgram, Corporal Adler, and Specialist Fromm slipped deeply and easily into a conditioned trance. The hypno-triggering had no effect on Sullivan; as an Individuated Officer, she had been exempted from military hypno-therapeutic conditioning. She dropped her rucksack in the shade of an old live oak tree and rested against it as she watched Milgram, Fromm, and Adler weave around the incursion site like drunks staggering home from a bender. Specialist Fromm stopped periodically to mark the ground with fluorescent orange spray paint whenever the mice reacted, and the circle of highly visible dots marked a relatively safe perimeter. Sullivan scowled when the team vanished behind the old campus library. If the perimeter was this big, the breach was dangerously unstable and something strong would be waiting on the other side.

Sullivan removed her helmet, her short brown hair pasted in sweaty curls to her scalp. Without the northern Florida humidity, the late summer morning would merely be unpleasantly warm. Her combat fatigues, damp with sweat, felt about five kilos too heavy. The material was supposed to breathe, but it felt like it was panting instead, hot and moist, directly against her skin. She lit a cigarette and shifted her attention to the buildings surrounding the commons. For a University campus, it remained in reasonably good shape. No burned husks of buildings, not much vandalism. No scent of smoke or decay; only the floral, herbal and fungal aroma of a sub-tropical summer day, spiced with a hint of unwashed troopers. Perhaps the students evacuated of their own volition once it was discovered that incursions occurred most often around universities, think tanks and research facilities…something about the Archetypes being more active where large numbers of thinkers converged to think. She took a drag on her cigarette and fought to suppress a coughing fit. She was new to the habit, and hoped to live long enough for it to kill her.

She missed her college days before the first incursions. Back then, she'd been a filmography major and her biggest concern was determining whether Hitchcock or Kubrick had influenced del Toro to the greater degree. No one knew she had an Individuated psyche, herself included. No one cared. But then, Delhi fell, the city flattened and over twenty million casualties within the span of minutes. Video footage in cloud storage showed a gargantuan, ever-shifting mass of eyes, teeth, and pseudopods phasing in and out of existence, crushing structures and humans indiscriminately. The trauma shredded the sanity of millions more. Six hours later, Beijing suffered the same fate. Then Sao Paulo. And Manhattan.

Military powers assumed extraterrestrial invasion. Many pundits cited H.P. Lovecraft like it was holy scripture. It wasn't until the anomalies appeared – Quetzalcoatl over Mexico City, Baba Yaga in Moscow, among others – that scientists began to theorize that perhaps these invaders were linked to humanity's cultural zeitgeist. Quantum physicists collaborated with Jungian psychologists and hypothesized that the Collective Unconscious wasn't an abstract concept but a hyperspatial field generated by sapience, a bubble surrounding Earth now over pressurized by nearly ten billion human minds dreaming ten billion human dreams.

The theory worked on several levels. The invaders matched specific Archetypes, concepts common to the Human Experience made manifest. Their shape and solidity would be inconsistent as the Archetype struggled to conform to the conception of millions of viewers. As for the anomalies, something must be present at these incursions that locked down the Archetype's form into one coherent reality, but what was it?

Apparently, it was Sullivan, and others like her. Folks who had an innate conception upon seeing an Archetype. Folks who could watch recorded footage of the amorphous monstrosities and still discern what it was supposed to be, what it was *trying* to be. Jungian psychologists slapped the label "Individuated" on these people, and the Military drafted them as soon as they were identified.

Her hike down Memory Lane ended as approaching footsteps and a polite throat-clearing indicated a presence behind her.

"Report, Sergeant," Sullivan said, leaving it somewhere between a question and a command.

"Platoon's at rest, Chief," Bandura replied. "Light trance, mild dissociative state. You could shoot their family dogs right now, and the most you'd get out of them is a heavy sigh."

"Good job, Sergeant," she said.

Bandura scowled. Sullivan didn't take it personally. She suspected Bandura started scowling when he got his first stripe and his face had frozen in the intervening decades.

"If I may, sir," Bandura said, "Is it really a good idea to have most of the platoon tranced this close to the breach? S.O.P. requires a squad on alert."

Sullivan suppressed a sigh. Bandura was a good man and an excellent non-commissioned officer. He'd tackled the required PSYOP training and certifications, and intellectually, he understood the differences between traditional warfare and the new reality of fighting Nightmares, but in his gut, the rules he learned while fighting insurgents in Iraq still applied.

"That's the old operating procedure," Sullivan said, "and it's gotten more platoons killed than I wanna count." She gestured toward the library. "That's a helluva big incursion, which means the Archetype on the other side is powerful, the barrier is weak, or both. It's risky enough just having those three establish a perimeter. The last thing we need is an entire squad with hyperactive, nervous minds this close to ground zero. You should grab some chow and rest, yourself."

When Bandura made no move to depart, Sullivan turned and asked, "Something eating you, Al?"

"Atlanta."

Sullivan grimaced. "Atlanta was a clusterfuck. We humped it pretty badly back there. But we know exactly how we humped it. We all stay sharp, focus on our responsibilities, and this won't be worse than any other monster hunt."

"I keep thinking about that…thing," Bandura continued as if Sullivan hadn't spoken. "It hurt to look at. Like it was trying out several shapes at the same time, without really having a shape at all."

"Was that your first time seeing an undefined Archie?"

Bandura nodded.

"Yeah, about the only way to describe an undefined Archetype is 'indescribable'. They're only quasi-real, you know," Sullivan couldn't resist. "The stuff that dreams are made of."

"Chief…what really happened in Atlanta? Not the official report bullshit. Howcome Lieutenant Rogers pulled the Archie over?"

Because Rogers was an arrogant West Point prick who couldn't stand the thought of not being the most vital member of the team, Sullivan carefully refrained from saying. Instead, she replied, "Lieutenant Rogers didn't go into detail with me, but he believed he'd discovered a better way to establish a safe perimeter than using mice. He must've been thinking too hard when he stepped too close to the breach. My guess," and she stressed the word, "is that his mental activity eroded what was left of the barrier between Realspace and the Collective Unconscious. He made a miscalculation. He paid for it with his life while we retreated. Nothing more to tell."

Bandura pulled a sodden handkerchief from his back pocket in time to cover a sneeze. "Fucking pollen," he mumbled. To Sullivan, he said, "There's talk in the platoon that the Lieutenant thought he might have achieved Individuation. He was real big on meditation, you know."

Sullivan ran her fingers through her curls. "Al, do you know what Individuation looks like? Can you spot the signs?"

The sergeant wiped his nose and returned the handkerchief before answering with a curt "Nossir."

Aannnd just like that, we're back inside the chain of command, Sullivan noted to herself. "Neither does PSYOP. Neither did the Lieutenant. Hell, neither do I, Sergeant. Jung says Individuation is the natural state of the self-actualized psyche, or something like that. It may be true, but I can promise you I've never contemplated my navel, stroked crystals or tattooed self-affirmations on my ass. All I know about Individuation is that there's something about me and a small percentage of other people that recognizes an Archie for what it is, and that locks them down into a solid form capable of being destroyed."

"If Rogers thought he'd achieved Individuation, he was wrong," Sullivan continued, a little too sharply. Bandera's scowl intensified, so Sullivan proceeded more tactfully. "If that were the case, Lieutenant Rogers' consciousness would've translated it into a solid shape during transition, and we could've shot it down. PSYOP hasn't reported any success in training people to achieve Individuation. Rogers knew that." *And yet he still thought he could impose a form on an Archie through sheer force of his indomitable will.*

Sullivan stared at the ash hanging from her cigarette. "Get some food, Sergeant, then get tranced, yourself. I'll need you in top form shortly."

"Yessir," Sergeant Bandura saluted and returned to the troops.

She scrabbled to regain the warm nostalgia from minutes before, without success. "Fuck it," Sullivan grunted to herself around the cigarette's filter. "It's not like del Toro's making movies these days anyhow."

Sergeant Milgram emerged from behind the library, Adler and Fromm in tow. Sullivan bogarted the remains of her cigarette, triggering another coughing fit. By the time her lungs were following orders again, Milgram was waiting to report.

"It's a big 'un, Chief," Milgram said. "Couldn't get an accurate reading, not without finding a back way into the library, but if the breach is near the center of the perimeter, that'd place it about three meters in front of the library steps."

Sullivan dropped the butt into the weeds that had overtaken the campus commons, and crushed the ember with the heel of her boot. While she was technically in charge, had been since the Lieutenant bought it back in Atlanta, she knew better than to let her accelerated stint in Officer Candidate School delude her into thinking she was qualified to make command decisions. "Suggestions, Sergeant?"

Milgram stroked his narrow chin as he thought. "Well, Chief…kinda depends on where the breach turns up. If it's inside the library, I'd suggest we burn it down. Might be able to collapse the structure, seal the breach away. Detonation charges would be best, but after what happened in Atlanta…" Milgram shrugged. "If we get it outdoors…" the sergeant scanned the terrain. "Those two buildings flanking the library, and just a tad south of it…a good rifle on each roof with an escort to guard them, and the rest of the company inside, shooting out from cover."

Sullivan pictured it. "That leaves me standing in two fields of fire."

Milgram snorted. "You'll be standing at Ground Zero, toe to toe with a nightmare, and you're fretting about a few bullets? Me and Bandura know our jobs. We'll ride herd on the companies. No one'll shoot without a clear line of fire."

"It's a plan. At least, it'll pass for one from a distance. Take squad A. I want Thorndike on the roof with her M-40. Give her Adler and Erikson for support, and have `em take a radio. Tell Sergeant Bandura that he has squad B. I want Skinner on the other roof with the rocket launcher and a radio as well. Fromm and Kohlberg can guard him. Get the rest of the platoon indoors and under cover. Find some good windows, and give me all the suppressive fire you can."

"Roger that," Milgram said. As he left to relay orders to Bandura, Sullivan retrieved her radio and headset from her ruck. Nailing down the breach, finding the exact location where the barrier between Realspace and the Collective Unconscious was weakest rested entirely on her shoulders, and required a relaxed, receptive mental state. She found it hard to maintain a Zen vibe, though, when actively seeking out a monster's lair. The centering techniques taught at OCS were less than effective in the field, so Sullivan had developed her own. She put on her headset, plugged it into the radio, and looked around for a jumping-off phrase. She found it on the sign identifying the campus commons as Landis Green. She crossed the perimeter, heading toward the center.

Landis Green. John Landis. American Werewolf in London bridge is falling down, down to goblin town you go, I go, Iago, Othello, Desdemona Lisa hangin in da parlor, a dollar, a twelve o-clock scholar and a gentlemen prefer blondes have more fundamental things apply a little make-up, make sure they get your good side of the angels in the Outfield of Dreams, if you build it they will come all ye faithful joyful and Triumph Tr-7, Double-Oh Seven Samurai, or just one samurai if he's the size of a water tower like the Osaka Incursion...

Sullivan stopped the moment her stream of conscious word association collapsed into structured thought, and noted the location. She was at the base of the library stairs. She backed away, and moved to another point on the perimeter. She checked the progress of her two squads, noting that Milgram had taken his squad to shelter in the southeastern building marked as Cawthorn Hall.

Cawthorn hall, Hawthorn Fallout Boy yer gonna carry that wait for the beat goes onward Christian soldiers' creedence clearwater runs deep in the heart emoji-I-Joseph and the Amazing Spider Mannheim SteamrollerBlade Runner in the night of the living daylight's out of your cotton-pickin' mind your peas and `scuse me while I kiss the Blarney Rubble and Fred Flintstone temple pilots do you copy, over? Roger, Rogers, if you weren't such an idiot, we wouldn't be in this mess...

Her path marked a second line back to the stairs. Triangulation put the potential breach roughly four meters ahead, atop the landing.

She keyed the radio. "Corporal Thorndike, do you copy?"

"I copy," Thorndike's detached contralto voice rang clear through Sullivan's earpiece.

"Specialist Skinner, do you copy?"

"Affirmative," Skinner replied.

"Bandura, Milgram…are you in position?"

"We're in position, Chief," Milgram replied, followed by Bandura's simple "yessir".

"Okay, Wednesday platoon, stay relaxed, stay focused. Shit's about to get Real…"

Sullivan stepped across the breach. The barrier between realities, worn thin by decades of students intent on their studies, reacted to contact with Sullivan's focused cognition like a water balloon caressed by a power sander, and as it disintegrated, a shock wave of primal emotion crested and rolled across the campus like a psychic tsunami.

Sullivan had prepared for rage. Rage was fairly common, with fear the next likely gift from the Collective Unconscious. This was neither, and her ego defense failed to compensate. Her legs buckled and she stumbled, squeezing her eyes shut against the heartbreaking misery slamming against her identity, eroding and subsuming it. No loss she had ever experienced, from the death of her pet hamster when she was eleven to the passing of her grandfather, compared to this. Her rational mind withdrew, incapacitated by raw sorrow, but her Individuated psyche, conditioned to assign relevance and identity to experience, recognized the emotional signature. This was Medea's grief, the

Madonna's grief, the grief of any woman forced to sacrifice her children. This was a Mother's grief.

The protean thing on the library steps trembled and phased into non-mutability as Sullivan, still weeping uncontrollably, regained her feet. She wiped the tears away and focused on the Archie on the steps above her, a three-meter-tall figure dressed in unbleached linen robes and resembling a mature woman of undefinable ethnicity. Its oval face was framed by waves of dark brown hair, and the eyes, a deep brown bordering black, gazed down on Sullivan with sorrowful regret.

It wanted her dead.

The compulsion enveloped Sullivan, resonated through her psyche.

It loved her, cherished her, and wanted her dead. It grieved for the pain she'd endured, the losses she'd suffered, and knew with perfect certainty that life would be an ongoing cycle of grief and loss unless death intervened.

Sullivan's resolve crumbled. Her hand went to her sidearm, slipped it from her holster. She worked the action, chambered a round, and pressed the muzzle beneath her chin.

The dead no longer made mistakes. The dead couldn't fuck things up. The dead were venerated by the living, their errors forgiven, their flaws forgotten. Guilt, shame, regret…these plagues tormented the living. The dead were beyond them. Wave after wave of *destrudo* emanated from the Mother, triggering Sullivan's death drive, poisoning her psyche.

Sure, why not? Sullivan thought. *It's not like we aren't all gonna die anyway, and some love and glory would be sweet! Better than marching and fighting and struggling, rinse and repeat. Life ended when I was drafted, really. Three billion people have died since, and I don't hear them complaining. We've lost this war; it won't make a difference if I fight another day or call it quits. Going out on my own terms may not be a victory, but from here, it looks close enough.*

Her ears registered the sound of gunfire, but it didn't seem relevant. Perhaps Wednesday platoon was putting up resistance. Perhaps they were committing mass suicide. It was all the same, and none of her concern. Sullivan thumbed the safety off.

On the steps above Sullivan, the Archetype stepped back as wave upon wave of high-powered ammunition slammed into its chest, tearing bloodless holes through the garments, ripping out of the Mother's back and striking sparks from the library façade. It turned its visage to the members of Wednesday platoon, a look of tender disappointment upon its gentle face. The platoon, detached and insulated from their emotions, continued their assault.

Milgram coordinated squad actions with Bandura. Sullivan, oblivious to the noise in her earphones, gripped the barrel of the pistol with her free hand, ensuring the weapon was properly angled.

They'll forgive me, Sullivan reassured herself. *If they can venerate Rogers for screwing the pooch as badly as he did, they'll find a reason to turn me into a goddamn martyr.*

Bullets screamed past Sullivan. A neat hole appeared in the Archetype's forehead. Another bullet struck it in the temple, colorless ichor geysering from the exit wound on the opposite side of its skull. Tears ran silently down the Archie's flawless face before its material form dispersed into unreality.

"Target eliminated. Chief, please confirm the kill," Thorndike's voice came through the earbud. "Chief...please respond. Do you copy?"

The psychic assault vanished with the Archie. Sullivan slipped her finger through the guard and onto the trigger. Perhaps the motivation had been external, but the suicidal ideation...the rationale had been all her own, and still made a lot of sense to her battle-ravaged psyche. *What's the other option? Standing down monster after monster until I either lose my mind, get torn apart, or soak up some friendly fire? Is there any cause to hope this shitstorm will ever blow over?*

"Chief...?" her headset buzzed.

Thorndike survived the assault. That's nice, Sullivan thought. *She's a good kid. Volunteered for this shit. Most of them volunteered.* Her finger rested gently on the trigger, as the faces of Wednesday platoon cycled through her mind. None of them had the quirk of Individuation, and none could take on an Archie without it, yet they volunteered to face down psychic horrors, armed with little more than blind mice, small arms, and faith in her irreplicable ability. They won't quit, she realized. *If I do this, they'll head to the next target, hungry for payback, and wind up as dead as Lieutenant Rogers. I'm not just killing myself. I'm killing them as well.* Sullivan waited to see if that realization mattered to her.

Several long moments passed before Sullivan mustered the will to lower her weapon. She thumbed the safety back on, replaced it in her holster and promised herself *Tomorrow. It's still an option. I can always consider it tomorrow.*

"Kill confirmed. Good job, Wednesday." Sullivan took a last look at the old campus. "Get 'em loaded up, Sergeants. If we hustle, we can make it to Gainesville by nightfall."

C.E. Barnes

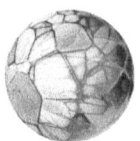

C.E. Barnes is a transplanted Floridian, now living in the shadow of Pikes Peak. His interests include gaming with friends, pontificating to his critique group, surfing Netflix for anything worth watching, and occasionally working his day job as a technical support engineer. You can find samples of his work in the 2021 anthology, *Fresh Starts: Tales from the Pikes Peak Writers* and *Street Magic: An Urban Fantasy Anthology*. If you see C.E. Barnes in public, ask him about his dogs.

The Bunker

Scott Kerby

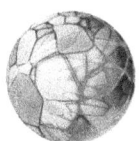

The sound of gunfire outside shatters my restless sleep and tears me from my only refuge. I am not safe here.

Time is running out.

How did this happen?

It wasn't like this when I was young. There was a world where everything was all right. Time and worry had no authority over me. They would just melt away. Happiness was free and it came easily. I miss that so much. I ache for the peace and safety of my childhood home.

All that has been taken away from me. The world is cruel. It devours the weak. I feel lost. Sleep, even though it bristles with nightmares, saves me, if only for a few moments at a time.

I would do anything to get out of this hell.

My body has turned to stone after only five minutes on the cold concrete floor. Letting your guard down can be a fatal mistake.

Static from the radio fills the cement shelter. There has been no news for at least three days, and the last news was bad. Every moment of uncertainty drains my will to continue. I draw a deep breath, searching for the rush of revitalizing oxygen that I need to survive. It is not to be found, only the stale, restrictive air of my cramped enclosure. What I wouldn't give to breathe clean air again.

But I can't risk it. I can't let *them* get in.

Just sitting up exacts a heavy toll, but one I reluctantly choose to pay. The endless battles exhaust me. How much longer can I endure this? I survey the dim room.

Everything is the same. Nothing has changed.

The rations will run out soon. I've gathered all the weapons I could get my hands on and have more ammo than I could ever use. Too bad I can't turn some of it into water or toilet paper.

I feel as though I'm all alone, but unfortunately, I'm not.

Gaylon. He's still here, not like there's anywhere for him to go, and I don't know anyone who would want him. He's supposed to protect and guide me, but he won't help me. He won't even fight. He's useless. He just sits there. He looks at me with that same stupid smile and says, "Did you think about it?"

"What difference would it make?"

"All the difference in your world."

"You guys are all the same. A bunch of dreamers. You have no idea what's out there. What's out there is real, not some ridiculous made up fantasy. How can you believe that crap? The world doesn't work like that."

The radio cracks to life and a panicked voice stabs through the air. "Is anyone out there? We are surrounded, and there are more of *them* coming. Prepare to defend yourself. Don't let your guard down. Do not go Outside."

"Did you hear that?" I jab a finger at the radio. "*That's* real."

"Your thoughts are your true reality, and you can choose to change them whenever you like."

"Yeah, a lot of good that will do. Who's going to change theirs?"

"You can, with your beliefs and actions."

"That's bullshit. You're clueless, man. I'm surrounded. They're in every district."

"Do you know who they are or what they might want?"

"I don't know, man! I don't know anything about them. Didn't you hear the radio? They will take everything. They can't be trusted."

Gaylon looks around the room and grins. "I see. Losing this way of life could be devastating. Did you ever consider going out there and talking to them?"

"Are you fucking nuts? They will cut me to pieces. This is the way it is, and it will never change. You don't get it."

"You don't kno—"

Gaylon lit up with a blinding flash of light. A scorching concussion erupts from the wall behind me. Something impacts my vest like a cannon ball and the backs of my arms cry out with a dozen hornet stings.

I regain my balance. "The shit's going down, man! Arm up. This is it." I chamber check my rifle and sling it. "Rockets maybe.

Maybe random artillery. If it's rockets, they know where we are. The wall can't take another hit like that. They will be on us soon." The battered barrier allows a spike of sunshine to penetrate the dark bunker. I move to the breach to see the enemy. It's like looking into a laser. "I can see some movement, but I can't make it out." I try to shove the muzzle through the hole to get off some rounds, but it won't fit.

Gaylon stands up. "Perhaps you could take a minute to think things through? Maybe you can let them in and reason with them. It could all be a misunderstanding. Give them a chance."

I turn to face him so I can tear him a new one. "What did you say?" Light falls upon him, dispelling the darkness as he smiles. An unexpected sense of calm invades my thoughts. He extends a hand to me. I hesitate. I want desperately to reach for it, but I can't. I force the possibility of a life without torment from my mind. It would never be like that. I must not show weakness.

The door bursts in behind him.

I raise my rifle. "It's the Silba! Get out of the way!"

Gaylon doesn't move. "You can end this anytime you want." The delicate cotton threads of his tunic part as the Silba's katana slips through his body. The fibers drink the crimson liquid as the blade withdraws. Gaylon's expression never changes as he sinks to the floor, his breathing even and peaceful.

The Silba towers over his body, clad in an impervious exoskeleton.

I level the barrel and open up. It is deafening. The air in the constricted space compresses with every round. Each muzzle flash illuminates the Silba's polished armor, revealing his true mass.

The bolt locks to the rear and the weapon ceases to pound against me. Temporarily blinded by the strobing of automatic fire, I am left with only the cacophony of ejected brass raining to the floor and the scent of burnt powder. My support hand races to another magazine as I search for confirmation that my desperate defense was not in vain. The faint haze from spent propellant clears the shaft of light to reveal the Silba remains unfazed.

It is hopeless.

The Silba advances.

I glance down at Gaylon. His eyes meet mine with a total lack of fear. An iron boot obstructs my view of his ever-present smile just before it drives down on his skull, shattering it like porcelain, spreading its contents across the concrete floor.

The ringing in my ears morphs into a scream of rage. A twelve-pound maul finds its way into my hands as I seek a target. A rivet at the base of the Silba's helm. Every blemish of the craftsman's hammer is clear.

The sledge has no noticeable weight as it flies over my head. Like a contained lightning bolt, I draw all the energy from a lifetime of suffering. My entire body contracts to bring the iron billet to its mark. The armor conforms to the sledge.

The Silba staggers backwards.

I pursue him. The maul rises and falls repeatedly. I slip in Gaylon's blood. I can't stop now. I have to win. I stomp forward, needing secure footing to inflict as much damage as possible. Gaylon's limbs roll under my boots and the bones break within.

"I. Will. Destroy. You!" A strike punctuates each word. I force the Silba against the wall. The helm begins to fail.

A booming voice shakes the bunker. "Michael."

They found me! They're coming.

A final blow dislodges the visor. The Silba's body relaxes as it twists to the floor.

The voice comes, louder this time with more conviction. "Michael, I'm going to count to three and snap my fingers."

The Silba comes to rest and the missing visor reveals his identity. My own face stares back.

My enemy is me.

A crack as loud as a rifle shot jolts me from my reality and places me in a different one. Incense and soft light fill the room. My therapist is saying something, but her words are lost in the revelation of an existence in-between what is and what can be.

I am numb.

My mind races. There is a tingling sensation in my fingers. I can sense everything, but can focus on nothing. I fight the fear that I must find a desperate foothold in this new place, or I will plunge back into the abyss of my old reality.

There is nothing here I need to cling to. I'm on solid, level ground. The foundation for a new way of life. A life that does not demand that I take it on alone. I am not alone and faith is not a weakness.

I go Outside. I am surrounded. Surrounded by the frantic chaos of daily life. Speeding cars. Horns violating the air. People everywhere. They are all around me. A few smile and make eye contact. I smile back. I feel at home. I realize that I am one of *them* and we are all together.

I am where I belong.

I notice a young family spreading their picnic across a red plaid blanket on the emerald grass. A child stares with wonder at the golden rays of sunlight gliding through the trees. A gentle breeze touches my face. I take a long, deep, restorative breath of fresh air cleansed by recent afternoon rainfall.

I feel alive.

I have accepted that I do not need to control anything. I have the freedom to choose how I feel about everything.

I am free from the crushing weight of fear.

Everything is the same. Nothing has changed.

And it's all right.

Scott Kerby

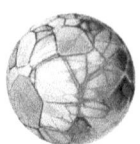

Scott Kerby is a special effects coordinator with over 43 years experience in blowing things to tiny bits. The art of movie making isn't all fun and games with explosives. You get to crush, dismember, and disembowel things, too.

After nearly half a century bringing to life everything that the Hollywood writers could imagine, Scott realized that they missed some stuff.

He lives with his beautiful wife in a log cabin in the Rockies with dogs and horses and all the Rocky Mountain critters.

His joy is sharing the wonders of life and the magic of a meaningful story.

Dream On

Lauren Lang

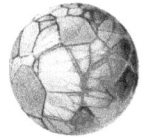

Dream on, dream ye for me
Dream for those that can no longer see.
Dream for those that have been slain.
Dream that we have not died in vain.

Live for dreams, die for dreams
It's all the same or so it seems.

So dream on, dream ye for me.
For I, I can no longer see.
And it's all the same in that eternal sleep
Blackness true, dark, and deep.

Lauren Lang

Lauren Lang is a former broadcast journalist and current freelance photographer and videographer living in Denver, CO. In her spare time, she writes fiction, cooks, bakes, crochets hats for stuffed animals, gardens with the intent of taking pictures of the flowers should they live and terrorizes residents by pretending to be a wildlife photographer and running through area parks with her camera screaming, "Birds!". Occasionally, she does take a picture of a bird.

More information about Lauren and her work can be found by visiting her on Facebook.

Der Traumlicht

John Christenson

Excerpt from: Nuremberg Transcript A27-38667
Dated: 27 April 1946
Subject: Written deposition of Leah Solowitz, age 16
Classification: MOST SECRET. All documents contained herein are
placed under court interdiction for 75 years.
Notes: Subject experiences brief periods of lucidity alternating with
bouts of profound terror and dementia, making conventional testimony
infeasible. The attached record, written by the subject, is submitted to
the court in lieu of said testimony. However, it is considered unreliable
pursuant to introduction into the subject's system of a variety of
psychotropic and psychotomimetic drugs administered during
internment at Auschwitz. Recommend permanent commitment to a
high-security facility. Prognosis for rehabilitation: none.

***

My name is Leah Solowitz. I will tell you about Der Traumlicht, but
only because the one who should tell this story died in her moment of
triumph, and because it was her dream that I become a writer like she
was. I will tell you of the horrors that Doktor Mengele inflicted on us,
but I will also tell you of Anne, of the hope she brought to us, and the
light she gave us. Her wonderful, joyful light.

     My mother died of typhus the day I first saw Anne. The women
in our barracks hid my mother's body, hoping the guards would not
find out she had died and cut our food ration. They knew that trick,

though. The barracks leader, a redheaded matron named Sybil, was stripped and tied to a post. Two guards took turns flogging her to death while Der Blockführer forced the rest of us to watch.

The scene twisted until the blood-soaked figure hanging like a rag doll from the whipping post was my mother. I screamed and ran toward one of her executioners. He dropped his whip, grabbed me by the wrist, and slapped me over and over. I only screamed louder. He pulled out his pistol and pressed it to my temple.

"No, wait!" The other guard stayed his hand. "Herr Doktor could make use of this one in his experiments."

That is how I was taken to Joseph Mengele and Der Traumlicht, the Dream Light. I found myself in a narrow, white-washed room that stank of urine, lined up with a dozen other girls around my age. A stooped, gray-haired man with a ragged scar on his left cheek, whom Doktor Mengele addressed as Caleb, announced our names from a roster. Herr Doktor walked past the others, as if inspecting the troops, then paused in front of me and caressed my cheek. Jet-black hair, square chin, aquiline nose, handsome as a movie star. He smiled and licked his lips as his face moved closer to mine. "You are terrified of me, yes?"

I nodded.

"Good. We will harness that terror for Der Führer." He nodded to Caleb. "Take her first."

As Caleb took my arm, I sought out the girl he had called Anne while reading the roll. Unlike the others, who trembled and cried, Anne regarded me with enormous, dark eyes, infinitely sad, yet with a spark of life that touched me in this moment of terror. I thought of how we might have been friends, even as Herr Doktor administered the first of many injections and sealed me in a bunker deep underground with only a cot and a thin blanket.

The injections must have included a sleeping potion, because I was unable to stay awake no matter how hard I tried. My slumber was anything but peaceful, though. At first, I dreamed of my fourteenth birthday party a year ago, of my family singing and joining hands around me, enclosing me in the circle of life. They vowed to protect me, now and forever. Then a guttural voice cut through the singing, a voice calling my name. My parents shoved me to the ground and turned me over. A blood-red creature with the legs and horns of a goat stood astride me. Its black lips pulled back to reveal long, yellow teeth, sharp as daggers. I screamed and screamed as the monster fell on me and tore me to pieces. Momma and Poppa held me down as they laughed and jeered. I pleaded for them to save me, but they only laughed harder.

<<Written testimony discontinued due to hysteria experienced by the subject>>
<<Written testimony resumed, 29 April 1946>>

I apologize for my behavior. When I experienced such episodes during the Traumlicht experiments, Doktor Mengele tied me down and injected me with sedatives, just as the court-appointed American doctor did after this latest outburst.

After several more of these sessions in the underground bunker, each worse than the last, Herr Doktor said, "You are progressing nicely, Leah. Your dreams are becoming more vivid." He had me describe the goat monster in detail. "Splendid," he said. "The hallucinogenics are working perfectly. They have been adjusted after a long process of trial and error to ensure that all test subjects experience the same fearsome vision. I cannot take credit, though. Reichminister Goebbels had the brilliant idea to weaponize dreams. Soon yours will be strong enough for our purpose."

One day, Herr Doktor had liquor on his breath and told me in a slurred voice that he doted on us, his Traumlicht Mädchen. "Unlike the endless supply of twins they bring me, mere genetic fodder, you, Leah, are special." He gave me fruit, a good orange and a ripe plum, I remember them . . . and sweet marzipan . . . and when I told him it was my fifteenth birthday, a sparkling diamond bracelet with the inscription "From Herman to Sybil, Happy 50th Birthday." I gasped when he gave it to me because I had never seen anything so beautiful. He laughed and said, "It is only a Jüdin bauble. I have mountains of them, mountains that grow bigger every day."

When I awoke after the nightly doses of drugs wore off, the headaches and nausea were so bad I could do nothing but lie on the pallet and sob. Nightmares of the goat monster had completely obliterated the cherished dreams of my loving family.

I did not see Anne again until the second week of dreaming. One of the girls had died during the night, and Herr Doktor told us he would suspend the tests until we were stronger. We were taken to the commandant's house, where his wife had hastily set up cots in the large anteroom. Her husband, she explained, would not allow inmates or any other vermin in the main part of the house. She fed us savory stews with carrots and potatoes, rye bread, and fresh milk. The headaches grew less frequent.

I was toying with the bracelet one morning, watching sunlight sparkle through the diamonds, when Anne sat on the edge of my cot.

"My favorite is *Top Hat*," she said with a smile that showed blackened gums and gaps where teeth had fallen out. What was left of her raven-colored hair had streaks of white that weren't there two weeks ago, but I still thought she was beautiful.

I returned the smile. "Your favorite what?"

"Movie, silly. Fred Astaire and Ginger Rogers. What's yours?"

Speaking was difficult, since I had almost bitten through my tongue during the last session. "My parents took me to movies before the war," I mumbled, "but I've never heard of Fred Astaire or Ginger Rogers." I wanted more than anything for Anne to stay and talk with me, so I asked her about *Top Hat*.

She told me the story of *Top Hat* and tried to imitate some of the dance steps. Then she stopped and put her hands on her hips. "This will *never* do," she said with a pout like a small child. Against my protests, she hauled me to my feet and spun me around the floor while singing a tune Anne called "Cheek to Cheek." We crashed into the other cots, but the other girls clapped and laughed. Suddenly, I was crying and hugging Anne so tightly she finally had to pull away from me.

We talked the rest of the day, discovering that we both wanted to be writers and live in America. Anne said she'd wanted to be a film star in Hollywood when she was thirteen, but now, three years later, her goal was to publish a book about her time in hiding. Her sister was also in the camp, but Herr Doktor wouldn't allow them to see each other. Anne told me how desperately she missed Peter, her boyfriend before Auschwitz. When I said I'd never loved a boy, she winced and took my hand. "Dear Leah," she whispered.

After listening to Anne talk about her family, about how they had lived in the Secret Annex until they were discovered, I asked why she wanted to write about such a terrible time. "Because when I write my courage is reborn," she said. "It's how I keep my dreams alive."

"But our dreams have turned into nightmares," I said. "There's nothing left."

She gave me a long, searching look. "They haven't taken everything, Leah. They haven't taken what is deep in our hearts, yours and mine. Whatever happens, you must find a way write about it. Writing is how we go on living after death."

We didn't dare sleep that night, fearing we had only a few precious hours to live out the friendship of a lifetime. Guards came in the late afternoon of the next day to escort us to Herr Doktor. As we left the commandant's house, Anne said, "They haven't won yet, Kitty."

"I'm Leah, not Kitty," I said. "Who is Kitty?"

Anne shook her head. "Leah, yes, of course. Kitty is . . . never mind. All that matters is that she's far away from here and always will

204

be."

As the sun began to set, Herr Doktor, accompanied by two Nazi officers wearing swastika armbands, took us to a gigantic searchlight in the center of camp. Its mirror was perhaps ten feet in diameter, many times the size of the searchlights in the guard towers. A cold feeling of dread squeezed my throat when I saw red lightning bolts painted on its side. A special detail of soldiers surrounded the light, with the same red lightning bolts emblazoned on their helmets. Wires snaked from the base of the searchlight, disappearing into a concrete portal in the ground.

Herr Doktor turned to the pair of officers. "Behold Der Traumlicht," he announced in a solemn voice. "Goering's precious Luftwaffe is all but gone, but the Traumlicht Mädchen will protect the Fatherland."

One of the officers glanced at the other and cleared his throat. "We are here at Reichsmarschall Goering's request in order to discredit this ridiculous charade. Do you really expect us to believe that this pathetic gaggle," he flicked his hand at us, "can protect us from Allied bombing raids? Do you think we are fools?"

Herr Doktor's nostrils flared and he clenched his teeth. "This is the crowning achievement of Germany's greatest scientists. Did you read the technical documents I sent you?"

The officers smiled and shook their heads.

"Der Traumlicht is the ultimate defensive weapon!" Herr Doktor was shouting now. "And soon it will also be an offensive weapon, able to destroy the enemy even more effectively than Von Braun's V-2s."

"Are you saying this thing is some sort of rocket?" one of the officers asked.

"No, it is based on telekinesis, the ability of the mind to control matter. It transforms the monsters of the subconscious into a most effective weapon, as I will now demonstrate."

He led all of us, including the officers, down concrete steps into a bunker far below the searchlight where he selected a name from a shiny silk hat. I looked at Anne, hoping to take strength from her, but only saw the dread in her eyes I knew was in my own.

A small, frail girl named Eliana was chosen. She collapsed when Herr Doktor called her name, so Caleb had to carry her to a steel table. She stared at him like a trapped animal while he strapped her down. We cringed in sympathy as Herr Doktor administered the injections we all knew so well. Eliana began whimpering and calling out to her mother.

"There are no mothers here," one of the other girls said in a loud whisper. Herr Doktor gave her a sharp look, and then turned his attention back to the procedure. It did not end with the injections this time. With trembling hands, Caleb shaved her scalp and placed a metal cap on her head connected by wires to an opening in the ceiling. I realized it must lead upward to Der Traumlicht. Caleb started to connect more wires to Eliana's temples and fingertips, then paused and stared at Herr Doktor with a look of abject despair and hopelessness. I thought the earth might open up and swallow us all. Herr Doktor seemed to reflect that despair for moment before ordering Caleb to proceed. He finished quickly and left the room.

"I am sorry," Herr Doktor whispered to Eliana. "Please forgive me. You girls are like my daughters, but the effects are irreversible." He kissed her forehead and followed Caleb.

Several girls began sobbing, and a low moan escaped me as the guards escorted us back up the steps. Night had fallen, and I shivered in the bitter cold. Herr Doktor left us with Caleb and took the Nazi officers to the top of a tall observation platform. I studied the wires running from the large searchlight down into the bunker where Eliana lay in darkness. If only I had a knife, I would've tried to cut them before one of the guards killed me. But I didn't.

Herr Doktor snapped his fingers, and one of the soldiers with red lightning bolts on his helmet started the motor powering Der Traumlicht. At first, an oval of white light swept across the sky, just like any other searchlight. Even so, my sense of dread grew worse.

The oval of light turned blood red.

Herr Doktor spoke into a telephone. "Launch the unmanned plane, directly over the camp."

The high-pitched whine of a small engine came from the distance. As it grew louder, the beam of light from Der Traumlicht took form and became solid. It was the goat creature that stalked my dreams. Several of the girls screamed and pointed, obviously recognizing the apparition as I did. Some hid their eyes, but I couldn't turn away.

Conventional searchlights tracked the small plane as it flew over the camp. When it reached the red beam of Der Traumlicht, the monster from my nightmares used teeth and claws to rip it to pieces.

The light faded and the goat creature vanished as the remains of the plane crashed to the ground. Caleb disappeared into the bunker, then returned and announced in a shaky voice that Eliana had died. Several girls began wailing, but Herr Doktor ignored them and raised his fist to the sky. "Enemy aircraft will be no match for Der Traumlicht!" he proclaimed.

The officers looked at each other, their eyes wide with amazement, or maybe horror. One of them swallowed hard and said in a weak voice, "The Reichmarshall will be here for your next demonstration." They saluted Herr Doktor and left in haste.

I would have given anything to be the next of the Mädchen to die, but Anne was chosen for the demonstration the following night for Reichsmarschall Goering of the Luftwaffe. The following day, she was separated from the rest of us. I despaired of saying goodbye to her until, just before dusk, Caleb led me to the Traumlicht bunker where Anne awaited her fate. He explained that Herr Doktor had given her an extremely high dosage. Blood and spittle dribbled down her chin, and her breathing was ragged.

"They have taken the light," she whispered. "All is darkness."

I embraced her, then pressed my birthday bracelet into her hand and kissed her cheek. "I love you, Anne," I told her, as Caleb escorted me from the room.

Too soon, Goering and his entourage arrived. A full-length greatcoat and cape protected his enormous bulk from the icy wind cutting through my tattered smock. He spoke tersely to Herr Doktor, who gave a curt bow and instructed the attending soldiers to commence the demonstration. Exactly as it had done the night before, the searchlight beam turned red and the goat monster began to form. But, as Herr Doktor ordered not one but three unmanned planes launched this time, the ghastly creature began wavering like a candle flame. It split in two, each half dissolving and reforming, until finally a pair of enormous faces appeared above us. Two faces I knew well, even though I had never seen one of their movies.

Gasps rippled through the spectators as bodies appeared with the faces. Fred Astaire stretched out an arm to Ginger Rogers, who lit up the night in a flowing ice-blue gown. They danced across the sky, whirling in time to music only I could hear.

Two guards grabbed each other and began a grotesque mockery of the sky dance. Everyone else watched in silence. As the three planes passed without harm and faded into the night, Goering shouted an obscenity at the apparition as he pushed through the crowd and stormed off to the touring car awaiting him.

Anne kept the dance aloft as long as she could. When Fred and Ginger finally parted, stars appeared through their faces. Silently, I mouthed the words Anne had sung to me, wishing I could caress her cheek and comfort her.

The faces grew fainter. Der Traumlicht faded to black. There was a brief flash, though, before the light disappeared forever. Anne had given me one last smile, as pure and precious as morning light reflected in diamonds.

<<A27-38667 END TRANSCRIPT>>

John Christenson

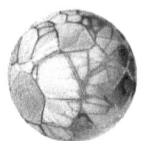

John Christenson lives in Boulder, Colorado and writes fiction for children and adults. His short fiction has appeared in the *New Mexico Review*, Flash *Fiction Magazine*, and several anthologies. His story "A Tree Grows in the Man Cave," published in *Rise: An Anthology of Change*, was nominated for the Pushcart Prize.

Damn The Dream

Sandy Reay

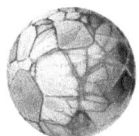

I'm sitting in my car, afraid to start it. *Damn The Dream*.

The Dream wasn't normal, fuzzy bits of muddled memories that melted when the alarm screamed.

It wasn't like premonitions I'd had. In third grade, I dreamt my braces broke. That day, when I bit into a soft chocolate-chip cookie, the bracket holding the wire popped off and slashed the inside my cheek. In eighth grade, I dreamt I fell on my head. That afternoon, playing volleyball in gym, I jumped up to block a shot. My teammate ran into me, flipping me backward. I landed on my elbow, which shattered. My dreams didn't match reality, but they were close enough to spook me.

After I dreamt about falling, I fell down the basement stairs and broke two toes. *My dreams have power*. I'd stare out the window at night until sleep sneaked up on me.

My friends followed their dreams: found careers, got married, bought houses, had children, and traded their sports cars for SUVs. They described trips they would take when they got old.

I was in my twenties. Old was thirty. I never had dreams like theirs.

I got The Dream, instead.

In it, I drove a sports car over a mountain pass, checking the gauges and feeling the tires hug the pavement. My hands and feet moved in sync with the road. In a tight turn, my car went straight and flew soundlessly two thousand feet to the bottom of the valley, where it exploded.

My screaming woke me. My skin burned. I gasped for air and

smelled burning metal and flesh. *Am I going to die before I turn thirty? Is that why I can't see my future?*

Dressed for work after a cool shower, I sat in my car, too shaky to start it. The gauges didn't look like the car in my dream, but my childhood premonitions hadn't cared about precision. I called in sick to work.

After a good night's sleep, thanks to warm milk and Bailey's Irish Cream, I felt stupid for letting a dream hold me hostage in my home. My hands shook while I drove to work, but I made it. Mile by mile, my life went back to normal.

A few months later, The Dream showed me the same car, the same tight turn, and my soundless flight to the explosion and flames. *Damn The Dream.*

I woke up gasping for air, shaking and crying. But, I forced myself to shower, dress, and drive to work.

The Dream came back four months later, and three months after that. I'd never had a recurring premonition. Something must have triggered it, but what? Nothing in my life looked like a trigger, except racing cars. But The Dream didn't return with race days.

I'm going crazy. I need to see a shrink. Before I made an appointment, The Dream stopped. After six months without The Dream, I felt cured.

The Dream woke me twice in one week. "Gotcha," it taunted.

I worked days, went to school at night, raced and partied on weekends, and died four or five times a year in my sleep. Every time, I woke choking on smoke, my skin burning. I joked about my new normal with my friends, but when I failed to laugh at their jokes, they knew that The Dream had left me shaking again.

When I was twenty-nine, I drove my sports car to a parking lot Gymkhana to race on a track outlined by chalk lines and orange pylons. Waiting for the flag person to signal my solo run, I took deep breaths and queued my mental pep talk. *Just go fast. You've had a full life. It's okay if you die.*

What? No, it's not okay to die.

The flag dropped. I sat with my mouth open. When the starter knocked on my windshield, I pulled out of line. A few strangers watched me pack up and leave. *I will never race again.*

When I had to sell my unreliable Triumph, I test drove a Saab Sonett III, but the black dashboard and white sloping hood looked like the car in The Dream.

"Sorry, I can't buy this car." I ran away.

After a few weeks, I found a Saab Sonett II, which didn't look like The Dream car. In the first autumn snow, a truck slid through a red

212

light and almost hit me. I took the bus to work, used the hour ride each way to do my classwork, and stopped going out on weekends. At the end of the semester, I gave up night school to watch cop shows on TV, but stared out the window during car chase scenes. After my bus slid sideways to the guard rail on an overpass in a storm, I found a new job closer to home.

I had to take a four-week training class across town, an hour commute each way. *I can do this.*

The Dream came back two weeks ago. For the last few days, I've pulled into a parking lot or down a side street on the way home, until I stopped shaking. *I'll be okay because I'm not driving in the mountains.*

Or will I? My early premonitions weren't precise.

I stopped twice on the way to the training center today, finished my class, and stayed until the janitor made me leave.

I'm sitting in my car, afraid to start it. *Damn The Dream.*

I need to drive home tonight to feed my cat. Tomorrow, I can ride the bus to work.

I slam the steering wheel with my fist. Clenching my teeth, I knuckle tears from my eyes and force my hand to turn the key. *I can do this.*

Tomorrow will be my thirtieth birthday. *I hope I live to see it.*

Sandy Reay

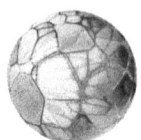

Sandy Reay worked in a full-service gas station, raced cars, ran rivers in rubber rafts, worked as a draftsman, programmed computers, lived on a horse ranch in the mountains, worked as a photographer, went pony-trekking along the banks of Loch Ness, wrote songs which other people performed and recorded (and got airplay), played bass in bar and bluegrass bands, worked at Renaissance festivals, adopted more than a dozen adult dogs (and five cats), and makes silver jewelry. She still hasn't decided what she wants to be when she grows up.

Dream Eater

Gregory Mattix

Iolanthe prowled the shores of the Dreaming in search of her next meal.

The Dreaming appeared as an ebon expanse filled with a universe of morphing constellations formed from the dreams of untold sleepers. Like the stars burning in the cosmos, some were spread far apart and others were in tight clusters. Some were bright while others were dim, their hues varying from the fiery crimson of violent dreams to the inky black of night terrors. Fairer colors were also in abundance—blues and golds and whites. But Iolanthe wasn't concerned with those. Pleasant dreams provided no sustenance for her.

The most recent nightmare she'd consumed had been typical, uninteresting fare: a young boy's unpleasant dream of arriving at the schoolhouse only to find out that the final exams were being administered—exams for which he'd completely neglected to study. He worried about flunking the tests and ending up on the receiving end of his father's angry fists.

The boy's nightmare had teased her with hints of the succulent fear of the wrath of his drunken pipe-fitter father upon learning of his son's failed exams. Unfortunately, the dream proved largely boring, bland, and unfulfilling. As it focused primarily on the boy's embarrassment as he fidgeted and sweated, staring cluelessly at the page while his classmates were hard at work, the nightmare didn't allow Iolanthe to plumb those richer depths. Plenty of her kind would be quite content with such meals, but not Iolanthe.

I'd like something more satisfying today, she thought.

Readying herself for her journey into the Dreaming, she threw back her head and gave a great stretch, her snout curling back atop her head briefly. She then shook herself to limber up, the effect much like a wet dog drying its coat. A shudder ran through her sturdy body, from the end of her snout down to her clawed tiger paws and culminating at the tip of her slender ox tail. One particularly foreboding constellation beckoned her, its sable and blood-red stars particularly numerous and intense.

I shall venture there once more.

She leapt from the shore and dove into the Dreaming. Within a short while, she was gliding through the grim nebula, briefly sampling the extraordinary horror and pain and anguish within each of the nightmares. The source, she knew from experience, was a great war brewing in the mortal world. No pleasant gold or blue or white dreams would be found here.

Iolanthe wouldn't admit it to others, but she did take some guilty pleasure in the euphoric dreams of humans, those that were filled with loving families, pride taken in achievements, passionate evenings in the arms of lovers, or being moved to tears by the beauty of a symphony. As much as she appreciated the happier dreams, because of her nature, they provided her no nourishment. However, even though her efforts might yield only fleeting results in the vastness of the Dreaming, she took pride in transforming the ebon and scarlet stars into cheerful ephemeral colors.

She shuddered at the intensity of some of the nightmares as she skimmed past. Many were unnatural in origin, being stoked by the dark ones. Unlike the baku, Iolanthe's people, the alpen were malevolent creatures who inflicted the worst kinds of nightmares upon mortals, delighting in their suffering as they consumed their psychic energies like parasites. Legend told that the two races were kindred, having originally been one civilization until many eons past when the alpen's twisted nature and penchant for evil had created a rift, eventually causing the societies to split asunder. Other than the rare inadvertent encounter within the Dreaming, the two races shunned one another.

Picking a nightmare at random, one without an alp present, Iolanthe dove straight into the heart of an intense, scintillating red-black star… and found herself inside a war zone, much as she had expected.

A small human village spread out around her, surrounded by a dark, mysterious forest. Iolanthe rather fancied forests. She felt as though one would have been her natural home had she been a creature of flesh and blood rather than a spiritual entity, a denizen of the Hidden Realm. She scented the air, tasting the lifeblood of the dream and taking her time to fully savor all the subtleties pervading its rich aroma. As was her custom, prior to sating her hunger, she first would satisfy her deep curiosity regarding humankind by taking the opportunity to observe.

A chill filled the air as a persistent gray drizzle saturated the environment. What might have once been a quaint, picturesque setting had become a scene of destruction. The narrow lane through town was churned into deep, stinking mud. Homes and shops lay in ruins, pulverized so that tumbles of bricks and stones spilled into the street. One lone roofless wall beside Iolanthe leaned precariously against its neighbor like a drunk heading home with a friend after the local tavern closed for the night.

Death was everywhere. A dozen or more bodies lay smothered in the clinging mud. Iolanthe stepped beside a young man who clutched an implement that she'd learned was called a rifle. His innards were strewn around him like grisly ribbons. Other dead men, in matching uniforms, held rifles as well—a group of fallen soldiers. Their helmets lay askew, some filled with rainwater.

Iolanthe moved through the dreamscape. Immersing herself fully, she allowed her paws to sink into the cold muck, feeling the way it squelched between her toes. She noted how the chill rain soaked into her fur. The cloying stench of death and acrid tinge of gunpowder filled her nostrils.

The dream's origin was easy for Iolanthe to discern as she homed in on the dreamer, who appeared to be located inside one of the few intact buildings, a large structure on the edge of town. A wooden sign affixed to a post named the apparent inn as The White Stag.

Before Iolanthe could reach the dreamer, a deafening thunder startled her. The sheer volume of the noise battering her eardrums came as a shock, though nothing could actually harm her within the dreamscape. The inn's side wall violently imploded, and an explosion rocked the building, causing the roof to collapse and rubble to rain down all around. A brick passed harmlessly through Iolanthe.

She tracked the source of destruction to an iron monstrosity on the road beyond the perimeter of the village, where a rumbling, smoking beast rode on odd elliptical wheels, a long, tubular nose protruding from its swiveling head—a machine of war.

The dreamer's scream drew Iolanthe into the inn. She passed through the front wall, which was about all that remained standing, and into a rubble-clogged common room. Within were several people—a family, evidently. An older man and woman were sprawled amid the debris, the quantity of surrounding blood indicating that they'd died from the blast. A large metal shard embedded in the woman's chest made an angry hissing as raindrops spattered it. One of the man's arms had been blown completely off. Two young sobbing children, miraculously unscathed, were clinging to each other amid the ruins of what had been both their home and their parents' livelihood.

Iolanthe spotted the dreamer—a pretty young woman almost of an age to start a family of her own. She lay prone in a pile of wreckage, pinned beneath a heavy beam and a large portion of the roof that it had supported. Judging from her pained expression and soft whimpers, the woman looked to be in great distress, both physical and emotional. Her hazel eyes, glazed over, seemed locked on the dead couple.

Iolanthe moved to the trapped woman and perched on some fallen bricks beside her. She inhaled deeply, absorbing the dream's heady essence, sifting through it until she gleaned a more complete picture of the situation. The distinctive flavor of a memory infused this nightmare.

Unable to resist her curiosity any longer, Iolanthe probed the dreamer's mind, made possible because the Dreaming bridged the physical and spirit worlds. Marie Arnaud was sixteen years of age and worked as a serving girl in her family's inn. She hoped to find a husband soon, but prospects in the village were slim. None of that information was particularly notable outside of the fact that Marie was dying in the physical world.

The realization gave Iolanthe pause. She'd never encountered such a situation before. For a moment, she simply stared at the dreamer, unsure of what to do. The fact that she was experiencing some of Marie's final moments before she expired was greatly unsettling. To an immortal being like Iolanthe, death had always been a vague concept, something experienced in the dreams of mortals, much like fear or shame or guilt. It was simply one spice among many flavoring her meals, another ephemeral element that she could consume, which both quelled her hunger and relieved the dreamers of their deepest fears. Only now, Iolanthe found herself powerless in the face of Marie's impending demise.

The vast majority of Iolanthe's kind regarded humans as nothing more than a source of sustenance, mere feed stock. But Iolanthe had always felt differently. Mortals fascinated her, with their brief lives so rich with the vibrancy of their emotions and experiences. She particularly fancied their creativity in producing wonderful works of art, music, and poetry, while their capacity for cruelty and kindness, hatred and love, in equal measure never failed to surprise her.

Iolanthe couldn't help but be impressed by Marie's inner strength, as the girl fought back her own agony and terror to focus on her siblings. "Marcel, Muri," she called, voice hoarse with pain. "Come here."

She had to repeat herself before the pair responded. The two young children hugged their older sister, at least as much as was possible with Marie being buried from the chest down.

Iolanthe scrutinized Marie's predicament further. The young woman's legs and pelvis were crushed and broken, and Marie worried that she was bleeding internally, the excruciating abdominal pain a sure sign of some dreadful injury to her innards. Iolanthe thought it a cruel misfortune that her back hadn't been broken, which might have spared her the awful pain. Such had happened to Alphonse, one of the local men who had fallen off his roof and broken his spine several winters ago. The accident had robbed him of both the use of his legs and any feeling below the waist.

Poor girl. I wish there was something that could be done to aid her.

Marie gathered her brother and sister into her arms as best she could and held them as they sobbed. She tried to act the strong older sister they needed in that moment, determined to look after them for as long as she could, which she feared wouldn't be much longer.

Distant booms and tremors spoke of the invading military's continuing assault, though at that point, little remained standing for them to destroy. A great conflagration was raging across the countryside. The German army had assaulted Marie's village, Fréssonne, where a small contingent of French soldiers had been holed up, recuperating after a devastating battle to the northeast, five days prior. When word reached town that Wehrmacht troops were pushing through the Ardennes, the dozen soldiers, though wounded and drastically overmatched, had shown exemplary courage in doing their best to hold off the enemy and buy the people of Fréssonne time to escape.

The Arnaud family had tarried too long, Marie's parents being intent on equipping their friends and neighbors with food and supplies as they fled into the forest.

Marie had dallied too, hoping the handsome young soldier, Luc, would survive the fighting. Over the past week, while tending to Luc's wounds, she'd fallen in love with him. She knew he fancied her, as well, and an innocent, hopelessly romantic part of her had dreamed of a future together.

Iolanthe felt a stab of sympathy, having seen Luc's corpse sprawled in the mud among ribbons of his entrails, while Marie slowly expired. At least Luc probably hadn't suffered for long.

The ground shook as the inexorable war machine drew near. The collapsed inn trembled. Loose bricks tumbled free and wood cracked as the remainder of the roof sagged even lower. Harsh foreign voices could be heard in the street outside as Wehrmacht foot soldiers searched through the destroyed Fréssonne.

Marie didn't understand any German, but Iolanthe could comprehend every human tongue in existence. Dreams were universal. Her comprehension, however, didn't mean Iolanthe could communicate flawlessly. Nor would she—as a mere watcher, she would never take such an action. Communicating with humans served no purpose.

Ikelos, eldest among Iolanthe's 999 brethren, had always warned them not to become involved in human affairs. "The wolf does not converse with the lamb before he feeds, does he?" he'd said when Iolanthe had questioned his warning many ages past. The answer was neither true nor satisfying, but Iolanthe, as one of the younger baku, had accepted it at the time, figuring his wisdom was much greater than her own. After untold centuries of experiencing human dreams and gaining an appreciation for humankind, however, she had developed serious doubts regarding that particular maxim.

My brethren would certainly show no such interest in Marie's plight, but merely gorge themselves on this fertile nightmare and then move on without a second thought.

"Don't worry, my loves." Marie stroked the children's hair while they sniffled and clung to her arms. "Everything will be fine. Mama and Papa … they're just sleeping. In a few minutes, they'll take you to see your friends again, all right?"

Murielle, who was only six, murmured acquiescence, but her eight-year-old brother protested. "No, they won't, sis," Marcel said with some heat. "They're dead."

Marie's eyes filled with tears. "Shush. I need you to be strong for Muri, you hear? You're the man of the family now, Marcel."

Iolanthe watched, fascinated, as the scene played out, affected more than she would have thought possible by the plight of the dreamer and her family. The knowledge that these were likely Marie's last moments in life gave the dream an added solemnity.

Boots tromped loudly just outside. A powerful blow knocked the inn's sagging door off its hinges, and a trio of Wehrmacht soldiers cautiously entered the section of common room still standing. Dressed in their black *stahlhelms* and bulky, dripping rain slickers, the men looked monstrous looming over the cowering children, giving the impression of some type of great beetles wearing the guise of men.

Murielle shrieked, then began sobbing harder. Marcel looked belligerent for a moment until one of the soldiers casually kicked his dead mother in the head as he stepped past. Then Marcel broke down again too.

"*Kinder,*" one of the soldiers barked, beckoning the children. "*Kommt hierher!*"

"Don't you harm them," Marie said, tears in her own eyes. "Please don't harm them."

The soldier repeated his command. When the children didn't obey, he gestured curtly to one of his comrades. A hulking beetle-man with tiny black eyes lumbered forward. He shouldered his rifle and seized both children by their skinny arms. Murielle squealed in fright. Marcel struggled, kicking at the man's shin. Terror bled off Marie as she shouted a protest, squirming and struggling futilely to free herself and protect her siblings.

The soldier cuffed Marcel hard enough to knock him to the floor. Marcel stared up in shock at the huge man, one hand going to his jaw, where a red spot was forming. The man shoved Murielle to one of his companions, who took her by the arm. The girl, unresisting, stood and wept quietly. The brute reached for Marcel, but the boy grabbed a shattered brick and heaved it, striking the soldier in the side of the helmet when he reflexively turned his head.

With a bellow of outrage, the big man reached again, only to receive another brick, this one striking him squarely on the nose. Marcel, heartened by his success, scrambled farther away amid the rubble as the soldier cursed and clutched his bloodied nose.

"You're dead, you little shit," he snarled in German. He unslung his rifle, put it to his shoulder, and fired a round just as Marie screamed.

Iolanthe had seen enough. She leapt forward, interposing herself between the child murderer and his prey. As a lodestone attracts iron filings, she drew the bullet into herself, where it blinked out of existence. She then threw her head back and took the nightmare fully unto herself, drinking deeply of Marie's pain and sorrow and dread. The nightmare inundated her, making her feel as if she were draining a river dry.

The hulking soldier wriggled like a dry leaf clinging stubbornly to a branch in a strong wind. Then he was swept away in a maelstrom surrounding Iolanthe, followed by his two companions. The ruined inn followed, collapsing into Iolanthe as she reared back on her hind legs, front paws spread wide in a humanlike pose.

Bricks, debris, raindrops, a torrent of mud, corpses, more enemy soldiers, and the terrible war machine were all sucked away into Iolanthe. She didn't stop until even the gloomy clouds were gone, allowing sunshine to warm the village.

Little remained of the previous dreamscape save for a clearing amid the trees and a hovel or two that had been spared the destruction. The day was warm and lovely, the sun shining down. It felt much like the first break of sunshine following a harsh blizzard. Iolanthe grinned upon seeing birds fluttering around and chirping. Even a colorful butterfly bobbed around a clump of wildflowers near the road.

Now that Iolanthe had consumed Marie's nightmare, she had a full belly and felt infused with boundless energy from the richness of the meal. She imagined how the dream's hue would have shifted in the Dreaming to one of the joyful, eye-pleasing colors.

"Much better," she pronounced.

"Is someone there?" Marie asked.

Iolanthe turned to see the pretty maid standing a few feet away, uninjured. Her brown hair was tied back with a ribbon, and a clean red-and-white-patterned dress covered her slim body. All of the hurt and sorrow had been drained from the girl's nightmare, leaving only this pleasant reverie in its wake.

Now is the time for me to take my leave so I can appreciate this bright new star amid that morbid constellation.

And yet she paused, something holding her back. It pained her that this young woman was dying. If Marie woke from her dream, it would be to a world of lingering suffering and agony. Iolanthe wished she could save Marie somehow, but she was a spiritual being with no corporeal form and no agency in the physical world.

On impulse, Iolanthe shifted into a human likeness and allowed herself to be seen.

Marie gasped. "Who are you? Where did you come from?"

Iolanthe had taken the form of a Milanese woman whose dream she had fed on some years earlier, a fashion model considered a great beauty, though her fair countenance concealed an ugliness inside. Iolanthe had fancied the woman's lovely gold-hued eyes, flawless skin, and lustrous black hair. The fashionable dress and fancy shoes with shiny buckles, she thought, were cute.

"I'm just a visitor here. My name is Iolanthe."

What am I doing? I should have left once I ate the last of her nightmare. Ikelos's admonishment not to become involved with dreamers rang out in the back of her mind, but she pushed it aside.

Iolanthe probed Marie with her senses. The young woman slept fitfully, having gradually succumbed to exhaustion after more than a day trapped in the wreckage, but her dream still lingered, as fragile as a butterfly's wing.

The reality had played out just as in the dreamscape. Marcel had been shot dead and Murielle dragged away, her fate unknown— perhaps a prisoner or, as Marie feared, something much worse. Marie herself had been ignored, a victim of casual cruelty. She had been less than nothing in the enemy's eyes, not even worth a slug of lead as a small mercy to end her suffering. The Wehrmacht had departed the village, pressing their advance deeper into France, with the young woman left to die a slow, lonely death.

Iolanthe found herself in what a human might have called a crisis of conscience. She should have stolen away the moment she absorbed the entirety of the malaise from Marie's dream. Even though her hunger was thoroughly sated, the experience had left her feeling ill.

She couldn't help but think of one of the alp-infested dreams she'd glimpsed earlier. A human bound to his nightmare, forced to relive the gruesome murder of his family over and over again as the alp gorged on his terror and suffering, gradually draining him dry of psychic energy until only a mindless husk remained.

We baku are not much different from the alpen. All we do is take, take, take. It is what I do, even as this poor girl breathes her last.

Iolanthe knew the baku relationship with humans was mutually beneficial. She took away their nightmares and in turn gained nourishment for herself. All the other humans she'd encountered had woken after dreaming, either blissfully unaware in their forgetfulness or, for those who remembered, grateful to realize their nightmares had not been real.

But once Marie woke, the nightmare would still be very real.

Fate is cruel to deny Marie the small blessing of solace in her final moments—to be free of pain and fear for just a brief time. After all, she has nothing remaining to her. A deep well of sorrow surprised Iolanthe with its intensity. *But perhaps I do have the power to help her, in a way.*

"No, that would not be good," Iolanthe muttered to herself. "Not good at all."

Interfering would in all likelihood mean banishment from her people—provided her actions were detected. She had heard stories of other baku being banished eons ago but didn't know if that was true or not, having never encountered any exiles before. Perhaps it was simply a fable concocted to frighten inquisitive baku into obedience.

"Excuse me? Mademoiselle, are you well?" Marie approached, a tentative smile on her face.

Iolanthe met Marie's gaze and smiled back. It was easy to do, as she basked in the contentment now radiating off the vibrant young woman.

"Fear not," Iolanthe said. "Your nightmare is over. The bad men are depressed now with their machines of war."

"Pardon?" Marie's eyes went wide, and she giggled. "I think you meant they are departed."

"Ah, just so." Iolanthe grinned, glad to see the humor sparkling

225

in Marie's pretty, hazel eyes and her overall change in demeanor. Although her vocabulary might be lacking, she still felt a tiny thrill to be speaking with a human for the first time. "Yes, they are gone now. You have no cause to be afraid."

"That is wonderful. I was so scared… I thought…" Marie wrinkled her brow. "I-I… how embarrassing! I've completely forgotten what I was even frightened of in the first place." She gave a nervous laugh.

"All is well," Iolanthe said. "Will you join me here, out in the garden, for a bit?" She knew Marie took pleasure in tending her flowers in the garden behind the inn.

The two strolled through a sun-drenched floral garden more impressive than it had ever been in reality, with neat rows of flowers stretching out of sight. Every plant was blooming to its fullest. Marie sighed happily as she studied the rainbow bouquet around them, the various scents weaving a complex perfume in the air. Butterflies fluttered, and honeybees buzzed around them. A bluebird chirped happily from the bough of a nearby tree. Marie paused to sniff a pink rose. The stray thought came to Iolanthe of Marie's wish that Luc would someday offer her a lovely rose as a gesture of courtship.

The dream suddenly shuddered, a mighty reverberation passing through everything around.

No! Not yet!

Marie was waking up, only to return to her suffering back in her body. The dream began collapsing, the distant forest falling away in waves as though a gigantic abyss had opened. It grew closer like massive ocean swells about to roll over them and sweep the dream away.

Poor Marie. She doesn't deserve to suffer anymore—to have her last moments in life be filled with pain and loneliness. I won't be like the alpen. Now is my chance to give something back.

And for the first time in the untold millennia of Iolanthe's existence, she used her own abilities to alter the natural course. She couldn't prevent the dreamer from waking or the dream from ending. But she could draw Marie into a dreamscape of her own devising. As the tsunami of dissolution washed over them, wiping out Marie's dream, Iolanthe drew her into a parallel dreamscape of her own construction—a daydream. Marie no longer slept, but the end result was the same. Her consciousness was now contained here.

Iolanthe, in a creative storm, replicated the surrounding landscape, flower garden, and Ardennes Forest, then returned Fréssonne to its intact state prior to the invasion.

"What's happening?" Marie asked, looking around in surprise.

She must have sensed the change, though she displayed no uneasiness, merely curiosity.

"Simply a change of… view?" Iolanthe shrugged, not finding the word she wanted. She wiggled her fingers and painted an image in the air, that of a stage play with the curtain descending and reopening to reveal a different backdrop.

"Ah, a change in scene. I love my home here." Marie's smile grew wistful. "But to confess, I feel a bit strange, as if I must leave it all behind and travel to someplace else." She massaged her temples.

"There's someone here to see you, Marie," Iolanthe said.

"Oh?" Marie brightened, and it was obvious who she was hoping to see.

She turned just as he approached, striding down the narrow path leading into the garden behind the inn. The sun shone on his tanned, handsome face, and his blue eyes were bright. He was clean and whole again, with no signs of the injuries he'd suffered.

"It's wonderful to see you again, Marie," Luc said. With a flourish, he revealed a single, perfect red rose he'd been concealing behind his back.

"Luc, my love!" Marie clasped her hands to her breast, and her cheeks colored, though she was smiling.

Luc captured one of her hands and kissed it tenderly, then gave her the rose.

Iolanthe sensed Marie's body finally succumbing to death in the physical world, her heart slowing and stopping. *It is now time.*

"Would you care to walk with me a way, *chérie*?" Luc held out his hand. "I shall escort you home."

"I'd be delighted." Marie took his hand, a glowing smile on her lips. Hand in hand, they strolled across the sun-dappled field, the young woman radiating joy up until the moment she faded away.

Iolanthe withdrew from her dreamscape construct, letting it evanesce to sparkling glimmers, well pleased with her efforts. Back in the Dreaming, she admired the lovely incandescence that had been created, which banished a scintilla of the gloom amid the ugly dark nebula. The fleeting burst of warmth and cheer was a vast improvement, in her opinion—a defiant speck of happiness among the nightmares.

An unusual sensation suffused her being, different from the contentment after a particularly satisfying meal. An effervescent feeling of warmth and lightness that felt both strange and wonderful.

It's as if I'm filled up with those pretty, glimmering stars myself. She smiled at the thought.

If her actions were to be condemned in the eyes of the elders and deemed worthy of banishment, then so be it. Here, amidst the innumerable stars of dreamers, she need never feel truly alone.

Iolanthe left the Dreaming behind, new possibilities unfurling in her mind like Marie's flowers welcoming the morning sunshine.

Gregory Mattix

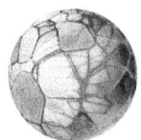

Gregory Mattix enjoys all types of speculative fiction and writes a variety of stories under that broad genre. He grew up in the blazing heat of the Arizona desert. He obtained a degree in Business Administration at the University of Arizona, served in the military, and lived overseas for a time. Currently, he lives in Colorado with his wife. He is the author of *Remember Tomorrow* and the *Extensis Vitae and Nexus of the Planes* series.

Seedlings of Reality
Karen Fox

Dreams are seedlings of realities. ~James Allen

"I'm going to quit my job." Kinsley Hamilton dropped into the chair opposite her best friend at Panera, their favorite restaurant. Though their jobs kept them busy, they made it a point to meet once or twice a week for lunch.

Piper Brown didn't react with any kind of amazement. "So you've been saying for a year now." Pausing, she waved the fork in the air. "What happened now?"

Kinsley *had* been threatening to quit for several months now. She'd been so excited to finish her degree in structural engineering and had dreamed of building things that made a difference. But it hadn't happened that way. True, her well-paying job at Markson Corporation allowed her to buy her first house, but designing huge, monolithic warehouses for storage and distribution of products was far from challenging...or satisfying. "They passed me over for the new housing project."

"I'm sorry." Piper reached across the table to touch Kinsley's hand. "I know how much you wanted that."

The position would have allowed Kinsley to design and help create low-cost housing close to the city's bustling downtown. To make the complex effective enough for its tenants, artistically pleasing, and affordable offered her a chance to actually do something worthwhile. She grimaced. "I should have known." She squeezed Piper's hand in gratitude. Thank goodness she had a friend who was there through thick and thin. "I really need to look for something else."

Her friend shook her head with a smile. "You've been saying that, too. Have you actually looked?"

"Some." Other diners chatted around them, oblivious to Kinsley's conversation. Wouldn't it be nice if someone overheard and jumped in saying *I have a job for you*? "I can't find anything that I'd like better without moving out of Colorado, and I don't want to do that."

"I don't want you to either. I'd miss you too much." Piper tucked a strand of her short, blond pageboy cut behind her ear. "Something will come along that's perfect."

Now Kinsley grinned. "And you've been saying that for months, too."

"Have faith."

Yeah, right. Kinsley had given up on that a while ago. Finding a new job and finding a good man both fell into the almost impossible category. At least she had a great friend and an awesome house to balance it out. Where would she be without either of those? "I have faith in you," she said. Piper was the ultimate optimist—something Kinsley needed and appreciated.

"Of course." Piper grinned as she raised her drink and drained it. "I'm going to have to run. It's pretty chaotic at work right now."

"I understand. Will you still make the concert?"

"I wouldn't miss it." Piper stood, gathering her dishes onto her tray. "I put that on the schedule months ago. They better not try to make me work that night."

Kinsley and Piper had managed to purchase tickets for a massive concert with several noted bands to be held in the football stadium in Denver in just over a month. But Piper worked at a 24/7 medical clinic as a nurse practitioner, which involved long shifts and numerous days, both scheduled and unscheduled. "Great. How about lunch Friday?" Kinsley asked.

"I'll see how it goes." Piper quickly hugged Kinsley. "Don't work too hard."

She hurried away just as Kinsley's pager vibrated signaling her meal was ready. *Figures.*

***

By the time Kinsley finally fell into bed that night, she was ready to cry. Work had been even worse that afternoon. There was another warehouse looming in her future paired with the threat of working with Mike Davis, who imagined himself God's gift to women and treated her as if she didn't have a brain. A little of him went a long way. She really needed to find another job--soon.

She'd barely closed her eyes when she found herself in a lush green meadow, dotted with dancing colorful flowers—daisies, violets, and black-eyed Susan that melded into a lush, green forest, thick, towering pine intermingled with leafy maples, ash, and more she couldn't identify. The scent of the flowers drifted by on a caressing breeze, tickling her nose and tousling her long auburn curls at the same time.

This place was beautiful. Soothing. Perfect.

Part of her realized this had to be a dream, yet it felt like more—more solid, more real.

Shielding her eyes against the brilliant sunshine, she surveyed the area. Nothing stood out. Shrugging, she chose a random direction and started walking.

She'd only gone a short distance when an animal headed toward her. As it grew closer, she could tell it was a dog, but unlike any she'd ever seen. Its face resembled that of a Labrador, but different, more alert. It stood as large as a Great Dane with uneven patches of black, brown, and white on its thick fur. Its large, pointed ears stuck up like those of a German Shepherd while its large curling tail reminded her of an Alaskan Malamute--an interesting combination.

The dog slowed upon reaching her and cocked his head. "Hi there."

Kinsley blinked. Had she heard right? "Did you just talk?"

"I did. I'm Diogee."

"D-O-G?" she repeated, with emphasis on the O as he had done.

"That's right. I'm your greeter. Follow me, please." Turning, Diogee started up a gradual slope.

As Kinsley followed the dog, she struggled to find words. Good thing she was dreaming. This made no sense. "Do all the animals here talk?"

"No, just me." He glanced back, giving her what had to be a toothy smile.

"Where am I?"

"Here." He spoke as if that was obvious.

"Does *here* have a name?" Kinsley shook her head. She was talking to a *dog*.

"Not yet. I imagine it will soon--when enough of you get here."

Enough of...? She frowned. "Why am I here?"

"You were selected."

"For what?"

"Liam will explain." Diogee looked at her again with what had to be humor in his brown eyes. "I'm just the greeter."

Kinsley doubted it. He seemed like more than that.

A squat box-like building appeared ahead, silhouetted against the azure sky. Built of uneven logs, it wasn't square and leaned to one side. As Kinsley drew nearer, she spied another similarly styled building, and one that looked to be in construction. The architect in her frowned. The buildings were wrong, not sturdy enough. The loads were off. Someone could get hurt.

A man approached them. He appeared slightly older than her age of twenty-seven, tall with wavy dark hair in an unruly cut. His clothing looked odd, like worn leather, his shirt and pants not quite in the right proportions. Even before they met, she sensed the air of authority around him. She didn't recognize him. Should she? She felt immediate attraction, but it was more than that, a knowing of some sort.

"Hi." He extended his hand. "I'm Liam Snyder. Welcome." He glanced at Diogee. "Thank you for guiding her."

"My pleasure." Diogee nodded, then trotted off to where other people grouped around the partially built structure.

Liam's grip was firm, his palm callused. His smile revealed a dimple in each cheek. "Yes, I know a talking dog is unusual."

"He said you would explain."

Liam's gray gaze locked on hers. "How open-minded are you?"

"I listened to and followed a talking dog." She grinned. "I think I qualify." This place held questions that she needed answered. "Diogee said I was…selected."

"We all were. We meet the criteria to come here."

She didn't know which question to ask first. "What criteria?"

Liam held up his hand and ticked his fingers with each word. "Kindness. Intelligence. Responsibility. Willing to work. A particular skill."

"Ah." That explained the misshaped structures. "I must be the structural architect you ordered."

Liam nodded. "Structural architect. Yes, that's good. We definitely need that." He pointed to the building in progress. "We're faking it right now."

"I can see there are problems." She'd have to be blind to miss them.

His smile warmed her. "Come on over."

This building was similar to the others, constructed from roughly hewn logs stacked on top of each other. She didn't see any form of nails being used at all.

They were only a few feet away when the logs collapsed with a resounding crash. Screams reverberated from beneath the logs. Kinsley gasped, her heart jumping into her throat. "Oh, my God!"

Kinsley hurried toward the accident, rising terror lodged in her throat. If they moved the wrong log, the rest of the walls could fall. The cries from those trapped echoed across the area. "We have to help." Liam was already moving with her.

Everyone rushed forward, tugging at the logs.

A beeping sound rang vaguely in the distance, but Kinsley blotted it out. This was more important.

"Don't move that one," she called to a young man trying to raise a log. Recognizing the points of failure, she took charge, directing where to lift the heavy logs to set them aside without endangering the people beneath. Diogee indicated where people were buried. Others lifted the people to safety as they were freed.

Many of them were covered in blood. Others had broken limbs, concussions, cuts. The cries diminished to moans as everyone was rescued.

Kinsley turned to assist as best she could, using a wet rag to clean blood off a young man's shoulder, who groaned at every touch. He needed stitches. "Do you have a doctor?" she asked Liam.

Liam shook his head, his frustration obvious. "Not yet."

Damn. If only Piper was here. "Seems like medical care would be a necessary skill."

"We'll get one." Liam didn't elaborate but returned to setting an obviously broken arm.

Broken limbs were painfully set, then bound to pieces of wood by tied strands of a roughly woven cloth. No one died. At least, not yet, but Kinsley wasn't sure about one young man still unconscious. A log had struck his head. He still breathed, but they had no way of knowing the unseen damage.

"I'll watch over him." A solemn young woman moved into position by where the man now lay on the grass.

Kinsley moved over to Liam's side as he finished giving instructions to some of the workers.

"Let the building go for today. We'll look at what we're doing tomorrow." Liam glanced at Kinsley. "We might have a better way to build these things." They left and he focused on her. "Thank you for taking charge. This could have been worse." He hesitated. "Can you help with our buildings?"

"Maybe." She'd already designed ways to build better structures in her mind, but needed to write it out, see it. She looked at the small group tending to the injured. "Is this everyone here?"

"For now."

Of the twenty-two people of varying nationalities, were in the twenty-to-forty age group, and they honestly appeared to care about each other. "I'm impressed at how well they worked together."

"That's one of our goals--to become a family. I think that kindness and willingness to care about others is one of the main selection criteria."

"I think I need to know more." This felt more and more real by the moment, yet it couldn't be. She'd never experienced such a lucid dream before.

"Come, sit with me and we'll talk." Liam led her to a grassy bank along a swift flowing blue-green river, and they dropped to sit. "Okay, now I'll explain."

***

Piper approached the door to Kinsley's quaint Victorian, her heart pounding. When she'd called Kinsley's work number to confirm Friday's lunch, she'd been told her friend hadn't come in that day. Nor had she called in. That wasn't Kinsley--at all. Her friend breathed responsibility. Something had happened to her.

Worry grew through the day until Piper finally had a chance to rush to Kinsley's place, leaving work as early as she dared. Thank goodness she had a spare key.

Letting herself in, she found herself greeted by silence. Her throat tightened. Silence had never felt so completely empty before. The rooms on the lower level looked undisturbed—Kinsley's sweater hung over the back of a chair, her briefcase sat by her desk, papers spread across it. The coffee-pot had brewed but sat there untouched. "Kinsley?"

Swallowing hard, Piper climbed the staircase and approached Kinsley's bedroom. "Kins?"

She opened the door to the room and stepped in. She gasped and rushed to the queen-sized bed where Kinsley lay, unmoving. Piper held her breath as she took her friend's pulse. It was slow, but beating. Kinsley's breathing was equally slow, but unlabored. Her skin was still warm.

Piper shook her shoulder. "Kinsley, wake up!" Getting no response, she shook Kinsley harder. "Wake up!"

Kinsley remained sleeping, but her eyes moved rapidly behind her eyelids as if she was caught in the REM stage of slumber. Her lips were parted, almost smiling.

"Kinsley." Piper sobbed out the name, then reached for phone and pressed 911. Something was very, very wrong.

***

"You're in the future."

Kinsley jerked back at Liam's words. "What?" Of all the things she'd expected him to say, that wasn't one of them.

"It's approximately three thousand years in the future from our time."

"Three thousand years?" She stared at him. "Come on. That's impossible." She looked around at the beautiful wilderness, the tall, waving grasses, abundant spreading trees, clear water—untouched, pristine. "No, it can't be."

"I know it sounds incredible. I had a hard time believing it myself." Liam leaned forward. "But I promise you it's the truth."

Kinsley sat quiet for several minutes, her brain trying to process his words. She didn't think he'd lie to her, but at the same time... "I'm dreaming, aren't I?"

"Yes and no. The dream is a portal to bring you here."

"A portal." She nodded. There was a certain logic to that. It explained her feeling of actually *being* there. "Can I return that way, too?"

His expression turned grave. "Once." He hesitated. "We've all been called from the same year to come here."

"So, we're all from twenty-twenty-two?"

"I believe so. We've only started arriving over the past month."

She stared at him. He appeared sincere. She wanted to believe he was telling her the truth. "I need to know more. *Why* are we here?"

"We destroyed ourselves and this planet long ago. It's slowly come back to life, and we're being recruited to rebuild it."

Kinsley blinked. Sadly, she could believe it. "Who told you? How do you know all this?"

"I was the first one called, brought in via a dream. Like you." At her nod, Liam continued. "Diogee met me, told me the purpose, the reason for coming here, the mission to be completed. I was given a choice—to stay and carry out the mission, or return back to where I'd been."

So far that made sense, if one overlooked a talking dog. "What is the mission?"

"We all have skills that will help in building this world faster than the first time. We know how to farm, how to hunt, how to build— more or less. We're not starting from scratch like cave men."

"Do you have tools?"

"No, just what we build ourselves. We've made a crude ax to chop the trees and fishing nets woven from grasses. For hunting, we use bows, arrows and spears." He gave her a slight smile. "I won't say we're good at it, but we're getting there."

She shook her head, disbelief warring with his words. "What skills do you have here already?"

"Farmers, cooks, hunters, weavers, seamstresses. We have food now, clothing. According to Diogee, the weather is supposed to stay consistent—warm with occasional rain—but I wanted to get shelters built. I think that's why you're here. You can help."

"I could." She'd studied primitive log cabins in college while pursuing her degree. She never thought she'd actually need to use that knowledge. "And you believe a...dog?"

"I really don't have another option. He hasn't been wrong yet."

A dog was guiding this crazy project. Yep, she was dreaming. But even her most wild dream had never approached anything like that. Where did a dog fit in? "Is Diogee the only dog?"

"The only one I've met." Liam shrugged.

She raised her gaze to Liam, studied his handsome face. "What's your skill?"

Liam's smile was almost sheepish. "Leader, I guess. I tend to think of it as organizer. I oversaw massive projects in my job. I guess that qualifies me for this one."

"Who chooses the people to come here?"

"I don't know. I know about them when Diogee brings them to me."

"How does it work?"

"People appear, called via dreams. Each has a skill we need. Some stay, some don't." He reached out to touch her hand. "I hope you stay, Kinsley."

His touch stirred an answering warmth, but instead of replying, she watched the water dancing over the worn rocks in the stream. Part of her still struggled to believe this was real.

Maybe this was just a dream--a crazy dream.

But if not, if Liam was right, what a challenge. Every day would be new, exciting, and open to all possibilities. It wouldn't be easy. She could see that already. At best, they'd start with near pioneer days knowledge and functionality. Still, she couldn't deny the rising anticipation inside her.

"What will happen if I agree to stay?"

"You'll vanish from your current timestream." He met her gaze, his own steady, reassuring.

"As if I never existed?"

"No, as if you didn't exist from that moment on."

She'd lose her friends, her family, and her house. An ache crushed her chest, making it difficult to breathe. Never to see Mom? Dad? Piper? Her younger brother? Could she do that?

"Can I go back to tell my family first?"

"I'm sorry. No. If you go back, you stay there."

Kinsley pushed to her feet to stare at the view of the nearby grassland and forest. "I need to think about it."

Liam nodded as he rose to his feet. "I understand. It's a lot to take in. I'll be in the village if you need me."

As he walked away, Kinsley shook her head. If this was only a dream, would her answer even matter?

The sounds, scents, and touches she'd experienced made this feel very real. The people she'd helped were truly hurt. She'd felt their warm skin, smelled the blood.

The idea of surviving without any of the modern niceties she was used to unnerved her. No showers. No flush toilet. No microwave. No medical care. Even perfect weather didn't make up for those things.

Could she stand to lose her family...and Piper? How could she desert her best friend?

She ran her fingers through her hair, tangling them in her curls. Anguish flooded her. Would she be able to help here? She had knowledge to guide them in building structures. Good structures-- weatherproof, permanent, even without nails.

"What do I do?" She looked to the heavens as if expecting an answer.

"What do you want to do?" Diogee appeared as if he'd been waiting for her to ask.

She startled. "That's the question." She sank down on the river bank and the dog came to sit beside her. "I know I can help."

"Yes, you can."

"But I can't just abandon my family, my friends, or my job." Her heart ached at the thought. Would they have any idea where she'd gone? They would grieve for her.

"You'll see your family and friends again."

She turned to him in frustration. "How do you know that?"

He didn't respond, but his gaze met hers, his eyes deep, holding more kindness and warmth than she'd ever experienced. She caught her breath. This was just a dog. Wasn't it?

"I have no guarantee that I'd survive. There's no medical help here."

"That's true, though I imagine some will arrive eventually."

She hesitated. That was possible. "Why are you the one guiding it?"

His mouth dropped open as if in a grin. "I believe people are worth it."

That wasn't really the answer she'd wanted, but she didn't think she'd get anything more. She dropped her hand in her hands. "I want to do the right thing."

"I know."

She stared at him. How did a dog get so wise?

He was more than a dog--much more. He was leading this, choosing the people. Who…*what* was he?

He continued, "What does your heart tell you?"

She'd be useful, needed, appreciated, vital even if this project was to grow. And there was Liam. She recalled the way he'd focused on her, as if he saw more to her than she knew.

Something in his eyes had called to her, promised more, a life that truly mattered. He made her feel something, a tingling warmth, that she hadn't experienced in a long time. Was that worth giving up her former life?

Maybe.

She rested her forehead atop her bent knees. She could make a difference here. A real difference, more so than building low-cost housing. Definitely more than building another warehouse. Wasn't that what she'd always wanted?

It would be a new job. A new life.

Certainty flowed through her. This was the right thing.

She stood and glanced down at Diogee. He stood as well and nodded. "You've decided," he said.

"Yes." She was scared, but she was sure.

Drawing in a deep breath, she turned toward the village. When she glanced back, Diogee was gone. Why didn't that surprise her?

She spotted Liam at once, apparently waiting for her. He must have seen something in her face, for he came over to greet her. His intense gaze met hers. "Will you stay, Kinsley? Will you help us create a new and better world?"

The right answer jumped out. "Yes, I'll stay."

***

Piper sat by Kinsley's hospital bed where her friend still lay unmoving. A coma, they said. But no one could say why. Kinsley appeared perfectly healthy—all the blood work looked fine.

Yet here she lay…unconscious…unresponsive.

The only sound was that of the monitors beeping, the single sign that Kinsley still lived.

Piper held Kinsley's hand, willing her friend to wake up. Medically, she knew better, but she had hope. "Please, Kins. Come back."

Kinsley suddenly took a deep breath and her eyes flew open, focusing at once on Piper. "Kinsley!" Piper leaned closer. "I've been so worried."

"I'll be fine." Kinsley squeezed Piper's hand and smiled--a smile that held warmth, knowledge, and caring. "I'll miss you."

"What--?" Before Piper could finish, a glow surrounded Kinsley as if she were lit from within. In another instant, she disappeared, the sheets collapsing to the bed as her monitor alarms blared.

"Kinsley?" Piper stepped back, her hands to her mouth, unbelieving. She shook from head to toe. This wasn't possible. What was going on?

***

Liam smiled at Kinsley. "I'm glad you made that choice."

"I think I can help." She *knew* she could help.

"You can. You also get to live."

"What?" She didn't understand.

"All those who come here have yet another selection criteria. They're due to die within the next few weeks in their current timeline."

"Die?" She stared at him. She was going to die? "How?"

"You were going to a concert," he said. "It will be bombed by terrorists. Thousands will die."

She stared at him. The concert? Terrorists? "How can you know this?" It meant foretelling the future. Well, seeing the past from this perspective.

"Diogee."

Of course--the mysterious, all-knowing dog. "Why didn't you tell me this before?"

"I couldn't. You had to make your decision based on wanting to be here, not as an alternative to death."

Kinsley gasped. "Piper is going to the concert with me. I have to go back and warn her."

Sadness marred his expression. "You can't. If you go back, you not only can't return, but you'll forget all of this."

"But...but why?" It wasn't fair. She had to help her friend.

"We can't allow history to change."

"Doesn't bringing me here change history?" She didn't bother to hide her anger.

"Not significantly enough. You'll be dead soon and your history will stop."

She closed her eyes, fighting back the tears that wanted to escape. Suddenly, a thought hit her that changed everything. "Piper is a nurse practitioner." Her eyes flew open. "And she's supposed to go the concert."

Liam produced a slow smile. "Is she?"

Kinsley grinned. And she knew exactly who to mention that to.

Liam slowly took her hand in his callused palm. "I'm glad you stayed for another reason as well."

Her pulse leapt and she couldn't stop her flirtatious smile. "Are you?"

"I think we're going to be friends, good friends."

"I'd like that."

***

Piper prepared for bed, exhausted. Throwing back the red, flowered comforter from her double bed, she sighed. She'd had to call Kinsley's family again. They'd already been on their way to Denver because of her first call. She tried to explain what had happened. No one believed her. There was no body. The hospital assumed Kinsley woke up and left. But Piper had seen her disappear. To where? Would she ever know?

Piper didn't believe it herself. People didn't just disappear like that. Why couldn't this all be a bad dream?

She sank into an exhausted sleep at last and found herself in a wide green meadow filled with scents of blooming flowers. Real scents. Bright colors. Swaying grass of the greenest green.

Drawn in one direction, she started walking. Two figures appeared—a person and a dog. A weird-looking dog.

And Kinsley!

Piper rushed to embrace her friend. "Kinsley. How? What?"

Kinsley simply hugged her tighter. "We have a lot to talk about." Releasing Piper, she smiled. "And I hope you decide to stay."

Karen Fox

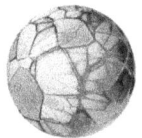

When not embroiled in the adventure and romance of her latest characters, Karen shares her house in the Colorado mountains with her husband and three cats. She has published ten novels, six short stories and one novella. Her second book, *Somewhere My Love*, was a 1998 RITA Finalist. *Buttercupbaby* was a winner of the Booksellers Best Award. She's been active in several writing organizations, serving on the Romance Writers of America board, the Pikes Peak Writers board and on PPW conference committee. She's also involved in the Novelists Inc. annual conference.

Dreamwater

Peter McQuade

Hyacinth Barlow died six days before the bulldozers were scheduled to arrive. My great-aunt's passing meant I now had sole responsibility for saving her bed-and-breakfast, the Inn at Barlow Springs. The feeling was beyond helpless—it was like balancing on one foot at the edge of the Grand Canyon.

Months before, Emerson County had decided it would be "in the best interests of the people of California" if Aunt Hyacinth would vacate her home and her land, and turn them over to a multinational conglomerate of land developers, the Eastern Provinces Investment Corporation—EPIC—under *eminent domain*, of course. In recent years, many state legislatures had placed severe restrictions on their states' ability to abuse eminent domain in this way. Unfortunately, California wasn't one of them. In our state, all a developer had to do was convince the county government that their proposed project would be for "public use" and would enhance "economic development." These two phrases were wide open for interpretation, especially when the potential for huge sums of tax revenue was thrown into the mix. When the county informed Aunt Hyacinth they intended to "condemn" the Inn at Barlow Springs and give it to EPIC, she dug her heels in with a passion. The next thing we knew, the ninety-six-year-old woman was being sued by the county.

So far, our hearing in the courtroom in Eagle City had dragged on, at intervals, for over four weeks. The judge still had to hear final arguments and make his ruling. Auntie and I shared a premonition that the next time we went to that courthouse, it would likely be the last—

one way or another.

When my family heard what was happening, they phoned Auntie to commiserate. But texts were all I got. One said, *Good luck, Toby old boy.* Another said, *Wish there were something we could do to help.* That was all they offered. Maybe it was because they knew that someday, when Aunt Hyacinth passed away, they would get her money, while the inn and the property it sat on would go to me. Nobody else in the entire extended family was willing to take on all the hassle of owning and running it.

I couldn't blame them. They just didn't understand what was really at stake. But then, none of them had ever spent a single night at the inn. If they had, they would have felt differently. They would have experienced the dreams.

And the dreams were what the Inn at Barlow Springs was really all about. Almost since the day Auntie became a widow at age twenty-three, she'd thought of her modest hideaway as a haven for troubled hearts to come and be healed in simple tranquility. Where they could dream beautiful dreams and rebuild their shattered, or confused, or uninspired lives. Not in massive numbers, but in ones and twos—maybe three visitors at a time. And so, for decade upon decade, her isolated mountain home in the wilds of the California Sierras played its role in making the world a bit less crazy. This was her passion, her reason for living. Now it was up to me to honor her deathbed wish to not let Barlow Springs die.

My hopes now lay in the hands of Judge Hugh Shackleford of the Superior Court of Emerson County. No stranger to cases like ours, he was famous for having once told a newspaper reporter that presiding over an eminent domain case was like performing a tonsillectomy on a porcupine. "Hurts like hell," he said. "And nobody appreciates you for doing it. Then, when it's all finished, people can't stand to look at your face."

The "Porcupine Judge" wasn't necessarily my last chance—if he were to rule against me, I could still take the case to the state Appeals Court, and even the state Supreme Court, if there was any energy left in me. But every day, I prayed the judge would deliver me from those long, hard struggles.

***

My attorney, Daniella Ramirez, was as smart and conscientious a lawyer as you'd find anywhere. And she was genuinely sympathetic to my plight. I'd retained her services eight months before, as soon as EPIC first tried to squeeze-play Aunt Hyacinth into selling Barlow

Springs. But I sensed Daniella's mind was just a little too logical to believe in the magic of dreams. I once invited her to spend a night at Barlow Springs. With a grimace, she said her hectic schedule wouldn't allow it.

Nevertheless, it was Daniella who'd first uncovered EPIC's real target: the *water* from Barlow Springs. Following her careful reviews of court documents, internet sites, and other public records, she'd concluded EPIC wouldn't have given two plug nickels for the bluish-gray, nineteenth-century Victorian inn itself, or its three flagstone patios with firepits, or the flower and vegetable gardens that Aunt Hyacinth nurtured and called her "babies." Instead, they were obsessed with the water. Presumably, because it was clear, pure, healthful, and marketable—the best thing since Perrier and Evian. Furthermore, as they'd stressed to the judge, the millions upon millions of bottles of it they planned to sell would bring *economic development* to our county and state.

That's not to say EPIC didn't have plans for every square inch of Auntie's twenty-six acres nestled in a valley in the middle of nowhere. It would all be transformed into the *Barlow Springs Pilgrimage Resort*. There would be a grand hotel, condominiums, well-manicured nature trails, and "Meditation Pavilions." There'd even be a planetarium for pilgrims to gain inspiration from the mysteries of the universe—at forty-five dollars per inspiration.

The most essential part of the resort, of course, would be the pair of small natural springs that for ages had been the source of Dusty Pine Creek, a two-bit stream so meager that only the locals had ever heard of it. EPIC planned to tap the springs within a gleaming, forty-thousand gallon-per-day bottling factory. The creek would flow no more.

Revenue from the bottled water was estimated to be over a billion dollars a year, assuming they could sell it all. And that didn't include the additional income from tourists, the condos, and special events.

But despite all their magnificent plans, there was no indication that EPIC was aware of the dreams. To them, it was all just Perrier and Evian. And I was happy to keep it that way.

***

"Toby dear, would you please take this tray out to the table at the waterside?" Auntie said that evening, thirty-one years before. *The waterside*: that's what she called the small flagstone patio overlooking the springs, as if it were a beach in Hawaii, rather than Barlow Springs

247

and Dusty Pine Creek. "Our guests are waiting," she added with a smile that belied the recent onset of arthritis in her knees and hips. She'd turned sixty-five earlier that year. But her French-braid ponytail conspired with a playful glimmer in her hazel eyes to make her look many years younger.

"Right away, Auntie," I replied as I accepted the china tea set from her. I turned and crossed the kitchen's fastidiously polished wooden floor, opened the screen door, and stepped out into the cool summer starlight. I was fourteen, and this was my first full-time, paying job. Mom and Dad had driven me out from Muncie, Indiana, four weeks before. I didn't want to go and argued with my parents the whole way. But after my first night or two there—and my first dreams—I never wanted to leave.

Taking meals and refreshments to the guests was one of my favorite responsibilities. I didn't mind the other chores: chopping firewood, painting the front porch, biking to town for groceries, bear-proofing the garbage cans. But getting to hobnob with Auntie's guests was a special treat, despite my horrible early-teenage shyness. There was something about the people who came to Barlow Springs—every one of them. They were just nicer and gentler than other adults. Even the ones who seemed grumpy and angry when they first arrived turned into very nice folks by the time their three-day stay was over.

That was Auntie's rule: all guest stays were three days and three nights. Never any shorter or longer. And nobody ever got to come back for seconds, because one visit to Barlow Springs was all anybody ever really needed. Besides, as Auntie said, "We must spread the wealth." Only I was allowed to stay longer—the entire summer season. And I would do so for the next three summers.

"Here you go, folks," I announced as I stepped off the darkened path and into the flickering orange that the firepit cast across the stones of the circular patio.

"Would you join us, please, Toby?" our guest Adriana asked. All three places at the table were taken, so she motioned toward the low red-brick wall that surrounded the patio and bordered the creek. I set the tray on the wrought-iron table and filled four cups with steaming jasmine blossom tea brewed with water from the springs. Then I took a spot on the wall, facing the guests. No one said anything at first. They all seemed mesmerized by the murmuring of the creek and the playing of the breeze in the pines and quaking aspens above us.

Adriana was a blonde-haired woman, probably in her forties. She was pretty, even to a young fellow like me. One of the other guests, Bob, had whispered to me that Adriana was a Broadway actress who'd been quite famous at one time. But producers and directors changed over the years, and now actresses who looked like Adriana just weren't in demand anymore. She grew bitter and resentful, obsessed with her own misery, not caring the least about anyone else. She came to Barlow Springs because somebody in New York had said it would help.

Bob, a man with reddish hair just starting to turn gray, owned a pro basketball team—one that used to be so great that sportscasters called it a dynasty. Now it was perpetually stuck in the basement of the NBA, a laughing stock. You'd never guess that, though, from the way Bob grinned whenever he spoke—at least since his first night at the inn.

The third guest, Howie, had been a police officer. His seat at the table was a wheelchair. A shootout at a grocery store in Houston had landed him in the hospital for nine months and ended his career at age twenty-seven.

Aunt Hyacinth stepped out of the shadows, carrying a plateful of her hypnotically aromatic cranberry-orange muffins. She smiled at everyone, then served each of us.

"My heavens…." Adriana murmured after her first nibble of muffin. Then she sipped from her tea cup and allowed the amber liquid to blend with the muffin's flavor and linger in her mouth. After a moment, she sat back and closed her eyes. Serenity spread over her face, highlighted by the wavering orange firelight. In that moment, I imagined how she must have looked on stage, with the spotlights on her and hundreds of adoring fans at her feet. Her smile told me she never wanted to leave Barlow Springs. She had dreamed there.

***

None of us knew exactly what caused the dreams. But every guest would tell you they slept more peacefully than they ever had before. Almost like magic, that serenity pulled them into a unique mental state that created dreams of vivid colors, warm textures, and soul-soothing stories. Dreams that inspired. Dreams that healed. Dreams that transformed.

People said that when you awoke from one of those dreams, you would never be the same again. You would be closer to being the best person you could ever be.

I knew what they meant. In the four-hundred-or-so nights I slept at Auntie's inn, never once did I have a bad dream. I had only nice, beautiful ones that made me a better person. I knew that to be true, because Auntie told me so herself.

***

Family lore had it that Hyacinth Barlow was born on a lovely April afternoon in her parents' and grandparents' Victorian house, just twenty yards from the springs. She died ninety-six years later, in the same room. The whispering gurgle of the springs was likely the first sound she'd ever heard—and the last.

Of course, EPIC couldn't have cared less about such sentimentality. Their plans were focused on the *future* of Barlow Springs.

And then one day, my attorney, Daniella, said she'd found evidence of what I most feared—EPIC knew about the dreams.

"Are you certain?" I pleaded, as my throat tightened with the feeling that a precious secret was about to be laid bare to the world.

"Yes," she said.

She explained that months before, one of EPIC's people had stumbled upon a glowing Facebook post by a guest who'd experienced the dreams. "It's like being in Heaven," the woman wrote, above photos of Auntie and the house. EPIC tracked down that guest—and others—and interviewed them. EPIC's board of directors became convinced the dreams were for real. And their profit potential was unlimited.

That must have explained why, shortly after Emerson County had decided Auntie must give up the inn and property, EPIC volunteered to assist the county in verifying the environmental safety of the place—the house, the soil, the air, the water. Everything. EPIC dutifully dispatched a small army of chemists, biologists, and psychiatrists on visits to Barlow Springs. To Daniella, their motive was now clear: EPIC couldn't market the dreams until they understood what caused them.

***

An owl hooted twice from the Douglas fir overhanging the waterside patio. Sitting on the wall next to the springs, I leaned my fourteen-year-old torso toward the warmth of the firepit. The tangy sweetness of Aunt Hyacinth's cranberry-orange muffin was making my mouth water, so I took another sip of tea.

Auntie smiled at her spellbound audience. "We saw so many shooting stars that night—dozens upon dozens!" She was sitting next to me and I could feel her warm, fragrant breath. "So brilliant and stunning. That was in 1969—the same year we landed on the moon. Oh my goodness, what a summer!"

Adriana, Bob, and Howie listened, nibbled their muffins, and sipped tea. But mostly, they listened—as guests always did.

Auntie pointed to a clearing near the house. "We lay on blankets, right over there—on both nights. In July, to watch the moon, knowing there were two men walking on it. And then a couple of weeks later, to witness the Perseids meteor shower. It was breathtaking, I tell you. *Fire in the sky*. That's what John Denver called it. *Rocky Mountain High*."

Then she fell silent, and all eyes turned upward, to the starry black dome above us. There was no moon or meteors that night. Yet the vastness of the glittering heavens drew everyone into their embrace.

"It's getting late," Auntie finally said. "Who's ready for sleep?"

Three smiling faces gleamed in the firelight.

***

The thoroughness of EPIC's scientists impressed the socks off Daniella, whose continuing research indicated they'd left no stone unturned in their quest to fathom the secrets behind what they called, "The Barlow Springs Phenomenon." They'd sampled the air inside and outside the house. They'd examined every type of plant and tree within half a mile of the inn. They'd captured and dissected a variety of insects and rodents. They'd set up magnetometers, photometers, and a dozen other kinds of "ometers," to ferret out any sort of waves that might influence the brains of sleeping guests. If there was a scientific test that could be performed on the place, they did it. And one by one, those avenues turned out to be dead ends.

The only exception was the water. That was the one thing their tests hadn't been able to rule out. For starters, EPIC's interviews of our guests found that every single one of them had consumed at least eight ounces of Auntie's tea before retiring each night. Their tests immediately dismissed her jasmine blossom tea leaves and petals as being just a very normal, store-bought variety. So, they analyzed the hell out of the water.

They almost came up empty-handed there, too—after extensive tests, it appeared to be just regular mountain spring water, with the usual traces of harmless mountain minerals. But one of their younger scientists detected tiny amounts of two rare chemical compounds with weird-looking names I couldn't hope to pronounce. Her report said the effects of those compounds on the human nervous system were "not yet fully understood." Apparently, that was good enough for EPIC's board of directors to declare Auntie's spring water to be the stuff of dreams.

I felt flabbergasted. Over all those years, I could never have imagined it was the water behind the dreams.

But this led to Daniella's most gut-wrenching discovery of all: the galley proof of an advertisement being prepared for EPIC's marketing department. Simple and alluring, it featured an opened twelve-ounce bottle of water and a champagne glass sitting atop a grand piano in an otherwise darkened room. The bottle's logo was a stylized lavender outline of a woman in a long dress; three-quarter rear view. Her hair was in a ponytail and she was holding a flower in one hand. Below her were the words, *Mystic Hyacinth Dreamwater: The Essence of Happiness.*

I wanted to puke.

***

Aunt Hyacinth's memorial service was small. But it was the best her sister Frieda could work out with the funeral home, in the little time allowed. Besides Daniella and me, only a handful of Auntie's closest friends attended at Three Peaks Church that morning. Had there been sufficient time, I'm sure an invitation to all our former guests would have brought a flood of well-wishers.

Afterward, her ashes were placed in the Columbarium at the local cemetery. She'd always told me she didn't want her ashes spread in some beautiful, nostalgic place—most especially Barlow Springs. It might make people sneeze.

The bulldozers were due in three days. Despite having such a brilliant attorney, I felt more alone than ever.

***

It was raining in Eagle City the following day, the day of what was likely to be the final court hearing. Daniella and I were sitting on the right-hand side of the courtroom. On the other side was the county's lead attorney, a steely-eyed man named Carboni. Next to him was his raven-haired associate, Miss Holloway. In the seats behind them was a platoon of dark-suited EPIC representatives—no doubt they all drove BMWs and owned multiple homes.

Above us, behind the bench, the slender, bespectacled, brown-haired Judge Hugh Shackleford listened intently to both sides for over an hour, occasionally scratching the back of his neck. I pictured him peering into the mouth of a porcupine.

We had gone first, and Daniella made our case as well as anyone could, emphasizing the rights of the individual citizen and invoking images of a quiet rural California region being destroyed and replaced by "Disneyland of the Sierras."

When Mr. Carboni stood to make the county's case, my heart rate jumped a few notches. The climax to my long struggle had arrived. He began by recounting that Emerson County had offered me fair market value for Barlow Springs. But just like my great-aunt, I was being intransigent, as well as insensitive to the needs of the people of California. Especially the youth, who would benefit most from the economic development of Barlow Springs. And all because I felt EPIC was out to destroy one person's legacy.

If he'd intended to trigger me, he was close to succeeding. I had to fight off an urge to jump up and demand an apology. Daniella could tell, and patted my hand to calm me.

Then Carboni gestured for the judge to look at me.

"Your Honor," he said in a nearly apologetic tone, "Emerson County isn't seeking to destroy the legacy of this man's great-aunt." A moment later, to drive home his point, the attorney called a witness: one of the EPIC representatives. The man went to the witness stand and took the oath.

After answering a few innocuous questions from the county lawyer, the beefy, dark-haired EPIC guy said, "That's right, Your Honor. Our plan for economic development of this property will *enhance* Hyacinth Barlow's image. Bring it to full bloom."

My slow burn was getting hotter and I couldn't keep from sighing audibly and rolling my eyes. The judge responded by giving me a dirty look and placing his hand on the gavel.

"Recently," the man continued, "EPIC has come to realize that Barlow Springs is even more of a special place than we had earlier realized—a magical place. One might even call it mystical."

This was it—they were about to play their ultimate hand. I leaned toward Daniella. "Damn!" I whispered. "He's going to bring up the dreams."

She glanced at me and pursed her lips.

"Please explain," the county attorney said to the witness.

The EPIC guy continued, "Our initial chemical analysis proved that the water at Barlow Springs possesses uniquely healthful properties. And this by itself justifies our claim that our resort and bottling plant must be placed in that particular location—to realize the desired economic development and its many concomitant benefits for the people of California."

The judge nodded in a way that said he'd heard all of this before and would like to wrap things up.

"However, Your Honor, we now have scientific proof that the water at Barlow Springs is healthful in more ways than just the physical."

He paused for effect. The judge leaned forward a little.

"You see, this water has certain *other* chemical properties that create a unique sense of inner peace in the people who drink it. You can think of it as tonic for the soul."

The judge's eyebrows shot up.

My hands balled up into white-knuckled fists. EPIC had so cleverly chosen this moment to reveal the true secret of Barlow Springs, to shout it to the whole damned world, when they had me backed into a corner—because if I denied the dreams, I would be turning my back on Auntie's legacy. And if I admitted they were true, I would publicly validate EPIC's *Dreamwater* advertising. "Object, or something," I whispered to Daniella.

"On what grounds?" she shot back.

"I don't know," I grumbled. "You're the lawyer."

Carboni smiled and took over from the witness. "Yes, Your Honor, as incredible as it sounds, this is all true. And we of Emerson County believe this amazing water should not be hoarded by one selfish man."

I began to sweat from the sensation that the hot gaze of every person in the room was boring into me.

"No, Your Honor, we believe this phenomenon should be shared with the whole world. Indeed, this could be an exciting, transformative step toward bringing about world peace."

Stunned, I gasped for air.

World peace? I wondered. My clenched fists softened. *How could I possibly fight world peace?*

Carboni continued speaking, but I was oblivious to it.

I struggled to regain my mental balance. But there was no balance to be found. *How did we get to this point? Does any of it make sense anymore?*

But the real problem was, I was now beginning to wonder if Carboni and his EPIC witness were right. Maybe I was being selfish and intransigent, an impediment to world peace. I lowered my head to the table and began to shudder.

Daniella placed a steadying hand on my shoulder.

While the judge asked Carboni some questions about proof of EPIC's startling claim, I sobbed over and over, "I'm sorry, Auntie. I let you down."

For the next twenty minutes, I was lost in the shipwreck of my thoughts. I never heard Judge Shackleford's final proclamation. I didn't have to.

As we left the courtroom, Daniella whispered. "Are you sure you don't want to appeal?"

"No," I mumbled, leaning against her arm. "No appeal."

***

The night before the bulldozers came, I stayed at Barlow Springs, with permission from the county and EPIC. I'd brought a sleeping bag and an air mattress that I set up in the kitchen. All of Auntie's furniture and possessions had been removed over the past two days, by order of a court that had correctly foreseen the final outcome of the case. The electrical power and water had been disconnected.

At dusk, I lit a fire in the fire pit and brewed a cup of jasmine blossom tea. Sitting on the low brick wall, I ate a muffin I had frozen before Auntie died. I listened to the music of the water burbling from the springs and watched the fire's reflection dancing in the ripples.

I didn't stay up late—that was one of Auntie's rules.

***

In the wee hours of the night, I dreamed I was balancing on one foot at the edge of a huge canyon. An owl hooted and a gust of wind brushed my back. I tumbled into space.

Bolting upright in the sleeping bag, I rubbed my eyes. Dizzy and shaking from the horrible dream, I struggled to stand and grabbed my cell phone to use as a flashlight. As light and shadows played on the floral wallpaper, I slowly regained my sense of balance.

Then it hit me like a slushball to the side of the head. In the hundreds of nights I had slept at the inn, I'd had only beautiful, inspiring dreams—until *this* night. And I had drunk the water of the springs.

In the darkness of the kitchen, a single indispensable truth now shone with the power of a thousand spotlights. The amazing, soul-healing dreams at the inn had nothing to do with the water. Or the food, or the air, or some mysterious waves. The dreams had sprung from Hyacinth Barlow herself—from the magic of her kindness, gentleness, and serenity.

And so, EPIC's grandiose billion-dollar plans were doomed to fail.

But it was equally clear that there would be another inn like Auntie's—somewhere, someday—because I would build it. And people would come there and have the best dreams of their lives, because I alone understood Hyacinth Barlow's magic, and would carry it within me all the days of my life.

Peter McQuade

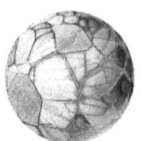

Peter D. McQuade grew up wandering the mountains and deserts of Idaho. When he was six, his parents made the mistake of letting him stay up late to watch *The Twilight Zone*—a mistake that led to a lifelong love of spooky storytelling. Now Pete resides in Colorado Springs with his wife, Marilyn, and their dog and cat, Jasper and Gauss. When he's not writing, Pete's a professor of Space Systems Engineering. But if the weather's right, he'll put aside both writing and teaching and head to the prairie with his model gliders, seeking the exhilaration of a sky-high flight.

Computer Genie

Marlene Fabian Stiles

Tony stared in slack jawed horror as his newly installed anti-viral program devoured every file on his computer like a velociraptor gorging itself at a red meat feast.

"No!" he yelled and pounded on the alt key. "You're supposed to neutralize viruses, not create new ones." Dang it, this was his wife Muriel's fault for sneaking into his man cave and using his computer to search for Caribbean cruises they never took even though they had both been retired for the past two years.

The door scraped on the laminated flooring as Muriel entered. "Tony, calm down. It's not good for your blood pressure to get all riled up." She handed him a pill and a bottle of water.

He took it then grumbled, "I'm trying to download this new program and it ate my files."

She stifled a yawn but still creased the greasy lotion smeared across her face. "Leave it until morning. You'll feel better if you get a good night's sleep."

He didn't like being told what to do: walk for exercise, eat five helpings of vegetables, and get eight hours of sleep. "In a minute. I want to check the instructions."

When she didn't move he looked her up and down from the old-fashioned pink rollers knotting up her hair to the faded chenille bathrobe and finally her fluffy blue slippers.

Sighing, she turned away. "Don't stay up too late." After she closed the door, he heard her scruffy house slippers shuffle down the hallway.

When he turned back to his computer, a Genie appeared that looked remarkably like the Disney cartoon character. Folding his muscular blue arms, the Genie said, "Your wish is my command. I am here to solve your every problem."

"All I need is a firewall on my computer so I don't get any more viruses."

The Genie's smile pulled up his pencil-thin mustache as he said, "Think big, Tony. What do you really, truly want in your heart of hearts?"

Startled, Tony leaned back in his swivel office chair. An invisible force rolled him closer to his desk as the monitor brought up the website for the last Caribbean cruise Muriel had researched. He watched dreamy-eyed as sun bronzed, bikini clad girls played volleyball on a beach beside a rolling surf.

A pent-up longing spilled into words. "I wish I had a wife thirty years younger than me."

"Done!" The Genie said and the monitor flickered. The screen went blank.

Tony rubbed his eyes. "Must have dozed off." He shook off his crazy dream and tried to stand up. Arthritic pain shot up his spine and he sat back down. Clutching his armrests, he started to stand again then noticed his skin was as dried and wrinkled as a prune. Panicking, he felt his face. His jowls were sagging, his nose was huge and his eyebrows had transformed into shaggy caterpillars.

He croaked like a frog, "What the hell happened to me?"

The Genie reappeared on the screen. "Your wish has been granted. You are now 98 years old."

"I didn't wish for that!"

"You wished for a wife who was thirty years younger than you. Muriel is exactly that."

Tony's panic morphed into terror. "Make me 68 again!"

"You will need to purchase another Genie Software package, only $49.95. All major credit cards accepted."

"Why you conniving, thieving—"

Muriel tapped on the door. "Tony! Are you alright?"

"I'm fine. Go back to bed."

"Your voice sounds scratchy, like you're coming down with something. Better gargle with salt water."

"I'll do that. G'night." He held his breath until he heard the scuffle of her blue slippers shambling down the hallway. Then he sneaked to the bathroom next to his man cave.

A decrepit old man stared back from the mirror over the sink.

He cracked open the door and peered up and down the hallway before creeping back to his computer as fast as his creaking joints would let him. "All right, you buzzard, I'm sending another $49.95. Now put me back the way you found me."

The monitor filled up with a ream of print so infinitesimally fine that it seemed like tiny black ants were crawling over a white page.

"Hit any key to sign our waiver," the Genie's voice purred.

"Why you—" Tony grabbed a pillow off his couch and smacked the computer.

"Tony!" the door scraped again as Muriel opened it without knocking. "Please! You'll give yourself a heart attack!"

Tony froze in mid-swing, afraid to turn around.

Muriel stepped up to him. He looked down, expecting her to scream with repulsion as soon as she saw he was nearly a hundred years old. When she didn't, he raised his eyes warily and met hers. They were still as warm and cinnamon brown as on the day he married her forty years ago.

As he lowered the pillow, he discovered his arms didn't ache. Hoping against hope, he followed her into the hallway then ducked back into the bathroom.

He looked like himself again! Except he had a funny sensation in his shoulder like someone was shaking it.

"Tony, dear, wake up!" Muriel's voice floated through his brain fog.

"What?" He woke up with a start in his swivel chair.

"Come to bed, Tony. You fell asleep in front of the computer."

As a fragment of his dream surfaced, he touched his face. "How old am I?"

She laughed. "We're both 68 and not getting any younger."

"You're right, Muriel, we aren't." He clasped her hands. "Let's take that Caribbean cruise while we still can."

Her mouth dropped open and for the first time in years, she seemed to be at a loss for words. Then the moment passed and she said, "Heavens, you've had quite a change of heart! Who let that genie out of the bottle?"

He took her in his arms and kissed her. "I had a crazy dream. I was old and you weren't."

In the halo of the overhead light she looked beautiful even with the rollers in her hair. It felt good to be young again, or at least younger than 98. "I love you," he said as he kissed her.

When he looked up, the monitor was flickering. The Genie appeared grinning broadly above a banner that read, "Another satisfied customer."

Marlene Fabian Stiles

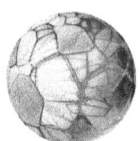

Marlene Fabian Stiles enjoys writing in multiple genres and has published a science fiction novel *Moon Life* in partnership with her geneticist brother Hank as well as a first person Alzheimer's account *Elderchild* based heavily on personal experience. She and writing partner Alice Hill will be publishing their children's book *Tulip-o-mania* and *Sistors*, a narrative of sibling rivalry.

Marlene also publishes short stories and poetry on www.storystyles.com.

As President of the nonprofit "The I Will Projects" (theiwillprojects.com) Marlene supports innovative approaches to education including a family caregiver program developed in partnership with Hospice and an aquaponics program with the Boys and Girls Club.

Other Lives
C.S. Simpson

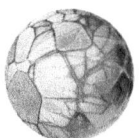

The sails were trim and taut, full of the Atlantic's salty offshore breeze. I angled the boat northeast, away from Miami, away from my tax-time CPA responsibilities, away from everything but my thoughts.

My new forty-foot Bermuda sloop had been expertly outfitted with all the pulleys and winches needed for me to handle her by myself. I stood at the helm, holding it loosely, for the day offered an easy sail. There's nothing like a brilliant spring day alone out on the open sea. I was the king of my own little watery world standing there in blue trunks and flip flops, as my Hawaiian shirt fluttered in the breeze, my tanned chest exposed for more sun. I reached down and flipped off the radio, choosing to hear the natural world instead.

The wire rigging creaked with every movement of the ship, and the rhythmic slap of the bow waves against her hull lulled me into a sweet, calming peace. I closed my eyes to enjoy nature's soundtrack and felt myself drifting away.

***

The unmistakable sound of a gunshot startled me awake.

I dove to the teak wood deck and threw my hands up to protect my head. Except, the deck was no longer teak, it was a pitted, dark oak. A glance up to the mainsail made my heart stop. Gone was my single aluminum mast and two top-of-the-line Dacron sails. Instead, I found myself frowning up at two wooden gaff-rigged masts, with yellowed canvas sails towering high above.

Another *boom* and the deck beside me splintered again, throwing up shards of wood that stung when they hit my bare arm. I noticed footsteps and shouting around me and moved backward, scuttling like a frightened crab. I *was* frightened.

My sleek, modern fiberglass sailboat was gone. I was cowering on the busy deck of . . . what, an old schooner? A brigantine?

"Come now, man. Don't just lay there. Ya ain't shot, is ya? Go!" a rough-looking bearded man bellowed down at me, pointing toward the bow.

I stood and wiped my pants clean before noticing my new garb: cutoff pants and a filthy blousy shirt. I was dressed like a . . . a pirate. A *pirate*?

"What the—" My exclamation was stopped short by the man's fist slamming into my solar plexus. As I bent over, gasping for air like a fish out of water, I faintly heard his stern voice again.

"Don't ya dare go backtalkin' now, ya hear? Get to the fore halyard and pull with the rest-a-yur lot. We gotta fend off them Spaniards or die tryin'."

He pushed me forward with the bottom of his boot, then spun aft as I stumbled the way he'd directed.

What the hell's going on? I thought, as I joined a line of five muscled men hauling a thick, fibrous rope the diameter of a large fist. Hand-over-hand, I pulled along with them, my palms bleeding from the effort. We all grunted and pulled, and I felt the ship heel to port as the sails caught a fresh wind, turning us sharply to the west. A glance out to the angry-looking sea showed a three-masted Spanish galleon just off our starboard beam, its square-rigged sails stacked high. From a gunport in its middle deck, a cannon barrel flashed brightly, sending a cannonball splashing into the sea just beside us. I pulled harder.

Thankfully, the new foresail was now aloft. The bearded man from before barked new orders and we followed them quickly and without question.

I heard snippets of conversation that informed me that we were off the coast of western Cuba, planning to take a cargo ship, when this Spanish galleon had sailed around the Cayos de San Felipe, surprising our captain. The plan was to out-sail them and get lost in the growing storm clouds to the south, toward the Caymans. I hoped we'd make it. Death by cannon shot was *not* an item on my bucket list.

Our schooner easily outmaneuvered its pursuers and the open sea was ours once more. I sat on the oak decking with a group of my fellow sailors, gnawing on a chunk of stale bread with my now-scabbed fingers.

"Must've been Spanish gold, not just cargo, else the warship wouldn't've been there," muttered a scruffy man to my right.

"Gold?"

"Aye. Why else ya think them Spaniards came after us? They was protectin' somethin'."

I didn't know how to answer him, so I just leaned back against the rail, shook my head and stared at my filthy bare feet, unblinking. *This is not the tranquil vacation I spent a month of overtime earning.*

I was completely worn out, body and soul. I hadn't worked that hard since the summer I spent mowing lawns and trimming bushes for my Uncle Rick up in Tampa.

I barely had time to fully contemplate my new predicament before I felt myself drifting off to sleep again.

***

The biting cold woke me. I was *freezing*. And shivering.

I knew I was aboard another ship. The tangy, salty smell of the sea was less intense than before, but the gentle rocking of the darkened cabin was just as unmistakable.

"Where the hell am I now?" I mumbled irritably. Throwing off a heavy wool blanket, I maneuvered myself to the base of a dimly moonlit ship's ladder. There were no portholes and no obvious light switches in the cabin. My thickly stockinged feet burned with the cold as I climbed up to the deck landing to peek outside.

Damn.

It looked like Star Wars' planet Hoth out there, as far as my eye could see. Icebergs and snow and ice and more ice littered my entire view. The natural light was eerie, as if there were three full moons outside, instead of one. *So cold.* I shivered and turned around, hurrying back down to the relative warmth of the hold.

By the dim glow from above, I noticed an oil lantern and a box of matches on a table at the bottom of the ladder. Lighting the lamp, I swung it inward to see the room. I was in the middle of a good-sized ship's main salon and had come from a lower bunk set against the inner hull. Two gimbal-mounted tables lay in front of me, the nearest one was where I'd picked up the lantern. A tall, thin stove of some kind glowed in the corner, no doubt the only thing providing heat to the salon. Again, everything looked antiquated, with not a hint of fiberglass or aluminum anywhere the light shined.

"You there, put that light out. It's not time for our watch, yet. Let us sleep in peace."

The voice came from behind and as I swung the light around with me, I noticed there were a total of twelve bunks, three pairs built into the hull on each side of the room. I mumbled a quiet, "Sorry," extinguished the lantern and slipped quietly back into my cold bunk.

Wide-eyed, I clutched the scratchy wool blanket to my now-bearded chin and listened to the scrape of icy water against the wooden hull. *What are these people doing in a boat in the middle of winter? Don't they know the ocean will probably freeze the ship in place?*

I tried to sleep, hoping I'd wake someplace warmer. But the cold was inescapable, which made me angry, which kept me alert. So I listened in the near-dark for clues to my new whereabouts. Other than men breathing and lightly snoring, there was the occasional scrape of a boot up on deck, or a gust of breeze rattling the rigging. Then I heard the rodents. I don't know if they were mice or rats, but I tried not to imagine one of them nibbling on my near-frozen toes. Not that I would feel it if they did.

By the time the light of a weak dawn appeared from the ship's ladder, the cook was busy in the galley next door and I had a plan to get out of this insane icebox as fast as possible.

"Wake up, wake up! B-Watch is on deck in one hour. Get dressed, get your meal, and get topside. Wake up, B-Watch."

The man's voice was firm, yet friendly. Whatever kind of vessel this was, it didn't feel hostile, like the last one—just unbearably frigid. I swung my freezing feet out of the bunk and slid them into waiting boots. Six of us had been roused from our bunks. A glance at my fellow crewmates showed pale faces, mustaches, and bushy beards. The fashion looked old, as did their clothing—mine too. We all wore some kind of sailors' uniform, thick and woolen. But the cold still seeped through.

After using the primitive ship's head, I returned to my bunk and caught the eye of the man next to me. "What's on the docket today?"

He answered as he finished lacing his boots. "I overheard the navigator say we're getting close to the Bering Strait last night, but winter's coming faster than anticipated. The captain thinks she'll freeze up soon, so they're going to fire up the steam engine again. I'm surprised he didn't rouse the crew to set sail hours ago."

The Bering Strait? I'm in the freaking Arctic and it isn't even winter yet.

Breakfast was some kind of pungent-smelling fish served with hard cheese on flat, crisp bread. And coffee. Oh, how the strong aroma and warmth of the coffee called out to me. I was so tired. But I couldn't risk the caffeine. Instead, I ate very little and rubbed my stomach a few times with a sour look on my face.

When the meal was over, everyone grabbed a fur coat, fur-lined gloves, and a thick, knitted watch cap before heading up the ladder.

Once topside, I was struck again by the biting cold, and watched my breath condense before me. An overcast sky did nothing to help my misery. *Where did the Atlantic's warm, benevolent sun go?* Yesterday's old pirate ship with its worn, splintered boards had been replaced by one much larger and cleaner. Its three empty masts towered over us in the morning gloom. A quick glance aft showed a steel chimney stack, which hinted at some kind of ship's engine.

"Let's get moving, lads. Huddle up," a deep voice called out.

As the six of us gathered around the man I assumed was the B-Watch Commander, I chose to stand next to a middle-aged sailor with a friendly face.

"We're going to try and make it through the Bering Strait before she freezes, so we need sails up to find this little breeze that just appeared," the leader said. "Now, A-Watch is headed down for their supper. Don't make them come up here and show you how to set a sail." He paused to let the group chuckle at his joke before continuing. "The boss wants to get underway as soon as possible, so get scrambling, boys."

I followed the bearded man forward, passing a large shore boat resting in the center of the deck. *Who in their right mind would want to get any closer to the freezing water?* I wondered incredulously, but I was still glad the ship had lifeboats.

As my watchmate reached out to grab a line on the foremast, I doubled over, clutching at my midsection, and groaned.

"What's the matter? Stomach cramps?" he asked.

I nodded, still leaning over, trying to look pained and pitiful.

"Go tell the watch commander. I'll rig this myself." He turned away and unwound a line from its mast-mounted cleat, clearly done with me.

I left him there and looked for the B-Watch Commander. I found him midship with another sailor, hauling lines to drop a square sail.

"Please, sir." I addressed him with a strain in my voice. "Stomach cramps. Can I please lie down for a bit?"

He appraised me carefully as they finished raising and tying off the sail. I stayed hunched over, grimacing.

"Fine," he answered, "You're no good to me like this. I'll check on you in one hour."

I nodded, trying to look grateful and sickly, then turned to go below deck. A-Watch was eating their meal around the main salon tables now, but I was sure their banter wouldn't keep me awake. I was beyond exhausted. *Whatever this weekend's been, it's definitely* not *anywhere near relaxing.*

Stripping off my boots and gloves—but leaving my coat on—I climbed back into the bunk and turned away from the sounds. Finally closing my eyes, I willed my feet to thaw so I could fall asleep.

***

A warm, salty breeze tickled my bare limbs, waking me gently. I could barely hear the steady thrum of a shipboard engine joining the sounds of the sea.

When I opened my eyes, I found myself cocooned in a linen hammock strung between two metal poles on the deck of a luxurious-looking sailboat. It was closer in size to my own forty-footer, with one tall, gleaming, aluminum mast holding two taught triangular sails. A glance forward showed a modest bowsprit with a third, colorful spinnaker billowing gracefully out front.

I sighed contentedly and lay my head back against the hammock pillow, luxuriating in the warm shade of the sails. No one disturbed me. The arctic was gone. I could feel my feet, fingers, and face easily.

Ahhh . . . this is so much better, more like Miami. I hope there's no back-breaking work to do this time. I can't believe I'm actually looking forward to sitting at my desk again—if I ever get back home.

As perfect as it felt, I was still tired, as if I had woken up here the moment I fell asleep in the Arctic. I was on the verge of sweet slumber when I made myself climb out of the hammock. I didn't want to risk falling asleep and ending up somewhere else unpleasant again. Besides, I wanted to learn where I was first. I strolled the deck of the impressive yacht in my tanned bare feet, touching the steel railing lightly, and gazed out at the brilliant blue sea.

I'd begun to think I was finally alone again, when a rattling sound from behind caught my attention. I walked around the deck-level salon to investigate, then stopped short in the doorway. There was a thin, petite woman dressed in a silver bikini top and a shimmering, sheer skirt, making a sandwich in the galley.

I froze. "Hello," I said, before I could stop myself.

"Hello, Love. Finished with your midday nap already?" She grinned at me sideways before giving her attention back to her task.

"Yes. It was wonderful." I was afraid to say much more and tip off this beautiful woman to the fact that I had no idea who either of us were.

"Good, good," she singsonged. "Now come sit with me while I eat." She laid a thick piece of bread on top of the piled meat, cheese, tomatoes, pickles, and sprouts, and my stomach rumbled loudly. "Well, now, if you're hungry again, why don't you join me?" she added playfully.

There was a bowl of fresh fruit on the counter, so I grabbed an apple and sat down with her in the cabin's corner booth. She eyed me mischievously, and I took a bite of the apple to silence myself. The woman was apparently comfortable with silence. We both chewed and gazed at each other, out the generous windows, and at the sea. Finally, I couldn't stand it any longer and blurted the first thing that came to mind.

"Why is the engine still on when we're at full sail?"

Her brow furrowed as she took the last bite and wiped her fingers on a paper napkin. She cocked her head a little to the side in the most adorable way before answering. "The saline drive does all the work, My Love. The mast and sails are holographic, you know that. Are you not feeling well?"

Holographic? My mind refused to move beyond this single word. I stared at her as if she'd just grown a third eye on the end of her nose. *Holographic?* The thought was a never-ending loop in my head until it seized on another phrase. *Saline drive? Damn. How far into the future is this?*

"Eric? Honey?" Her voice and gentle touch on my arm snapped me out of it.

I blinked and blinked, unsure what to say that wouldn't give me away. "I . . . I'm okay. I must've been stuck inside a dream," I said lamely. She didn't know how true the statement was.

"All right." The way she drew out the vowels, I could tell she didn't believe me.

She stood, taking her paper plate, napkin, and my apple core, and put them into a sleek cabinet drawer. She pushed a button on the counter and the drawer emitted a low hum briefly before quieting. *An incinerator? Cool.*

The woman turned and held out her palm for me to take. I grasped her hand like a lifeline, stood, and followed her back outside. The sun was high, the holographic sails still trim and taut, though there wasn't much of a breeze. Looking closer at the illusion, I realized I could barely see through the sails and mast—but I really had to try. The futuristic effect was almost perfect.

She sat on a padded bench and leaned against the stainless steel rail, still holding my hand. I sat down beside her, our bare knees touching.

"Eric," she said cautiously, "We're due to pull into the Rhodes Marina in a few hours. Would you like me to call ahead for a doctor to meet us there?"

I shook my head, then rubbed my clean-shaven face, hoping to awake some useful tidbit of information. "No, no thank you. I just had a moment. I'll be fine." Her hand was small and cool in mine. I focused on her brown eyes and light brown hair blowing in the breeze.

"Are you sure? You shouldn't address the New Mediterranean Consortium with an unclear mind. You've been writing and rehearsing this speech for months."

My heart seized. *A speech? My worst nightmare! I'd rather haul lines for pirates again.* Trying to keep my face serene, I nodded and pretended I was of sound mental faculties and knew exactly what she was talking about. "No, really. I'm fine," I answered hastily. "I'm . . . I think I'll lie down in the cabin this time, out of the sun."

I needed to get out of there, off the ship, out of this new reality. I couldn't give some impossible speech to a bunch of business people. As beautiful a life as it was, it wasn't mine, and I couldn't pretend to be some business or political man of the future. They'd all know I was a fraud before I even got onto the stage, or whatever form company conferences looked like these days.

She nodded and watched me go, with concern still in her eyes. How I hated to leave her sitting there alone.

I descended the ladder from the deck salon and stepped into an immaculate bedroom suite, complete with opulent bedding and pillows. Opening the door to my right, I found a closet, not the ship's head I was hoping for. An elegant silver dress and a black-tie tux hung there, each hanging safely underneath a clear plastic cover. *I really need to get to sleep before I have to put that thing on.*

Trying the other door, I found a fully appointed ship's head. There was even a bathtub—a *bathtub*—on a not-really-sailing yacht! I walked to the sink to splash water on my face and found myself staring in the mirror instead.

I was expecting a stranger's face, but it was definitely me—just a few years older. "How?" I asked my reflection. I looked tired. I *felt* tired, like I hadn't slept in days. Hanging my head, I leaned over, hands on the counter. *Am I an idiot wanting to leave this life?*

But there's no way I could pretend to be this Eric and pull off some fancy speech.

I lay down sideways on the king-size bed, not even bothering to pull back the duvet, and closed my eyes. The ship's saline drive offered a steady, easy thrum for me to focus on. I felt my body getting heavier as my thoughts slowed down.

***

"Ahoy! I say, mate, are you all right over there?" The man's voice was too loud.

My head throbbed as if a massive, beating whale's heart had been shoved inside my skull.

I groaned and opened my eyes to a bright, partly cloudy sky, before squeezing them shut again. I was lying on some ship's deck again, a Dacron sail flapping lazily above me, the boom spar swinging side-to-side with the boat's movement.

"Oi, you're alive, then." A relieved chuckle.

The elderly man I'd glimpsed sounded British. *Ugh, where am I now?*

"Your ship's been sailing madly, wherever the wind took her. Had to come see if there was anyone still alive over here." His voice was too perky for my pounding migraine.

When I cautiously reopened my eyes, I could see his smaller, older sailboat was tied to mine, its worn, sun-baked fenders cushioning our boats from the constant movement of the ocean. I sat up slowly, my hand going instinctively to the side of my head, where the ache was the strongest. My hair was warm and sticky. I pulled my hand away and saw blood on my fingers.

"Oi! That don't look good. Here." The Brit turned and grabbed a towel from a squat cabin before he stepped nimbly over the double set of wire railings and boarded mine. He knelt beside me on the teak decking, then offered the shabby navy-blue towel before sucking in a breath between his teeth. "You took quite the wallop there, lad. Did the boom swing 'round and get ya?"

I gingerly pressed his towel to my bloody head, stifling a groan, and looked up at him. "No, I . . . it was tied off. I swear."

He *tsked* and hurried to grab the loose jibe-guard line. While securing it on an aft deck cleat, he muttered softly, "It is now."

When he stepped back in front of me, the Brit asked, "Well, then, if you'd done it properly, how'd you end up face down on the deck of your fancy boat?" He chuckled and stared down at me with his hands on his hips, like some triumphant Peter Pan.

I shook my aching head slowly, in order to avoid dislodging my throbbing eyeballs. "I... I guess you're right. Thanks for your help."

"Don't mention it." The man patted my shoulder before crossing the wire railings to his boat once more.

With the towel still pressed to my wound, I watched him untie our boats and wondered what exactly had just happened to me. Were the Spanish galleon, arctic passage, and beautiful lady all just some concussion-induced dream? Or did I somehow leap between realities? Each one of the ships and locations had felt *so* real, so completely believable. My muscles even ached from all the nonstop work on that old pirate ship.

Maybe my overtaxed psyche was trying to tell me something.

I stared down at the deck of my fancy new sloop. I'd been chasing this—wealth, possessions, *things*—my whole life, working for whoever paid the best. I'd even chosen a career based on the salary it offered—not because I thought I'd enjoy the work itself. *And what do you have to show for it, Eric? Cars, boats, condos . . . and stress. You could've died alone out here today, if not for the kindness of this stranger.*

My muddled musings are interrupted by the British sailor. "You can keep the towel, mate," he called as he stood at his helm, ready to sail away. "We best be gettin' out of here as soon as possible. Your ship's wandered deep enough into the Bermuda Triangle that I don't suggest being here after sunset."

The Bermuda Triangle? My eyebrows shot up with an audacious new thought. *That's it.*

Standing slowly to avoid any dizziness, I waved to my rescuer and called out, "Got it. Thanks, again, man. You saved my life!"

He grinned in humble acknowledgment before turning his boat away from me and sailing westward.

My headache had reduced to a dull throb, so I dropped the bloody towel and checked my phone for the date and time. *Amazing.* My mind had lived days while my body lay here for only a few hours in the shade of a loose sail.

It was time to make a bold change. A quick check of the GPS at the helm confirmed my suspicions. I was actually closer to the Bahamas than Florida. I glanced at my compass, turned the rudder, and set sail for a tiny island chain in the natural shape of a triangle with white beaches I'd always wanted to see—Bimini.

It was time to leave Miami and the busy CPA life behind for good.

C.S. Simpson

C.S. Simpson is a multi-genre writer of several short stories, some poetry, and a novel. So far, her work can be found in *Shoreline of Infinity*, the Pikes Peak Writers Anthology: *Fresh Starts: Tales from the Pikes Peak Writers*, and her own self-published fables. C.S. likely has Diet Coke in her veins, loves reading, and hikes with her husband and dog under the Colorado skies she calls home. Keep up with her writing journey at www.authorcssimpson.com

About Pikes Peak Writers

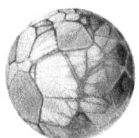

Pikes Peak Writers is one of the best writers' organizations in the country. Its annual writers conference has routinely been ranked in the Top Ten of Best Conferences by Writers Digest Magazine.

The brainchild of Retired Air Force Colonel Jimmie Butler, PPW started as a conference in 1993 with just 175 story-loving writers who wanted a place to collaborate. Today, PPW is a thriving and all-volunteer 501(c)(3) nonprofit organization with more than 2,000 members.

PPW is dedicated to providing quality education for writers, year-round. Beyond the annual conference, PPW hosts free and low-cost events. From monthly writing workshops to Writers Night, there are many fun and educational opportunities for writers of all levels to find inspiration, education, and lifelong friends.

For more information, visit the PPW website at:
https://pikespeakwriters.com

About the Editors

Kathie Scrimgeour, *Project Manager and Editor*, writes under the pseudonym KJ Scrim. She is a graduate of the University of Colorado at Boulder. In addition to serving on the Board of Directors with PPW, she is also the Managing Editor of Writing from the Peak (PPW's blog) and the Project Manager of PPW's anthologies, *Fresh Starts* and *Dream.* Her inspiration for blogging, flash fiction, short stories, and the long haul of novel writing comes from her many life experiences. You can follow her on her website, KJScrim.com and on Facebook. When she's not writing you can find her somewhere in Arizona biking, hiking, or finding Zen through Pilates.

***

Edward T. Raetz, *Senior Editor*, was born and raised in Colorado Springs, with stints in Germany, Boulder, and California. He graduated from CU Boulder (BA-English) and CSUSB (MA-Composition/ Rhetoric). His Master's Thesis was a psychoanalytic exploration of Lloyd Alexander's Prydain Chronicles. His writing is inspired by ancient myth and archetype, folklore, faerie, mycology, and bizarre natural phenomena. He loves world travel, surrealistic art, horror movies, music, and dark humor. He has dabbled in various vocations, including: college instructor, Postdoctoral lab researcher, and stay-at-home dad. He served on the PPW Board of Directors (2018-2020) and has published several Plant Pathology journal articles. He has been married to Carina since 1994 and is the proud father of 15-year old son, Rowan. Finally, Ed is an aspiring master potter and has exhibited his artistry at the Fine Arts Center.

***

Born in California, **Deborah L. Brewer,** *Editor,* moved around America and to Europe, before settling in the foothills of Colorado's Rocky Mountains. An avid reader, she holds a degree in liberal studies and is fascinated by both the history of daily life and mystery fiction, seeking to intertwine these interests in her own work. Debby especially enjoys well structured stories and whimsical poems that play with language and present ideas in unexpected combinations. She regularly volunteers with Pikes Peak Writers.

***

Jenny Kate, *Marketing Director and Editor*, is the founder of Writer Nation, an online space dedicated to helping writers market their work. With 19 years communications experience, she regularly writes on social media, internet marketing and face-to-face publicity. You can find her on her Website, Facebook, and Instagram

www.ingramcontent.com/pod-product-compliance
Lightning Source LLC
Chambersburg PA
CBHW071128200626
46817CB00018B/2472